Jerusalem Ghosts

Jerusalem Ghosts

A David ben Simon Mystery

MARTIN S. COHEN

RESOURCE *Publications* · Eugene, Oregon

JERUSALEM GHOSTS
A David ben Simon Mystery

Resource Publications
An Imprint of Wipf and Stock Publishers
199 W. 8th Ave., Suite 3
Eugene, OR 97401

www.wipfandstock.com

PAPERBACK ISBN: 978-1-7252-9523-0
HARDCOVER ISBN: 978-1-7252-9522-3
EBOOK ISBN: 978-1-7252-9524-7

06/30/21

Powerful men are lying in wait. . .

—PSALM 59

Author's Note

THIS IS A WORK of fiction and all the characters who play major roles in the story as told are imaginary personalities invented by the author.

Readers will want to recall a few historical facts. After Alexander the Great died on the eleventh of June in the year 323 BCE, his enormous empire passed not to his concubine's son—his only living son at the time, although another would be born posthumously—but to his generals, known collectively to history as the Diadochi, the Heirs. There were major battles and lesser dust-ups across the empire for a while, but eventually a number of smaller kingdoms emerged and established themselves. Of these, the kingdoms of Seleucus, who ruled over most of the Middle East, and of Ptolemy, who ruled over Egypt, are the relevant ones for this story because the Land of Israel, lying precariously between their domains, passed back and forth in the context of a series of wars that lasted more than a century. The precise story, which is a bit hard to follow anyway because most of Ptolemy's successors were also named Ptolemy and almost all of Seleucus' successors were named Antiochus or Seleucus, isn't all that crucial for readers to master. But readers will want to recall that it was at the great Battle of Raphia in 217 BCE (also known as the Battle of Gaza) that Ptolemy IV defeated Antiochus III, thus securing Israel as part of the Egyptian empire, and that it was at the Battle of Panium in 198 BCE (also called the Battle of Paneas) that that same Antiochus defeated the aforementioned Ptolemy's son, called Ptolemy V, and retook the Land of Israel for the Syrian Empire. And it was *that* victory that created the context for the so-called Maccabean revolt of the Jews against the Seleucids in the fourth decade of the second century BCE, the success of which is still celebrated annually on the eight nights of Chanukah.

As these various political upheavals were taking place, there was also great internecine tension playing itself out within the Jewish population and it is this tension specifically—which more than occasionally featured acts of extreme violence, including murder—that provides the background against which the story told in this book takes place. The narrator is a Levite, a member of Jerusalem's "second" priestly caste. When he refers to his brethren, it is to his fellow Levites that he is making reference. His enemies, mostly left unnamed in the narrative, are the priests themselves. The priests' book—the work that encapsulates their theology, their religious practices, and their version of the national epic—is the five-part book moderns call *the* Torah. The Levites' book, also presented to the reading public in five parts, is the book moderns call the Psalter or the Book of Psalms. (When the narrator makes reference to "the book" without further qualification, he is invariably referring to the Book of Psalms.) Most translations of the psalms are taken from my edition of the Psalter with English translation and commentary called *Our Haven and Our Strength: The Book of Psalms* that was published by Aviv Press in 2004. Translations that differ from the ones printed there have all been freshly prepared for this book.

Many passages in this book are based on biblical texts. Ketziya's oracle cited in chapter thirteen, for example, is taken from the poem that today is known as the fifty-second psalm, while the oracle cited in chapter forty-four is a reworking of several sections of the sixty-eighth psalm. Other biblical references are as follow. The inclusion of women as musicians in the First Temple is noted at 1 Chronicles 25:5–6. The verse from the Psalms attributed to David ben Levi in chapter eleven is known today as Psalm 34:9. The passage attributed to Assaf in that same chapter is today called Psalm 81:11, while the "Prayer of the Indigent" appears in the Psalter as Psalm 102. (The verse cited is number 25 by today's reckoning.) The passage from Isaiah mentioned at the beginning of chapter forty-seven is Isaiah 9:1–4. The citation from a poem by a David ben Levi in chapter fifty is a version of Psalm 37:35–36. The reference to a cadre of women drummers among the Temple musicians is at Psalm 68:26. The story of Doeg at Nob is told at length in 1 Samuel 21 and 22. Sprinkled throughout the narrative are references to some of the more obscure passages in the eighty-first psalm, here taken as references to specific rituals.

The passages describing the library at Pataliputra are wholly fictitious, as are those describing the *archayon* of ancient Jerusalem. The personal details mentioned here and there about High Priests of Israel and the emperors of Mauryan India are also mostly fictitious.

In ancient times, Jews did not have family names in the Western sense. Instead, they bore what moderns would call "first" names and were further identified through the use of patronymics formed of the Hebrew word *ben* (for men) or *bat* (for women) followed by that individual's father's name. Thus, the name X ben Y simply means "X, son of Y" and P bat Q means "P, daughter of Q." Also, it was customary for Levites and priests respectively to append the words Halevi (that is, "the Levite") or Hakohen ("the priest") to their fathers' names. Thus Reuben ben David Halevi means "Reuben, son of David the Levite."

I have tried to present a picture of life in old Jerusalem that mirrors the reality of ancient times, but have occasionally allowed myself to deviate from that policy for the sake of my storyline; as far as anyone knows, for example, there were no modern-style restaurants in ancient Jerusalem. Also, I have rather anachronistically called the various parts of public bath houses by the Latin names bequeathed to the ages by the Romans. Readers will also want to know that distances were mostly measured, at least as far as the narrative here is concerned, in handbreadths, cubits, parasangs, and mils. A cubit was roughly double the average handbreadth or, in Western terms, about eighteen inches. A mil was 2000 cubits. A parasang was four mils.

Dramatis Personae

David ben Simon, the narrator
Avital, his current wife
Zakur, his eldest son with his first wife, Deborah
Yehoram, his second son with his first wife, Deborah
Nathaniel and Asarela, twins, his youngest sons with his first wife, Deborah
Elzavad ben Shimri, Avital's late first husband
Uriel Gedalia ben Peretz, called Uri, Avital's brother
Meshullemet, his wife
Hephtziba, their daughter

Joseph, the narrator's brother
Joel ben Izri, his best friend
Yemima bat Zerach, his wife
Ethan, their oldest son

Bukiyahu ben Yerimoth, called Buki, a Levite
Shlomtziyyon bat Yakar, his mother
Yedutun ben Yakar, his mother's oldest brother
Assaf ben Yedutun, his first cousin, the son of his mother's brother Yedutun
Leah bat Yerimoth, his sister
Shaphan ben Gamliel, his friend

Eli ben Heman, called the Great One, chief of the Levites

Yaddua ben Korcha, their second-in-command

Uziel ben Jonathan, a Levite

Yoshbekasha ben Avraham, a Levite

Romamti-Ezer ben Assaf, a Levite

Onias II ben Simon, popularly called Choni, the High Priest of Israel

Benjamin Ginnethon ben Baruch Hakohen, the Vice High Priest called the *segan*

Naphtali ben Ahio, one of the two *katikolin* officials serving in the Temple

Zebulon ben Shashak, the other *katikol*

Esther Malka bat Shimon Halevi, Benjamin Ginnethon's estranged wife

Meirav Serach bat Baruch Hakohen, his sister

Ikkesh ben Tovim Hakohen, her husband

Tola ben Ikkesh, their son

Asa Gad ben Tovim Hakohen, Ikkesh's brother

Tovim ben Asahel Hakohen, their father

Tovim ben Yehoseph Hakohen, their great-great-grandfather

Dan Iddo ben Uziel, a local criminal

Ketziya, a local seer popularly called the Witch of Ein-Dor

Saul, the proprietor of a brothel in Beth Tzur

Migdania, a prostitute

Chandragupta (c. 340–c.290 BCE), first emperor of united India

Bindusara (c.320–c.272 BCE), his son and successor

Asoka the Great (304–232 BCE), the son and successor of Bindusara

Devavarman (reigned from 202–195 BCE), a later Mauryan emperor

Kadmiel ben Henadad Halevi, an author

Zebuda bat Shlomo Halevi, a drummer in the Women's Drummer Corps

Shlomo ben Elnatan Halevi, her father

PROLOGUE

"Let's walk together." The Great One took Buki's arm as they set off slowly down the Street of the Lambs in the general direction of the Three Angels. They had met many times over the previous three or so years, of course, but those meetings had all taken place in private and secure settings. And always indoors. This was the first time the Great One had proposed they meet outside or suggested a walk.

Buki said nothing, preferring to wait for the Great One to get to the point.

"It is a truly beautiful day, isn't it?"

The Great One sounded as though he meant the question seriously, so Buki answered it. "Yes," he said, "I love this time of year."

The Great One squeezed his arm. "I suppose you heard about Ikkesh."

"Of course," Buki said immediately. "Everybody's heard."

The Great One took his arm more tightly. "Everybody's heard . . . what exactly *has* everyone heard?"

Buki slowed their pace. "That he died, that he had a heart attack."

"You're sure that's what happened?"

"That's what everybody is saying."

"And that makes it correct?"

Buki stopped walking entirely. "He didn't have a heart attack?"

The Great One let go of Buki's arm and looked directly into his eyes. "I don't think so," he said.

For a quick moment, Buki could almost see Ikkesh in his mind's eye—a tall, robust-looking man who always appeared to be entirely healthy. "Then what happened to him?" he asked, speaking more slowly now, more thoughtfully.

"If you can, I'd like you to find out."

"Did it have to do with . . . with, you know, with his and my—with our—with his and our *arrangement*?"

"I have no idea, Bukiyahu. But I'd like to. Wouldn't you?"

ONE

I'VE GOT A LOT of stories in me to tell, but this is the one I've been carrying around inside me for the longest time, the one that got everything started. So it makes sense to begin with this one. But where exactly *do* I begin? Like all really good stories, this one starts in lots of different places, after all. But I think the right place to begin would have to be in the steam that first night as I lay still and said nothing at all while the boys talked among themselves about poor Buki's abduction.

In its own way, the bath on the Street of the Lambs was your everyday *hammam*, although one with an exclusively levitical clientele. It hasn't been there for almost three decades now, but some readers may recall it in its heyday and some may even have been there. But even readers who haven't ever heard of the establishment will be able to conjure up the scene easily enough. The evening starts out normally enough, I suppose. Two dozen or so men—all Levites, all brethren—are lying on their bellies, their heads resting on wet rags they douse periodically with balsam scent and only some few of them scrupling to keep their buttocks covered with torn, rough red towels of the kind usually used to keep camels' saddles from chafing. The air is heavy with wet steam as the sweat and the balsam combine to create the peculiarly evocative scent of men who have earned their rest. But one man is not lying on his stomach at all: the Great One, Eli ben Heman, is lying on his back with his knees raised and slightly bent. His arms are peculiarly white for someone who spends most of his life outdoors, as are his almost hairless legs and his muscular shoulders. His beard is also white, and so is the hair on his chest and what little he's got left on the sides of his head. He may be the leader of the Levites and their undisputed spiritual and intellectual master, but he isn't concerned with false modesty and his penis, slightly swollen

3

from the wet heat, lies nestled in a thatch of white hair like a fat albino worm snoozing peacefully on a patch of dead lemon grass.

"Is there anything about Buki?" It's impossible to see through the steam to tell which of the assembled has spoken, but it's more than obvious to whom the question is being addressed.

"Not a word." A strange sort of catch in the Great One's voice, as though he were suddenly afraid of some hidden meaning he might somehow be unintentionally investing in his own words. *I really do remember this as though it were yesterday.*

"So where does that leave us?" I'm not sure if it was Romamti-Ezer who had asked the first question, but I'm positive he's the one who carried things forward.

"Nowhere."

"And we just forget about him?"

"No."

More silence. Buki—or, as his mother surely called him, Bukiyahu—had been gone for about half a week at this time. What had happened, no one then knew. Whether he had run off on his own, as some imagined, or whether he had been kidnapped, as others theorized, no one could say. The note nailed to his front door ("Gone to hell for my sins") was not in his hand. But whether those words constituted the final insult of kidnappers intent on justifying their crime to passers-by or were merely meant as a joke of the kind Buki himself would have thought hilarious was hard to decide.

To say the truth, Buki had always been a bit of an enigma. He was usually a mess. His clothes were never all that clean. He hadn't ever married. He was far too fat for his own good. He had a good sense of humor, but there was a certain vulgar edge to most of his jokes—the kind that makes you nervous, not the kind that makes you laugh in spite of yourself—and, as a result, he wasn't all that popular with at least some of the brethren. Whom he was sleeping with—if, indeed, he was sleeping steadily with any one person at all—no one knew. He spent some nights in the dormitory with the younger brethren, but only when he was too drunk to go home on his own and nobody volunteered to go along with him in case he slipped and fell.

When he wasn't bunking down with the boys, he presumably slept in his own home, an attractive stone house just past the Sheep Gate on the north side of the Temple Mount which he had inherited, if I remember correctly, from his father's parents. But no one knew that for sure. And, as a result, no one thought much of it when he disappeared one night a few days before this scene in the bath I'm describing. He had gone off duty, said he was going home to bed (or so some of the boys later recalled him saying was his intention), and then he wasn't there when Yoshbekasha came to get him in the morning and this absurd piece of sheepskin was nailed to his front door.

Joseph told me that his friends—Joseph's friends, I mean—that *his* friends just assumed that Buki had run off with some woman, probably a married one or at least one whose boyfriend would have objected to their plans had he somehow found about them in advance. I don't remember hearing that rumor myself until Joseph shared it with me—he was my brother and my closest confidant in those years—but it wasn't all that improbable. It was well known, at least in our circles, that Buki had had any number of affairs over the years and that most of them had been with entirely inappropriate women. Although none of them, at least as far as I knew, had been actual married ladies, it certainly didn't seem that Buki would have drawn the line at adultery and never crossed it. And if he had gotten himself into that kind of trouble, then it didn't seem *that* unlikely that he would have had eventually to flee for his life. Was it possible that the note on this door was of his own composition? Could the woman had written it? At that point in my life, the only woman I personally had ever met who could write was Avital—that had actually been one of the things that had attracted me to her the most strongly when we first encountered each other—but why couldn't there have been others? I hadn't heard that theory put forward, but, really, who knew? If there *was* a woman involved, that was.

Other questions were even less simple to answer. Where Buki and this alleged woman might have gone—and when or whether they were planning to return—no one seemed willing to guess even tentatively. I personally didn't really know Buki intimately enough to feel right about taking a stand one way or the other. I suppose I wished him well, wherever he was. But the possibility that he had come to harm was also in the air and it was that notion that was driving the conversation forward more than any other, less unnerving theory.

"So what *do* we do?"

"We wait."

Now it was my brother's turn to speak up. "We wait? We wait for what?"

The Great One turned onto his side to look directly at Joseph before answering. Some translucent beads of sweat trickled down his nose and dropped off one by one onto his chest. His cheeks were red and slightly swollen, leaving him looking partially like a robust man with a ruddy complexion and partially like a stout athlete on the verge of collapse. For a long moment, he stared at Joseph and said nothing. But he eventually did speak. "Buki isn't a slave," he said carefully. "You ask what we are to do as though it goes without saying that we are obliged to do *something*. But are we really? Buki can come and go as he wishes. As can I. And as can you too."

"With all due respect," Joseph continued, commanding the attention of every man in the steam merely by standing up and facing the Great One directly to speak. "With all respect, the man leaves work apparently planning as usual to be back the next day. He's never just not shown up before, so nobody thinks twice as he takes his leave. But when Yoshbekasha comes to wake him the following morning, he's gone. There's this ghastly note on his door, but everything inside is tidy. The bed is made. The *traklin* is neat. The pitchers on the washing stand are filled."

Romamti-Ezer sat up abruptly, swinging his legs down to the floor and leaning forward to speak directly to Joseph as though Joseph had been speaking to him personally. "That sounds like he wasn't abducted then. Surely kidnappers wouldn't have waited for him to make his bed and fill the jugs on his washstand!"

"Unless he was taken on his way home and never got there."

"Unless he's somewhere on the coast in some lovely guesthouse trying his best not to feel guilty about the indescribable pleasure his new girlfriend is forcing him to live through."

"Unless there is no woman."

"Unless you don't know what you're talking about if you think Buki ben Yerimoth would go off without a woman by his side. It was all he ever talked about."

"That's not true."

Romamti-Ezer looked around quickly to see if the assembled were with him or against him. "Well," he answered, looking down his long nose at my brother and smiling just condescendingly enough to make his point clearly, "maybe it isn't what he talked to *you* about . . . but it was surely what he talked about with the rest of us. Constantly."

Joseph fell silent. If I had been able to think of anything to say, I would have defended my brother. But, truth be told, even though Buki and I hadn't been all that close, all he ever did talk about to me when we spoke was women . . . and the various fantasies he had about what he would do if the strictures of the world were somehow to fall away and leave him free to fulfill whatever desire might pop into his head first at such an unimaginable moment. So maybe, I thought momentarily, maybe we were getting all excited about nothing at all. Well, not really nothing . . . but nothing we could—or should—do anything about. I felt slightly comforted. But only slightly. And then there was the possibility, remote yet plausible enough to consider at least briefly, that Romamti-Ezer was wrong. And that Joseph was right after all and that something truly terrible had happened to our slovenly friend who really did weigh far too much for his own good.

TWO

THEY FOUND HIM TWO days later in the Wadi Kerith, just east of the Jordan, about a six- or seven-hour walk from Jerusalem.

A goatherd came across him and the report of precisely what the poor man found was ricocheting around the city within an hour of his return. Some of what was being said turned out to be false, but the reality was more than horrible enough all by itself without there being any need for it to be amplified with fictitious details. Buki was found stripped down to his underbreeches, his outer clothing—every stitch of it—turned into a pile of ash in a makeshift campfire built a few yards from where the body was found for the express purpose, we all assumed, of destroying his clothing while Buki looked on and was forced to contemplate the prospect of being left alone in the desert to die. He didn't die of exposure, however.

The fact that he wasn't drenched in his own blood suggested clearly enough that he had been decapitated posthumously and probably died when the murderer's dagger was plunged first into his heart and then into his gut. (It was still there when the goatherd found him, its copper hilt barely visible between the rolls of Buki's fat as though the latter were part of a sickening *tableau vivant* depicting old King Eglon sitting dead on his emerald-studded ivory privy pot after the young Ehud ben Gera pierced the royal bowel with his left-handed dirk.) Was the decapitation meant solely as an insult? It was hard to say *what* it meant, particularly since the cut was neat and more than clean enough to have been the work of a professional slaughterer. But *that* knife, certainly not the one jammed into Buki's belly, was nowhere to be found. Nor was it only the fact that he was found decapitated that garnered all Jerusalem's rapt attention (although that surely would have been more than enough to do the trick all by itself), but the specific *way* he was found propped up against an outcropping of granite deep in the lowest section of the wadi. What the point of posing the body in that specific way was, none could say. But neither could anyone imagine that there was no meaning to the fact he had been found in a sitting position near the campfire that consumed his outer garments, looking almost as though he were just resting in the shade for a moment before continuing his journey. Had he still had his head sitting on his neck, he might have looked like a weary traveler sitting calmly in the afternoon sunlight while his freshly washed burnoose dried in the midday heat. But his head was not on his neck—it was being held by two stiff hands that had been wrapped posthumously around its sides. What *that* meant, if in fact it meant anything at all, none could say either. The goatherd's opinion—that the murderers were afraid their victim's head was going to float off to heaven to indict them of their horrible crime before God if it wasn't held tightly in place atop its (former) owner's hairless, white belly by his own stiffened hands—was widely discussed and debated. The man had run for help. What he thought such help would be able to accomplish was unclear. But, whatever he was thinking, he *did* run for help—this part I really am sure about—and only came back an hour later with a motley crew composed of whomever the goatherd could convince to come along back with him.

Buki's head was gently pried loose from his hardened hands. Later, the man who did the prying, a Jericho potter named Chakliyahu, said he knew from the first moment that the head weighed much more than it should have. As far as I know, he never did say exactly how he had come to know how much a severed human head should weigh, but even someone truly possessed of that fascinating information could not have known precisely *why* poor Buki's head weighed as much as it did. Indeed, all the witnesses— the goatherd and the potter and the others—they *all* agreed that it was only when Chakliyahu lifted the head away from its body to put it in one of the goatherd's baskets that the thread holding his jaw shut snapped and the coins began to spill out. One after another they tumbled out through Buki's stiffened lips . . . thirteen in all, all copper double-drachmas minted by the Philopator in Egypt not twenty years earlier. Not especially valuable, it's true . . . but very mysterious. Why would anyone have done such a thing? Why Egyptian coins? And why exactly thirteen? And why stuff them into a dead man's mouth and then tie shut his jaw in a way that whoever did it must have realized wouldn't keep it closed very long at all once the head was found and moved? Assassins, after all, generally take money *from* their victims, but Buki's murderer apparently chose to leave money behind.

Had the coins been Buki's? There was no obvious reason they could not have been, although it's also true that you almost never saw double-drachmas in Jerusalem in those days. Still, they *could* have been Buki's . . . but why they were left behind—and, especially, why they were left behind in such an elaborate, provocative way—that was something for which no one outside our circles appeared to have even an *un*likely explanation. We, on the other hand, knew what it was all about. Or we thought we did. I'll tell you when we get there just how wrong we were.

And then there came a second revelation hard on the heels of the first, one more transparent and far more unnerving. Once Buki's head had been gently removed, all those present could see that someone had taken a knife—possibly the same one used to cut off his head—and carved four Hebrew letters into the hairless flesh of Buki's chest: an *ayin*, two *nun*s and a *yod*. All together they spelled out *aneini*, the Hebrew for "answer me" that was a constant refrain in all our lives in those days. The word that appeared in almost every one of our hymns. The single word that served as our one-word slogan *and* our motto *and* our constant prayer. It was a word we knew all too well was used out there to deride us and our aspirations, to mock our hopes and our dreams, to label us as blaspheming fools who actually thought the all-powerful God of Israel might, at least occasionally, be prompted to say something to those who devote themselves with enough dedication to the possibility of hearing a word of divine speech.

Some of my readers will already have forgotten about all this and others won't have ever known anything of it. But you can believe me that it was that particular word that galvanized the populace against us when our version of the religion of Israel became known to the masses. And it was precisely the word that children yelled out when they pelted us with pebbles as we walked along the alleyways and lanes of old Jerusalem on our way to the Temple. It was an insult all the more insulting for being drawn from the language of prayer, a term of opprobrium all the more sharp for being one we ourselves introduced to the world. And it isn't even quite right to label it a word drawn from the language of prayer because it actually *was* a prayer all by itself. And not only *a* prayer, but *the* three-syllable prayer that was the hallmark of who we were and what we were all trying to accomplish in those days before we finally lost our edge and slowly, although certainly not inevitably, joined our enemies and became more or less exactly what they said we were destined all along to be.

It's hard to remember what it felt like to hear that that word, that that *particular* word, had been carved into Buki's soft, white skin sometime very shortly after his death. (That this too occurred posthumously seemed consonant with the amount of blood produced by the deep incisions, yet another piece of the larger puzzle discussed *ad nauseum* in our circles—and I'm sure in many others as well—in the days following the discovery of Buki's body.)

But whatever the precise order of events, the whole picture was *still* plenty gruesome enough to give us all weeks of nightmares. That we were being played occurred to no one at all, myself most definitely included

When I force myself to think back to what I knew of poor Buki before his murder, I find that the image of him lounging around in the *hammam* on the Street of the Lambs is what comes the most readily to my mind. In fact, I can still see in my mind's eye how he looked lying flat on one of the belly stones, his huge stomach and swollen breasts reddened by the steam and dripping bead after bead of silvery sweat onto the alabaster. He wasn't the fattest member of our little group—although he was surely close—but he really was huge and I remember thinking, perhaps even discussing with Avital, how it was that some fat people look swollen and burdened by their blubber, while others manage to look robust and just as hugely healthy as they are hugely huge. Buki was definitely in the second category: unashamedly obese, but nevertheless able to appear well-fed and alive rather than burdened with unwanted poundage. I remember that belly from the *hammam* . . . but I would never have believed that I'd still be thinking of it, both with and without the sacred word carved just over its enormous swell, all these decades later.

But I'm getting away from the thread of my story. The people assembled in the wadi gathered up the coins, placed Buki's head in the basket and his body on a makeshift bier some of the others quickly fashioned from some of the goatherd's spare tent cloth and brought him home. I wasn't there when Buki's mother received her son's mutilated corpse, but all Jerusalem knew what happened immediately afterwards: breaking so many rules at once that it became a kind of informal contest to list them all in ascending or descending order of badness, his mother seized the basket containing Buki's severed head and fled with it into the Courtyard of Women at the east end of the Temple complex. The HP almost had a heart attack when he heard. (For readers unfamiliar with our customs and laws, let me explain quickly that the introduction of even the most inconsequential source of impurity into the sacred precincts of our Holy Temple was, and still is, considered both a sin and a crime in our country. And the human cadaver, or part of one, is considered the most potent source of impurity of all. Except for the odd time when someone actually keeled over dead while visiting one of the Temple courtyards, I can't think of a single instance other than this one in which the Temple complex was made impure by all or part of a human corpse. I suppose it could have happened. But I've never heard of it happening other than this one time.) At any rate, the priests on duty—mostly countryside types in town for their big week of service—had no clue what to do. Even *our* people were immobilized, but more by curiosity over what would happen next than by actual inertia. It must have been some scene. And, of course, the Temple itself remained silent as it stoically endured the contamination of its sacred stoa. What choice did it have?

Part of me wishes I had been present. But the other part of me—the normal, decent part—is just as glad to have missed the whole episode. But, whether I saw it or not with my own eyes, the mental image of Shlomtziyyon bat Yakar sitting huddled in a corner of the courtyard clasping the basket containing her son's pudgy head to her chest and alternately (and loudly) cursing his murderer and bemoaning her own sorry fate is still with me. I can see her still . . . which is doubly amazing to me since, as I just said, I wasn't actually present in the Temple to see her clasping that horrible basket to her disheveled bosom at all.

THREE

THE FUNERAL WAS TERRIBLE. Under the watchful eyes of hundreds of *them*, we were permitted to conduct a formal funeral on the civic side of the double balustrade that set off Temple from municipal property. I'm not sure if every single Levite in Jerusalem was present, but surely most of us were. I was there, of course. So was Avital. And so were Zakur, Yehoram, Nathaniel and Asarela, my four sons from my first marriage. And so were a million other people.

We were huddled up against each other in the cold wintry air. I was freezing—we all were freezing—but no one was in any particular mood to hurry the proceedings along. Buki's widowed mother Shlomtziyyon and her brothers and their wives and children, plus the late Buki's sister Leah and her husband and three sons, were sitting in the front row. The grieving mother was wearing—actually, I'm not sure precisely what she was wearing, but it looked like a huge sheet of black burlap wrapped around whatever she might have had on underneath. Her nieces—her brothers' daughters—were similarly decked out in black and her nephews were wearing the dark robes of the tasteful mourner. Buki's sister's sons, on the other hand, were rather peculiarly wearing the normal kind of white outfits a thousand other boys their age were wearing that day to school all over the city. In front of them, Buki's body lay in a box. In that the dead in Jerusalem were (and are) generally buried wrapped in nothing sturdier than a winding sheet, there had been some discussion about the use of a casket in this particular instance. There had been arguments put forth for and against, but Shlomtziyyon was absolutely clear about her wishes and, in the end, no one had the nerve to start up with her. Had Buki been found with his head still attached to his body, she would have been on far shakier ground. But, of course, if Buki had just had the heart attack he was undoubtedly scheduled to have eventually rather than being hunted down, stabbed, beheaded, mutilated, stuffed with coins, and then left to await whomever found him sitting up with his head in his hands, you can be sure no one would be writing about his funeral sixty years later.

By the time of the funeral, the coins were all anyone was talking about. They were universally deemed significant . . . but what, precisely, they signified, none could say with absolute certainty. The story had more than enough bizarre details to discuss endlessly even without focusing on Buki's mouthful of drachmas. And yet it was the coins that seemed fixed in the imagination of the public as holding the key to interpreting the event of Buki's death correctly.

It was Shlomtziyyon's oldest brother, Yedutun, who spoke the eulogy (which I've just realized that I can't recall even slightly), but it fell to Assaf, the oldest of Yedutun's sons, to compose the text of the funeral dirge. He can't have been more than seventeen back then, but he did a great job, weaving together themes from our ever-evolving hymnal with the details of poor Buki's death. The poem itself became famous. Perhaps you've heard it. I'm sure you've heard it, actually. Romamti-Ezer later set the words to the tune that everybody knows, but before his work became well-known there were other, less successful, attempts. Avital herself gave it a shot soon after the funeral, but her work—and believe me, I hate having to admit how docile we all were half a century ago about things like this—her work wasn't given its fair hearing because of she made the fatal error of not submitting it to Heman's daughters for their approval first.

I know I'm getting all balled up in details inside of details, but it's hard to recreate a world, especially one that no longer exists, without going off in a dozen different directions at once. Heman was the father of the Great One, our leader Eli ben Heman, and he himself was a decent sort—bald, muscular, generally good-natured, occasionally kind. But his daughters, the Great One's sisters, collectively known as the Three Bats because of their exceptionally irritating high-pitched voices, were none of the above: not bald or muscular, of course—Keren-Hapukh was as fat as Buki, or almost as fat—but also not generally good-natured and only rarely, if ever, kind. They were the heads of the women's division—a position no one, myself included, could ever actually say how they came to occupy—and they ruled their roost with iron fists: any woman who wished to sing with the women's chorus or to submit a composition to the women's chorus for consideration had to pass through their gate and impress them with her talent. I can't say no woman ever passed muster, but I can say with absolute certainty that none ever did so without suffering needlessly in the process. Now why am

I talking about the Bats? Oh yes, because Avital, the peace of God be upon her, because Avital had forgotten to pass her version by the daughters of Heman and simply gave it to one of the choirmasters to try out at rehearsal.

Now, theoretically, there was no real reason not to do this. The Bats only controlled the women's chorus and Avital set Assaf's poem in five parts for mixed choir and male soloist (she was thinking of me, I'm sure), so she really had no reason to involve the Bats in the matter at all. (In those days, the woman's chorus was independent of the mixed choir even though most of the women singers sang in both ensembles.) The Bats, of course, didn't like that one little bit . . . and pretended as best they could not to see it that way: in their beady eyes, the fact that Avital was a woman made her involvement in the musical life of Jerusalem, or at least of the Temple, their business. And it displeased them mightily to learn that she had attempted to bypass them.

And that was why the version she wrote, lovely though it was, ended up languishing in the choirmaster's notebook while Romamti-Ezer's version—which has its own melodic charm, but lacks Avital's adventurous sense of flourish and delicate melisma—became famous. Buki's funeral, however, was the occasion on which we first heard the words sung at all . . . and neither to Romamti-Ezer's music *nor* to Avital's, but to the standard dirge mode of singing our songs that was developed in the first place to suit a funeral, an interment, or, most dramatically of all, an execution.

Assaf himself was given the honor of chanting his poem and his deep, mournful chant was beyond effective. It was neither a true *maskil* nor a formal *mikhtam*—just your standard dirge, called a *kina* by the cognoscenti, punctuated by the occasional, traditional groan that was itself some sort of cross between a sob and a low moan. Given his age and level of experience, Assaf was unexpectedly great at performing his work and I can still remember being mightily impressed by his talent.

"O God," Assaf began, "I seek You, I long for You, I yearn for You . . . in a land parched and thirsty, in a place of no water."

The crowd murmured its approval. We had all been on hikes in the Wadi Kerith because all of us had, at one time or another, wanted to see the place where the ravens brought bread and meat to Elijah as he hid from King Ahab. Elijah was one of our true heroes—we talked about him all the time—and some of us had been out to the wadi dozens of times. We knew its parched ground and its waterless riverbed . . . and Assaf's reference to the soul that yearns for God in the manner of parched land yearning for rain was lost on no one.

Assaf, encouraged by the crowd's rapt attention, waded deeper into his poem. "For although I have seen You—both Your ineffable might and Your indescribable glory—in the sanctuary, because I have had these incredible experiences of Your goodness in my life, let my lips sing Your praise." Assaf, later admired as one of the supreme masters of this kind of writing, was in rare form that morning as he sang clearly about Buki by singing formally about himself. But the larger impact of his words had little to do with his literary art or musical talent and everything to do with the real subject of his poem. Buki had never become a real leader . . . but he was one of us and his fate was taken by us all as a crystal-clear warning. I realize I haven't really explained yet what this was all about . . . but just remembering young Assaf's dirge for his dead cousin—or, rather, remembering that terrible, cold morning when I heard it sung aloud for the very first time—somehow *remembering* that morning is bringing me back to my own first years in Jerusalem before I myself understood fully what this whole levitical thing was really all about. And those memories include Buki because he was one of the very first people I met in Jerusalem when I first got here and he was simply too goodhearted not to be kind to a newcomer he thought he might be able to help out. I remember him fondly for that. And I miss him still, even after all these many years!

FOUR

I CAME TO JERUSALEM almost seventy years ago—sixty-nine, to be exact—but my point isn't how much time has passed since then, but how hard it is to fathom the extent to which the world has changed in *just* sixty-nine or seventy years. Of my three Jerusalems—Egyptian Jerusalem until Ptolemy Epiphanes lost it once and for all to Antiochus the Slightly Great, Syrian Jerusalem until the other Epiphanes—Antiochus IV Epiphanes, master of Syrian Asia and perennial patron of lost causes, including his own—lost it to Judah M., and Jewish Jerusalem as we know it now and as it will, I hope, always be. Who knows? Maybe we will endure as our own people in our own place. Probably not, I suppose. (In my opinion. Rome only hasn't gotten to us *yet*. I know there are plenty of people out there who think otherwise, who feel we have a fighting chance. I wish them well. It won't matter to me once I'm gone from this world of dust and mud, but if I were fifty years younger, I'd be taking Latin lessons just to be on the safe side.)

When I came to Jerusalem, it was still an Egyptian backwater. Mostly, we were ignored. Other than the occasional tax collector or the odd prefect who showed up from time to time, no one ever came here from Memphis. Once in a rare while some matter of foreign policy required the Assembly to put its meaningless stamp of approval on one or another Ptolemaic initiative . . . but, for the most part, we were left alone to do as we pleased in our own place. Maybe that was the key to our success—in their hearts, *all* the Ptolemies thought of us as the aborigines here, as a nation living out its history on its own land. But that's not how they thought of themselves, which was as interlopers *pretending* to be Pharaohs, *pretending* to look natural in their phony pschents and psedjets, *pretending* that they didn't look ridiculous making believe they were the legitimate rulers of a land their own ancestors had seized when Alexander died not because they had some specific right to it or reason to think they did, but merely because they could. They paraded around decked out in as much old Egyptian finery as they could muster— but, in the end, they *all* knew that they didn't belong and that the real Egyptians thought they were clowns indulging in an elaborate dress-up party at which they were present solely because they had invited themselves. Us, on the other hand, they had zero interest in imitating and mostly left be other than when taxes were due.

I came to Jerusalem two years before Paneas, which is to say two years before our happy Egyptian backwater became the newest bauble in the archipelago of formerly Egyptian towns and cities won by Antiochus and made to serve as the southwestern outpost of his newly expanded empire. (That's the father of the Antiochus who later on—and, as it turned out, so ill-advisedly—started up with our people just when the Maccabees were itching for a fight.) Like most immensely powerful rulers, he was good at some things and only fair at others. But we welcomed him—we weren't so completely crazy not to know where our own interests lay—and figured we'd find out later on how to exploit the situation to our own greatest advantage.

At first, the change of regime didn't seem to make much difference. Everybody still left us alone. The tax collectors still spoke Greek, only they brought their money sacks to Antioch instead of Memphis. The bored officials sentenced to terms of office in our midst now dreamt of returning to their estates to the north instead of to the south. The coins that circulated had a different face on them and the face had a different name under it. Everything changed and nothing changed. Everything was about to change, but what did we know? When you ride on a donkey, you can see what's coming easily enough but you have to make an effort to turn and look at where you've been. But in life it's just the opposite: you can only see clearly where you've been, never where you're going. And we had no idea where things were on their way to going . . . only the idiot's pleasure of looking back and, finding the past to have been mostly peaceful and calm, imagining that we were looking into the future as well.

As I said, I came to Jerusalem two years before Paneas. Joseph had already been living in Jerusalem for a year or two. I remember those early days fondly. Avital was living in Jerusalem then too, although I was still married to Deborah in those early days. We were happy then, more or less, and ready to embark on the great adventure of life together. I was twenty-five years old—the very best age for a man to be, the one that effortlessly combines the choicest parts of adolescence and adulthood with neither the strictures of the former nor any of the real responsibilities of the latter.

Buki, even though he was a few years younger than me, was already present. I can still remember the first time I came across him, in fact. (It was, oddly enough, in that same bathhouse on the Street of the Lambs in which I would find myself thirteen years later listening to the guys discussing his disappearance and not quite knowing what to make of it all.) Well, maybe I can't recall *every* word we said. But it seems like seventy weeks ago, not seventy years.

Deborah and I found an apartment easily in those uncrowded, unhurried days. I can still remember the leisurely pace at which we unpacked our things and settled into our new digs. Joseph and Yemima were nearby. Yemima was pregnant. Things were going well. On one of our first nights in town, Joseph took me for a scrub-down on the Street of the Lambs. It was already a fine establishment, even back then. There was plenty of very hot water. The steam was clean. The cold pool was crystal clear. I hadn't ever seen a pool as well kept, actually . . . especially not one used by so many people. (There was apparently some sort of drainage system in place that kept the water moving through the pools and almost totally free of impurities.) The *mikveh* was separate . . . and dramatically less clean. I tried to avoid using it whenever possible—as did, I think, most people. But the rest of the place was first-rate. The marble pillars, the stone floors, the hot steam, the cool water . . . all of it came together in my mind to create an atmosphere of luxury and intimacy unparalleled in my limited experience. It's been closed for decades now, but there's a new place I go to bathe almost daily even though I can only take the steam for a few minutes these days before I start to wheeze. Are you hoping to grow old one day, dear readers? I suppose you probably are, but you can take it from me that you won't much like it when you get here.

That first night stays with me still. Buki was already huge, although not as immense as he ended up being by the time he died. His buddy Shaphan was with him—they were *always* together in those days—and the two of them were holding court, as they usually did, in the caldarium. It was the first time I had experienced anything like the kind of arch banter and clever repartee that came naturally to them both as they covered a million topics at once, passing effortlessly (or so it seemed) from Antiochan politics to municipal ones, from the latest in Greek foreign policy initiatives to the most recent developments in the court of the Ptolemies. They seemed to know everything and, even more impressively, to have an opinion about everything. That they were holding forth in a steam bath to listeners whose undivided attention they were able to command fully and absolutely made a deep impression on me. If other people resented their commanding presence in the room, I surely wasn't among them.

From Joseph, I knew that both Buki and Shaphan ben Gamliel were players. You know, it must seem now that we were all in on everything back then, that it was an "us" against "them" situation in which the very least you could be expected to know was who was on your side. The truth is that it really *was* an "us versus them" situation, but it didn't quite feel that way to those of us actually experiencing the situation all those years ago. I mean . . . we knew who we were. And we knew who the opposition was. But we still had hopes that they would see reason. That we'd form some sort of sacred alliance. That our different ships would somehow find haven in the same harbor and that we would live in peace. One of Romamti-Ezer's first songs was all about that notion, about us all dwelling together as brethren in good and pleasant fellowship. It was a short hymn, but it had a catchy tune and it caught on immediately. They still sing it now and then on the steps when the Great One is about to ask some favor and a reconciliatory mood needs to be established. It even works sometimes—although most often not—but we try it anyway, mostly as a boozy sort of round that implies by its very booziness the kind of uninhibited *camaraderie* that could prevail between the thems and the us's if the will to make it so were but there. It never happened—and I think I even knew back then that it wasn't ever *going* to happen—but it was a nice dream, a kind of a prayer made slightly less absurd by a little internal rhyme and some superimposed rhythm. But only slightly so, to say the truth. Really only very slightly so indeed!

FIVE

I MOVED FORWARD IN my studies at the normal pace. I was taught, retaught, instructed, re-instructed, tested and tested again. According to the curriculum then in place, I had to take classes in everything—choral singing (obviously), but also conducting and composition. I took lessons on the *sheminit*, a kind of eight-string lute that I doubt seriously anyone's played in public in half a century, and on the *gittit*, our own version of the twelve-string guitar. I took the Great One's famous course in the ins and outs of priestly worship—it would hardly do to have a Levite gawking at the priests as they dig the entrails out of an ox as though he didn't know the first thing about the laws of sacred butchery—and found myself enjoying it more than I would ever have imagined I would or could. (The Great One was actually capable of being very funny when he was in the mood and something about eviscerated oxen seems to have brought it right out of him.) I sat through the courses in meter and rhyme, as well as the ones in ancient and modern poetry and in martial arts (in case any vandals actually did ever show up with the intention of plundering the Temple treasury). I even sat through six months of lectures on the priests' *torah* and tried to get all their beliefs and opinions organized in my head. It was a daunting six months, but I managed—and I do have to say that being paid out of public money to go to school pleased me enormously. Deborah became pregnant shortly after Joseph and Yemima's first son was born, and that too made our first months in Jerusalem exciting and fun.

From Joseph, I learned that there were secrets. I didn't know what they were exactly, but I became aware, slowly at first and then with ever strengthening conviction, that they existed. Joseph himself gave me a few broad hints, smiling at certain things I would say or making cryptic comments to himself, comments that I could not explain but which seemed to point to a body of information to which he himself had already been admitted and to which he was endeavoring to gain entrée for me as well. I began to piece things together slightly, but I have to admit that I didn't really get it until I was formally told what it was everybody was always talking *around* without ever actually spelling out. I wasn't entirely wrong . . . only far too little daring in my thinking to have conceived even theoretically of the big picture as it actually did exist.

You have to remember this was *before* Paneas, *before* the Maccabees, *before* the whole Hellenistic circus opened to the paying public. I mean, of course we had *heard* about what was going on in the world. Occasionally someone went abroad and came back with stories about *gymnasia* and theaters and we were familiar—vaguely—with some of the big names that came back to haunt us with such a vengeance just a few years later, and not *just* Aeschylus, Euripides, Sophocles, Homer, and Aristotle, but the less bright lights as well. I guess the best way to express how things were would be to say that we were pre-hellenized, slightly like plump hens plucked clean and rubbed down with lime juice but not actually roasting on the spit just quite yet. Mind you, we didn't *feel* like chickens waiting for the skewer. The whole thing was interesting, intriguing, perhaps even slightly tantalizing—I know I wouldn't have hesitated for a minute before going to see a real tragedy or to attend some traditional Greek games or even maybe to participate in them—but it was also very far away, very much what was fashionable with other people in other places. That it would come to us seemed unlikely. The Ptolemies, after all, were no less overtly hellenized than the Seleucids, just less pushy about it. They had their gymnasia and their theaters, their tragedies and their comedies and their gods. They got together just like the Selx to watch naked guys twirling around and throwing plates as far as they could. They revered Homer without actually reading too much of his stuff. They drank *kykeon* by the gallons, pretending to enjoy it. But, truth be told, I think the PTs were always more deeply into the Egyptian thing than the Greek thing. The latter, they did, but without their hearts really being in it . . . and my guess is that they *all* turned to Memphis, not Athens, to say their prayers when they were sure no one was looking, or a lot of them did. And then there was the whole sex thing to boot . . . and, believe me, the PTs were *way* more Egyptian than Greek in that department too. But I'm getting off track again, this time probably fortunately.

At any rate, those first years in Jerusalem were good ones. I was semi-happily married to Deborah. (Is that what I mean? We got along best of all in the bedroom, followed by the *traklin*, followed by any venue in which we couldn't occupy our mouths with kissing or eating.) At any rate, she became pregnant three times in four years and I *was* wholly happy about that, even if the twins did—in the end, fortuitously—put an end to our plans to have a huge family. Joseph and Yemima were down the block and Yemima was often pregnant too in those days. (Their oldest, Ethan, is just five months older than Zakur.) I was being paid to go to school. I was living in the best place, doing the best thing. As noted above, I was the best age. I was lanky in those days, but—if I can say so after so many years—I was handsome. My stomach was flat. My eyesight was *excellent*. My hair was long and thick and the color of ripe chestnuts. My cheeks were always ruddy and if my legs weren't quite pillars of marble set upon sockets of fine gold, then they were certainly good enough to arouse at least some envy among the bald pot-bellies on the Street of the Lambs, none of whom, or almost none of whom, was above taking a good look—and, at least for some, a good *long* look at that—when Joseph and I would retire there for a good soak after school (for me) or work (for him) and wander around as though we were both so totally suffused with boyish insouciance so as to be utterly unaware of how good we both looked with our clothes off.

I suppose it must have been quite early on that I figured out that something was going on. I wasn't the sharpest *kashil* in the shed, I guess . . . but it didn't take a Ben Sira to seize the fact that there were all sorts of things going on just beneath the calm, placid surface of the lake in which we were all being trained to swim. A word here, a gesture there, a note furtively—but not quite furtively enough—passed from one brother to another in the shadows inside the Temple courtyard. Some of the gestures were just that—vague, veiled allusions to something even more veiled, even more well-hidden. But others were less obscure, particularly after you had already pieced together some parts of the puzzle. It's actually hard for me to remember when precisely I became aware of the larger picture, but become aware I certainly did. And my great step over the threshold between being aware and being fully in that picture came just about on the first anniversary of our arrival in town.

Zakur was about a year old. Deborah was pregnant with Yehoram, although she can't have been more than two or three months along. Paneas was less than a year off—only three or four months, actually—but who knew? For us, the PTs were *always* off somewhere fighting someone over some perceived slight or some disputed territory. (Readers to whom this is all ancient history will possibly not remember just how incredibly touchy those Ptolemies were in general. And Five, which is how everybody in Jerusalem called His Hellene Pharaonic Majesty, Ptolemy V Epiphanes, Ruler of Both Egypts and Firstborn Son of Ra—Five was the absolute touchiest of them all. Whether it's actually true that he once had the Cyrenian ambassador beheaded for farting in his wife's presence, I don't know. But we certainly all believed it. Maybe he was especially touchy because she was also his sister. Or was it his mother? Who can remember? And, speaking honestly, does it really matter?)

At any rate, Five never came to Jerusalem. Except when he came to lose at Paneas, I don't believe he ever even came here at all. He sent along his tax collectors, of course. And prefects and officials of various shapes and sizes. And maids for those people's wives and teachers for their children . . . but he himself displayed no specific interest in us. Of course, in retrospect the far more important detail was that, for all Five seemed only intermittently aware of our presence in his empire, Three (a.k.a. His Hellene Seleucid Majesty, Antiochus III the Great) was *extremely* aware of us. Mind you, the two of them were destined to duke it out one day or the next even if they didn't end up squabbling to the death over the Holy Land. Ever since Five's dad kicked Three's butt at Raphia (and that was a good fifteen years before I came to Jerusalem myself or had even heard about most of this), it was completely obvious that the day would come when Three would get his revenge on the PTs . . . or try to. And then that day came too.

Anyway, the basic story is almost simple: when Egyptian Five's father finally died, Syrian Three was good to go and immediately entered into an alliance with Phillip of Macedon (another self-righteous prig wholly unworthy of wearing the mantle of Alexander), the basic idea being they take Egypt, get Five's head on a pike before he had the time to realize what was happening, and divide the country up between them. It was a good plan and it probably would have worked if Three hadn't gotten attacked by the good king of Pergamon from the north when he was pushing his armies south, which gave Five a chance to seize back some of the land he had lost. Or rather to send in a general to do the deed for him (if he could). The general's name was Scopas, and he actually did do a pretty good job of it. That, however, is not the point . . . which is that Scopas' victories are what finally got Three's attention and prompted him to come down and whup the whole PT invasion force at Paneas and *that*, dear readers, is how we ended up part of the pseudo-Greek empire ruled by pseudo-Greek kings from their hideously ugly pseudo-Greek capital in Syria instead of the pseudo-Egyptian empire ruled by pseudo-Egyptian Pharaoh wannabees from their hideously ugly pseudo-Egyptian capital along the Nile.

And although that really is how the PTs lost control of Judah, what I really want to talk is what about happened in the couple of months before we saw any trouble brewing at all. I know that must sound funny to say, at least in retrospect. But you can believe me that we were busy in old Jerusalem plotting to do *each other* harm in far too involved and involving ways to pay attention to the fact that the largest armies in the world were gathering on either side of our tiny patch and planning to fight to the death over controlling it. And so, as we wallowed in our blissful ignorance, we really did have enough time to spend plotting against each other and trying to find more and more ways to weaken our people precisely when the nation's unity was about to be more crucially needed than ever before.

But let's go back to those months during which our story really begins. Deborah is pregnant. Zakur is a baby, as is his cousin Ethan. Joseph and Yemima are down the block. I'm in class most of the day. I'm doing my best to pass every course they're making me take and slowly things are becoming clear, or at least clearer, to me. The storm clouds are gathering on two horizons, but what did I know or care about that? I had coursework to contend with, all sorts of people to try to get in good with, a baby to play with, an attractive (if slightly crazy) woman to sleep with, and only the vaguest intimation of what I was getting myself mixed up in. The latter situation resolved itself, actually, almost without me having to do much at all. And that brings me (almost) to the incident that helped me over that particular hedge . . . and left me finally, if a tad suddenly, aware of what this game I was training myself to play was really all about. And also why it really did matter who won.

SIX

As far as I can recollect, the incident—this threshold incident I want to describe—began the third or fourth night that I was on real duty. In those days, Levites were basically Temple slaves. Well, not *really* slaves, but, if you ask me, as good as slaves. The whole initiation horror said it all. Can you imagine a grown man—can you imagine me, even divested of the dignity extreme old age has possibly conferred on me—can you imagine *me* being stripped naked in front of all of them (or rather, in front of as many of them as were interested in watching, which was usually more or less all of them) and having every single hair shaved off my body while my clothing was laundered to make sure it didn't contaminate any of them with anything that might affect the pristine purity deemed solely, or at least principally, to pertain within their priestly precincts? Anyway, that was my first day. So imagine me standing there in the breeze totally in the altogether having the hair shaved off my chest, off my legs, off—am I making myself clear enough?—off every damn place it grew while some priestly launderer guy washed my outfit to get the levitical nastiness out—and that wasn't the worst part. Not by a long shot.

So there you are naked and shorn of whatever hair you had and that's when they bring the oxen in. And the non-priests designated to represent The People. And then we get to the really weird part. The people—and this part still gives me the willies even after all these decades of trying to forget about it—the people come forward and lay their greasy hands on your head as though you were an ox about to be slaughtered—and, of course, that really is the whole point, that you *are* a sacrificial animal about to sign over your freedom to them against the slight benefit of not *really* being an ox that's about to have its neck cut and its eviscerated carcass burnt to a crisp on the

25

huge altar casting its long shadow on the proceedings at hand. For a long minute, you actually have this feeling that the whole thing might be some elaborate ruse and that you actually are going to be sacrificed. And then, just as you're wondering if you should be getting worried for real, that's when they bring the two real oxen in and you are led over to them—they're as naked as you are, but they don't seem to care as much—anyway, they bring you over to the oxen and now you lay your hands on their heads and then you have to confess your sins aloud. That's a nice touch too, if you ask me: they are the ones demeaning you, degrading you, and basically taking you into their service whether you like it or not . . . and you are the one who has to say out loud what an iniquitous lout you are and how you sin all the time and ignore God's laws (as conveniently codified for your regular inspection in their book) all the time. So then you finish—there's a script you can read in case you're too flummoxed to remember what to say on your own—so you finally finish and that's when the priests themselves come in and they stand behind you—one of them behind each initiate—and they sort of give you this horrible bear hug from the back so you can hardly breathe and they start swaying you back and forth like you were a huge (naked, hairless) puppet and that's when they say the words you remember your whole life: *tenufa, tenufa, tenufa*. And the worst part—the most galling part—is that they're right: you aren't an ox, but you're a *tenufa* forever now, an offering, a sacrificial man supposed always and for evermore to be thrilled not to have been slaughtered like one of those poor dumb oxen.

I remember my ceremony vividly. The man standing behind me was this really short bald guy. So he's doing his best given his height, but his arms are around my belly, not my chest—honestly, the guy was maybe three and a quarter cubits tall and he's actually straining to get his arms as high up as my stomach—anyway, he has his arms around my naked belly and he's standing on tippy-toes to get his mouth as close to my ear as it's going to get unless he actually finds a stepladder somewhere and that's when he whispers these horrible words that have stayed with me ever since: a pun of sorts, I guess, but a trenchant, scary, slightly vulgar one that I haven't ever forgotten. And what does he have the *chutzpah* to whisper in my ear as the others are chanting *tenufa, tenufa, tenufa*? I'll tell you what he whispers—he whispers *lo tinaf* right into my ear. The seventh commandment of the Big Ten. Thou Shalt Not Commit Adultery. Translation: You're ours now. You belong to us like any wife belongs to her husband except that divorce is not an option, that there actually *is* no such thing as divorce for a union as permanent and intimate as our own. Just the message anyone would want on the day of his initiation into the service of God's holy Temple! I can still feel his hot breath on my neck (he was really nowhere near my ear) and the implication of those two words still goes through me like a warm knife through *cheilev* every time I think of them.

But I'm not done just quite yet, because that wasn't all there was to the ceremony. So there I was with these stunningly horrible words still ringing in my ears when we have a slight deviation from the script. The ox—there were two oxen, but I'm referring to the one designated for totally immolation on the altar as the *olah* sacrifice—the *olah* ox drops a huge load on the floor just as we're laying our hands on it. And with that, that place goes nuts. The ox is designated for total immolation—it's going to be barbecued wholly as part of the ceremony—so you'd think they'd just clean up the mess and move forward. But the rules say that the aforementioned mess lying on the cool marble tiles was part of the ox when it was designated *totally* for sacrifice. So I—there were four of us that day—so we're all standing there without even a hair on our chest to grant us some dignity while everything stops and every single molecule of sacred manure is swept up and brought lovingly to the altar. I loved that. I *still* love it. I love it so much I'm writing about it here, aren't I? It's in their Big Book too, if you want to check—the whole thing is outlined in detail there so that our shame need not die out with us, so that future generations can have a good laugh at our expense. Well, why not? I'd laugh too if it hadn't been me. And that's the truth. I was a married man of twenty-five at the time, the perfect age to be stripped naked, shaved, and told you're actually (and permanently and irrevocably) married to your work. And there's basically no way out. And that when you're standing in the Temple courtyard freezing and completely naked next to a pile of ox apples, you're *second* on the list of things that requires the attention of your new masters.

So that was when I was twenty-five, four years before Paneas. And now it's a year later. I'm twenty-six, my hair's grown back (and don't ask how itchy *that* all was), and my dignity is somewhat restored. I'm still in class all day, but they're shorthanded—they're always shorthanded—anyway, they really are down a few guys at night and they need some of us to join the team. Basically (and in addition to everything else,) we were the night watchmen, the *shomrim laboker*, the security force. It's not hard work. It doesn't really require any training at all, just walking around and checking on things. We manned twenty-one different guard posts and each nighttime guard was assigned to one of them and was expected to circle back to that place repeatedly in the course of his hours on duty. It's true that the priests also theoretically served as guards. They had their own posts too, different ones from ours too although just three of them. We saw them occasionally wandering around, but, semi-amazingly, never when we needed the place to ourselves. Now I know why that was. But back then I thought what we all thought—that the lazier priests made a show of being on guard and then just went off to bed once they figured things were quiet for the night and no one would know if they were or weren't present.

So some of them knew. How can they not have? What they were told, I have no idea. Was it all about money? It could have been! Or maybe not . . . it's impossible even to guess after all this time. And how it can have been that no one *not* on duty ever came across us in the courtyard I *also* don't have any idea. Okay, it's true the older priests had their own homes off the hill and some of the richer, less old ones did too. But the younger guys *all* slept in the Hearth House dormitory within the Temple complex and all it would have taken would have been for one of them to get up, go out one night late for some fresh air and take a good look at what was going on. But that *never* happened. Or at least that's what we all wanted to think. Still, who can really say? They did have a ramp within the dormitory going down to their own personal toilet, the one reputed to be the only one in the entire city with doors on the stalls. (I had and have no idea if that was really true.) So they didn't have to go outside to take a leak and it's also true that there weren't any windows facing the courtyard. I also know for a fact they used to lock themselves in at night. As noted, I eventually found out how the whole system actually worked. But whether there were some among them who were sympathetic to our work or if this really was just about money—to that question I never really did find a fully satisfying answer.

Anyway, it was about a year after my initiation ceremony. My body hair had grown back. I was taking classes in the daytime and, at least occasionally, helping out at night. Nothing heavy, just standing guard and checking the gates and the doorways into the various chambers built into the wall around the courtyards. (For readers who haven't been to Jerusalem, the Temple consists of three adjacent courtyards lined up from west to east. The westernmost one sees most of the action. That's where the building is that houses the Holy of Holies, the inmost sanctum. That's where the great bronze altar is and that's where the animals get slaughtered. It's not far from where the choir—*our* choir—sings when we're not on the steps going down into the Women's Courtyard facing out at the people and trying to drown out all that lowing and mooing and bleating and cawing and tweeting and cooing going on just behind our backs. Anyway, all these courtyards were surrounded by a very thick wall and there were chambers of various sorts built into the walls—one for the priests' outfits and one where the priests disqualified for service by physical blemish—and there were a full one hundred and forty different categories of bodily defect that rendered a priest disqualified—where the temporarily or permanently disqualified used to spend their time looking for termites or woodworms in the logs used as kindling atop the great altar, one for the incense makers and one for the bakers, one for the younger priests to bunk down in and one for the Great Assembly to meet in . . . and a dozen others I won't bother listing here. Anyway, so there were all these chambers and each one had a door—some had two—but each one had at least one and we had to make sure they were locked, that no one was hiding in the ones that were supposed to be vacant, that everything was clean and in order for the next morning.) Anyway, that was the job. We patrolled in groups of three and there were generally somewhere between seven and ten groups walking around at any given moment making sure things were calm and secure. As I said, we had twenty-one specific guard posts and each one was manned by one or several of our people every day and every night of the year.

So there I am. I'm not really finished with all my post-initiation training, but, really, how much training do you need to check some doors and make sure no dastardly lamb thieves are at work pilfering tomorrow's daily offering? I do it one night, two nights, three nights . . . and then, on the fourth night, I get a glimpse of something marvelous. It's like a door has just opened and I'm seeing something behind it that I hadn't even thought to wonder if I'd ever see, something that I hadn't known about at all.

So I'm patrolling. It's winter. It's cold. I'm stamping my feet on the ground and hoping my toes don't freeze off in this unbelievable weather we were having that year when two men, two of our guys, suddenly appear in our path. I think we were—I *know* we were—standing in our traditional group of three just in front of the Chamber of Hewn Stone where the Great Assembly guys meet when suddenly, unexpectedly, these two appear in front of us and one of them walks right up to me and says that he's come to replace me. I ask why I need to be replaced, which is a reasonable question because I'm not sleepy and I'm not even really tired and, even if I had been, I'm still the one who signed on to patrol that evening. His answer, that I need to be replaced because he's come to replace me, makes no real sense at all. And then the other guy takes my hand in his and we start walking away from the others. We are clearly going somewhere, but I have no real idea where. I understand that something's afoot. And I also understand something else, and for the very first time: that I'm *already* involved.

SEVEN

AND OFF WE GO, the other guy—the one who hadn't come to replace me—leading and myself being led.

In the shadows, I can see about eight other guys trying hard not to be noticed. Or not to be noticeable, I should say. They're tucked into the northeastern corner of the Priests' Court, just behind the rows of post-and-ring things they use to hold the oxen in place when they're cutting their throats and, really, I myself have to say they're doing an *excellent* job. I had patrolled through there twice that evening and hadn't seen a thing. Maybe they really *weren't* there earlier on . . . but I somehow sense they were and that I just didn't notice them. And that the fact that I can see them now means that I'm being admitted into something exceptional. I just don't have any idea what it is. Yet.

I approach and make a quite count. Eight was right. My escort and I make ten. I don't see anyone I know at first, but then I do see someone . . . and it's Joseph. I'm getting some clear vibes to leave him be, but it's also obvious I didn't recognize him at first. Without knowing what I'm doing—or why I'm doing it—I stand back. He is chatting with some guy I can't quite make out in the dark and trying hard not to notice me. But I know he has. And so I pass my initiation without even knowing it: a man shall not recognize his own brother. The prerequisite, or rather, one of three possible ways in. Someone actually mutters those exact Hebrew words out loud—the ones for "he shall not recognize his own brother"—and they hang for the briefest moment on the frigid air of a Jerusalem winter's night as, for the very first time, it begins to dawns on me that I don't really have any clear idea what this is all about or what I've gotten myself into. Or what exactly Joseph has been holding back from me. Or why, now that I think of it for the very first time, the Torah—their *torah*, not ours—actually *does,* and in so many words, say that the mark of the true Levite, the one truly devoted to keeping God's word and keeping God's covenant, is his (I hope momentary) inability to recognize his own brother *or* to see his own parents *or* to know his own child. I had passed the test. But what it was all *really* about, I as yet had no clear idea.

The ritual continued. Let me describe it all to you in detail. Or at least let me relate the part I *can* tell, the part I feel reasonable about revealing. I'm standing in the courtyard. It's midnight . . . and it's cold. But I am so enthralled that I barely notice how late it is, or how chilly. As I watch on, they first blow the horn silently. I see the *shofar.* I see a man—my brother's best friend, Joel ben Izri, whom I recognize immediately—I see Joel pick up the instrument, put it to his lips and blow as hard as he can. I hear nothing. There is, in fact, no sound coming out of the horn. He's blowing into one end of the thing like his life depends on it . . . but how he's keeping any sound at all from coming out the other end, I can't imagine. But he's serious about it, that much is obvious. I can hear the faint whistle of his breath. Even more faintly, I can hear the buzz of his lips vibrating against the horn. But sound out of the other end comes there none. The sound of silence. The thin, small voice. The sound that is no sound meant to invite the presence of a God who exists and cannot exist, who is and who cannot be, whose very reality is predicated on being so totally other than the world that even thinking about divine existence should bring either apostasy, insanity, or blasphemy in its ruminative wake. As well it does. For most. Or at least for some. But not for all.

So that's the second step. I didn't recognize my brother and now I've heard the soundless blast. Third step: I see another Levite—a big man, not Buki-size but huge enough—I see this *large* man comes in carrying this . . . what do I call it? A cauldron makes it sound too big. An urn, too fancy. Maybe it was most like a clay chamber pot of some sort, not that it was a *real* chamber pot, but it was that size and shape . . . made on some potter's wheel, no doubt, but otherwise indistinguishable from a thousand other clay pots used every night of the year in every house and dormitory in the city *other* than the Hearth House with its fancy underground privy. So, anyway, the huge guy carries this thing in on his shoulder and Joseph—I can see this like it was yesterday—Joseph takes it from his shoulder, saying "I take this burden from your shoulder" loudly enough for all to hear, words everybody nowadays knows by heart but which were at that moment totally unfamil-iar to me. And the rest respond, quietly but unmistakably, in the name of God: "You have called out in time of trouble / I shall answer you with secret thunder." I find myself so engaged that I realize I'm actually listening for the thunder, but, of course, all I hear is the wind howling through the courtyard. And so concludes the third step. We're almost there. But, of course, I wouldn't have known that then.

Finally, the fourth part. Done silently and without explanation or commentary. Without any words at all, actually. The pot on the ground, this humble clay pot that really does look like it was created for people to fill when it's too cold to leave their warm beds during a frigid Jerusalem night, *that* pot sits on the ground now and all the assembled, myself somehow included, bend down to place our hands on it. I remember that horrible man placing his hands on my head when I was initiated into the service of God in the first place, but I displace that unsettling recollection by wondering if anybody else is having the same association. Whatever . . . we form a circle around the pot and bend over to touch its rough upper lip and then, as though responding to some unheard command, we all take our hands away at the very same moment. The pot disappears into the shadows. We turn slowly to face the door into the anteroom that leads into the *devir* that leads into the Holy of Holies . . . and that's when I realize just how hot the fire we're playing with actually is.

I can't tell you what happens next. I want to. I even think I probably *should* tell you. But I can't. And I won't, even if that means that this bit of our collective past dies with the last of us who personally experienced it. But let me just say that it worked. We heard the silent blast of the shofar. We saw the shoulder unburdened. We took our hands off the pot. We turned . . . and we began to recite the prayer over and over. I can still hear the opening cadence, which consisted solely of words I knew by heart, but which I had never really considered as possibly constituting a serious request something specific actually happen. Was it possible, it suddenly struck me to wonder, that the One Who Rides the Cherubs might actually deign to self-manifest in the actual presence of people like ourselves who spent their *lives* praying for that specific thing actually to happen? I wouldn't have known then even what that *could* mean, let along what it actually *did* mean. But, I'll tell you this much: I saw the light. Not like in the way people say they saw the light when they finally get something they had previously not understood. I mean I *really* saw the light. Am I the only person of that whole generation left alive who can say that? I wonder—I've outlived all of my friends from that part of my life by a decade now, even my poor brother. Yemima, his widow, is still alive—she's eighty-seven, although almost totally detached from her moorings and more or less utterly unaware of the world—but, of course, *she* never saw the light. Our kids did, of course . . . for as long as the whole enterprise continued. But of the people from back then that I became close to, I think there's a reasonable chance that there's just me left to tell the tale.

They say most people don't get anywhere at all their first time out, but I surely did. It was faint, that's for sure. But it was fully real—and I can say that absolutely and without the slightest hesitation. The frigid wind, the peculiar odor of the Priests' Court (some sort of residual combination of incense, manure, barbecued meat, baked bread, and human sweat), the sudden realization that we were *guarding* the Temple for them at the same time we were *seizing* it for ourselves . . . all of it together *plus* the sudden, undeniable perception that things were not even slightly as they seemed during the daylight hours, it *all* came together to create an ambience that can hardly be transmitted in words to anyone who never actually experienced it personally. I'm doing my best. But I'm not even coming close.

Yoshev hakeruvim hofia, the song goes: Appear, Thou Who art enthroned upon the cherubs. And suddenly the rest began to make sense to me. *Lekha lishuata lanu*. Come to save us! *Ha'eir panekha venivasheia*. Illuminate Thy face that we be saved. *Tehi yadkha al ish yeminekha*. Press down Thy great hand on your most devoted servant. *Hashiveinu*. Bring us close to Thee. *Hashiveinu*. Bring us near to Thee. *Hashiveinu*. Bring us back into Thy presence. The same hymn, over and over and over. How many times? I have no idea. A hundred. Two hundred. *Ha'eir panekha* over and over. Shine forth the *light*. Shine forth *Thy* light. Shine Thy light over *us*. On us. To us. At us. Save us. By the time we were done, I think we must have recited the song at least a couple of hundred times. Maybe more—I know for sure that I lost count at a certain moment. Save all of us. Save *some* of us. Save *any* of us. Some of the rest of the details, I'll keep to myself, but you already know enough to sense how it worked. The same hymn over and over. The loneliness of the courtyard. The occasionally bleat from the Chamber of the Lambs over by the Hearth House. The lingering odor of burnt meat and manure. The sense of danger and the intense excitement combining to create a clear sense that this, at least ultimately, was the whole point . . . that it only appeared that *we* were *their* servants, but that the reverse was actually the case: that *they* served *us*, that their elaborate ritual existed to maintain public support for an institution that really existed for us . . . and possibly even because of us.

Was it all some sort of mass delusion? I can't say, but I know what I felt and I know what I saw. And I saw the light. At first, only a slight glimmer, but then, as I began to mutter the prayer on my own, independently of the others—although they were all doing it too, of course—as I began to feel myself shifting into the zone, hurtling ever higher towards the celestial spheres at the very same time I felt myself burrowing deeper and deeper into the inmost chambers of my own heart. Is it weird to say it that way? Even I think so! But that's more or less *exactly* how it felt. And I really did see the light, the light they call the light of God's face. And, yes, maybe that's what it was and maybe that's not what it was, but what I saw, I saw. And I'm writing this whole story down because I want to die knowing that at least some among the people I leave behind will know that this whole thing isn't just a fairy tale you hear from time to time from people who themselves can't say for sure if it's true or not. And that this happened to me not once or twice, but, eventually as the years passed, dozens upon dozens of times.

The oblong building that houses the Holy of Holies has an anteroom at its eastern end that you enter through a great doorway. Who fit the door to that doorway, I have no idea. No one I ever asked seemed to know either, so I suppose it must either be original—which I doubt—or else a replacement made so precisely to spec that the fact that it wasn't the original door set in its place back in the time of Zerubavel didn't seem to be a big deal. Whatever, it was a nice door . . . but a detail I had never noticed now presented itself to me for my contemplation: it wasn't as good a fit as I had always thought. It did fit in its frame, of course, but the bottom of the door was just a fingerbreadth higher off the ground than it needed to be for it not to scrape along the threshold when it was opened each morning for the High Priest's entrance. I hadn't ever noticed that before. (Who would have?) But now it seemed to me a detail of crucial importance. And although I know for a fact that the building was empty, that no one was inside, that no one *could* have been inside . . . I also know I saw light flickering out towards me from the narrow space—possibly not *even* a fingerbreadth, now that I think of it—from that *supremely* narrow bit of space between the bottom of that door and the threshold. And that first experience of the reality—not the theory or the hopeful fantasy—but the absolute reality of the light, of the divine presence in that place and at that moment . . . it was more than enough to change my life forever. As it did the lives of the rest of the brethren who experienced it once they finally managed actually to experience it, and not merely to believe that other people sometimes did.

We didn't do it all that often at first. But we became more brazen as the months and years passed. Later, I found out how it was that none of *their* patrols ever came by while we were at it. I'll tell you that story too when we get there—but at this point I would just have thought it was our tremendous good fortune never to have been seen, never to have been discovered, never even—I thought—to have been noticed. I'll tell you the rest when we get there, but now I want to get back to poor Buki and the story of his horrific end. So just bear with me for another few pages and I promise that the pieces of my story will start to come together.

EIGHT

THEY HATED US. I don't mean they didn't approve of us (which they certainly didn't) or that they disagreed with us (which they certainly did), but that they loathed us almost beyond the telling of it. We were more like trained dogs than men in their eyes, servants not truly worthy to serve, slaves lucky to have some meaning granted to our miserable lives through the unearned, undeserved good fortune of having them as our masters. They must have known we had names, but they never used them. And they liked not using them too. When I'd hear "Hey, *tenufa*, come over here," I knew the point was partially to get someone to sweep up some sacred ox dung and partially to enjoy the experience of insulting us to our faces. So why did we put up with it? It's a good question, but it's a little like asking an addict why he doesn't just stop smoking *ganjha* and get a job. I remember when one of Assaf's kids—Dan, I think—wrote that in that step-song of his that he hated them with ultimate loathing and how none of us, myself most certainly included, found that excessive or overstated. But what we got for taking all that contempt, for being treated like dirt, for letting ourselves be stripped and shaved and forced to let them burn our own clothing to ash and to call us names—and taking it all without complaining too loudly—was this indescribable experience I've only succeeded in talking about vaguely, not really in describing precisely or even all that accurately.

Seeing the light. Feeling the heat. Experiencing the closeness of God—the *real* God, the One who speaks and hears and appears (occasionally) to the faithful, not the One who exists merely to be served, to be worshiped, to be *acknowledged* as Sovereign of the Universe. Hearing the divine voice—and that happened too, and to almost all of us in the course of our years on the hill—that was part of it too. You've all read our book—you probably own a copy even if you call the poems "psalms," the name the Alexandrians dreamed up to label our sacred songs and which somehow stuck—and so you know that we didn't just see, that we heard as well. Some of what we heard appears in several of the poems in the book, of course, but there's a lot that never made it into any specific poem. And we did *very* well with that book, incidentally. I still remember when Joseph told me there would be a day when no home in all Judah would *not* have a copy of our book in it and how I thought that was the craziest thing I had ever heard. But, amazingly enough, it actually did happen. And it's been the profits from that one book, our Tehillim, our Psalms, that have kept us afloat for years.

But I'm getting way ahead of myself. We knew they didn't like us or trust us—that, they made clear enough every single day—but we also knew that they crossed the line regularly from *just* not liking us to seeking actively to do us harm. And we also understood that things were getting worse. Still, many of the guys continued to hope for the best and, for a long time, that was how I felt as well. But even my optimistic self eventually seized the fact that they would stop at nothing—or some of them wouldn't—to preserve the power structure they had created to justify their own place at the peak of the pyramid.

There were stories even when I first came to town about what we delicately called "incidents." We all knew, for example, about the time the Great One's half-brother Shevuel ben Heman was ambushed just outside the Tadi Gate and confined against his will in the *mikveh* under the Hearth House for almost three weeks or the time Zevadyahu ben Yatniel was jumped behind Solomon's Stables and his legs so severely beaten that he couldn't walk without a stick for the rest of his years—but most of us, myself possibly included, wanted desperately to believe that these were isolated incidents we could regret all we wished, but which we didn't need actually to take too seriously to heart. For a while, that seemed reasonable, but things began to get worse, not better, and all of us—probably with no exceptions at all—we *all* knew at least on some level that we were heading into the kind of trouble from which only the luckiest of us would escape unscathed.

At first, it was mostly petty things. More patrols by *them* meant more of *us* found dozing on the job, hence more of *us* stripped in the moonlight and forced to watch while they burned our cloaks and either sneered or laughed at us, or both. And more mysterious stuff would happen too. A brother would be holding a pan of boiling water (of the kind used by *us* to skin the big animals so that *they* could take home their leather pelts) only to have the handles come off in his hands and the pan of boiling water fall to the ground and scald his feet. Another would be standing on the *dukhan* and singing only to have a sharp shard of broken pottery jammed into the flesh of his buttocks by a passing priest all too aware what the punishment would be for a Levite to decamp to the Chamber of First Aid during the sacrificial service to get someone to pull the shard out of his behind and administer some salve to the wound. Or even more mysterious stuff than that. We would be dining together in one of our private homes on a meal we ourselves had prepared, only for all of us to come down with food poisoning within hours . . . despite the fact that the food never left our gaze while it was being prepared or consumed. Or an amazingly high percentage of our people would develop warts on the soles of their feet within the same few months or rashes on their thighs or some sort of itchy scaling on their forearms.

For a while, it was just upsetting. But then, a few years before Buki's murder, things began to degenerate seriously. I suppose the first "incident" in that series of horrors would have been when Eliashiv ben Bilga was jumped on his way home one night and beaten unconscious, then left to live or die in the street for most of the night. But that was only the beginning. Within the following three or four months, we all lost count of the incidents of brethren being ambushed, jumped, beaten, even abducted. People were confined in various dungeons around town for a day or two, then mysteriously released. Eder ben Micha, one of the sweetest guys you'll ever want to meet, was seized on his way home one night and left for dead hanging upside down by his heels over the Upper Shuk. Yoshbekasha's little brother, Eliata, was on his way home one night with one of the girls from the Olive Grove only to find five or six of her "brothers" waiting for him when they got there. He was never the same afterwards, although even now I'm not entirely sure what they did to him. I know some of it, however—eventually, I saw his back and buttocks in the bathhouse on the Street of the Lambs and the welts were still terrifying, even months later. Worse, they shaved him— everywhere—and told him he was to keep himself hairless permanently . . . and that if any of them ever ordered him to strip and saw that he had let some of his hair—any of it—grow back, they would kill him and his mother for real the next time. He was a big, burly boy . . . and it was hard to decide, at least for me, if he looked more ridiculous or more terrifying when he stripped down to bathe and exposed his totally hairless body. I think it was probably after that specific "incident" that we started to understand that we were never safe.

And then Buki disappeared, only to be found dead a few days late in the Wadi Kerith. I was already an old-timer by then—this was about thirteen years after I arrived in Jerusalem—and considered as such by most of the younger pups. Despite all the trouble outside, my family—even with all the upheaval involved in my divorce from Deborah—was thriving. Zakur was already a bar-mitzvah. Yehoram was eleven. The twins, God bless them, were ten. Deborah had taken her *get* and her pay-off and gone off with some man she claimed to have met only days earlier (which, if you believe that, I have a used incense censor—made of solid Phrygian gold, I swear!—I'd like to sell you) and I met Avital—who really *was* made of gold—only a few months after that and married her almost on the spot.

NINE

I SUPPOSE I SHOULD say something about the end of my marriage to Deborah. There's not really all that much to tell. In fact, it's a sign of just how tenuous her place in the boys' emotional structure was that they didn't seem to have any difficulty welcoming Avital into our home as their stepmother. Part of that probably had to do with the fact that Avital is actually older than Deborah by about two years. So it wasn't like I sent their mom off and brought some teenager in to take her place . . . and I think they all understood, even the twins, how much grief Deborah had given me over the years. She was constantly disappointed—in the boys, in Jerusalem, in her father, in the size of our house—but mostly she was disappointed in me. Whatever I did, I couldn't ever quite get it right. I was too fat, so I limited my eating severely and lost weight. But then she said I was too bony and had only made myself unappealingly thin. We made love too often—I was hurting her, she said regularly, without ever explaining precisely how—so I backed off. Then she complained that I was neglecting her and not living up to my conjugal duties. (I loved it that she used just that expression—"conjugal duties"—to refer to sex. It took me a while to realize that she called it by that name because that was precisely what it all was to her: an obligation to be avoided whenever possible and lived up to when unavoidably necessary. Just what every husband wants to hear!) I wasn't spending enough on her, so I began to shower her with more and more expensive gifts. But then, when I started spending more and more, I was just being a show-off and squandering our money on the off chance it might help me—I love this part best of all—on the chance a pair of lapis lazuli earrings imported directly from Crete might help me get her into bed slightly more often. I could go on, but I'm sure you get the picture.

Our home was the stage upon which all this misery played itself out. Deborah would cry for hours on end, then become weirdly elated and run around trying to cheer everybody up as though we were the ones who were depressed. She would deny me for weeks, then want to make love at the strangest moments—at dawn, for example, or at midnight. Or in peculiar places. (Her greatest wish, to penetrate one of the courtyards or inner chambers within the Temple complex to which women were never admitted and to make love there, was never fulfilled. Or at least not with me it wasn't.) She conceived the desire to make love with our mouths gagged and our eyes blindfolded. Or, at least once, with a burning candle held sideways in my mouth so that the wax would drip down onto her chest. She accused me of out-of-control spending, but she was the one who would go out and spend three months of grocery money on an Egyptian mirror. I was the one who was too skinny or too fat, but she was the one who would go on these weird diets, spending months at one point eating only *hummus* and olives, and then, a few months later, going for sixteen weeks—and I mean *precisely* sixteen weeks—without eating anything made of any grain other than spelt. There was even stranger stuff too, but I think I've said more than enough to give you the general impression. Things went from strange to weird to screwy to completely nuts, and then we just crossed the line and I just couldn't take it any longer..

She got odder and odder with the boys too. I do have to say that Deborah was a caring, devoted mother in many ways and it was always clear that she truly did love her sons. That much I have to give her, but she had no idea how to express that love reasonably or normally. She wanted to continue to nurse Zakur, for example, until *after* he was in school. And she never quite stopped taking it personally when the boys stopped feeling comfortable being naked in front of her.

I never stopped hoping things would improve, but we got to a point at which I just couldn't take it any longer. I hated the bickering, the yelling, the constant stream of invective (most of it vulgar) that flowed from her mouth like blood from an ox's thick neck. Nor was the verbal abuse a one-way street only—she brought out the worst in me as well. And so, in the end, we needed to wrap things up. And I think she knew it too. The boys were unhappy. *I* was miserably unhappy. Even Deborah herself was sad most of the time . . . not only when she was being sad-depressed or sad-miserable about her rotten, horrible life and her shiftless, useless husband and her ungrateful, prudish children, but also when she was blessed (or do I mean cursed?) with a moment of insight into the way things actually were for her and for us. And I suppose she thought she couldn't take much more of it either.

The divorce was painless. I know all the scribes in town, but I had Yoshbekasha's oldest brother, Uziel, draw up the papers because he was the one connected with the *beth din* that met in the Fish Gate and that was where I wanted the decree executed. By the time I was ready to tell Deborah the bad news, I think she had already guessed what was coming. It really wouldn't have been hard for her to guess—unexpected comings and goings, visits from a scribe, messenger boys arriving from the Fish Gate (and you could always recognize them because they wore these very smart deep-blue jackets with a golden fish on the back)—and so it really can't have been much of a challenge to understand that something was afoot. And I suppose she wouldn't have had any difficulty knowing what it likely was. Well, I don't *know* any of that . . . but I do know that when the messengers arrived to summon her to the *beth din*, she went along willingly and didn't seem amazed or all that upset at all.

The proceedings were cut and dried, almost (I thought) to the point of being peculiarly so. The *av beth din* said his part. I said mine. She answered the questions put to her easily and apparently without malice or rage. I gave her the *get*. She accepted it calmly. I gave her the money coming to her. She took it . . . and that, more or less, was that. She was forbidden from sleeping any longer under my roof, but she went right home to pack her things and to wait for the boys. What happened when they got home, I don't really know. But when I eventually showed up, Deborah was long gone and the boys were eating *pita* and radishes with Joseph. (I had asked him to stop by shortly after I figured Deborah would arrive and he ended up staying on to help them with their homework and then to set out supper for them.) No one was crying. No one even seemed all that upset. Deborah had handled it well, I suppose.

There were bad moments later on, times when the boys—all four of them, including Zakur—cried for their mama. But she was never too far off . . . and I made sure that she understood that her access to the boys was not ever going to be impeded, even if I did marry again. Which I did . . . and, I'm sure, in less time than Deborah would have thought possible given my countless peculiarities, faults, and deep, ineradicable flaws.

I suppose that there's a kind of a contest when people get divorced to see who remarries first. And, according to the rules of the game, *that*, almost more than anything else, is supposed to show which of the two was the normal one, the desirable one, the one some totally unbiased outsider would be delighted to have as a spouse. I imagine the competition is more or less real in the case of most couples, but for us it hardly existed. Deborah announced to the children when she stopped by the day of the divorce that she was done, that she would never remarry or have any more children. She didn't say why, but she didn't appear—so say the children *and* Joseph, who was present for this part of the speech—she didn't appear to have even the slightest conflict about her decision. I considered it so much empty rhetoric, but she ended up keeping to it. And, indeed, as far as I know, she remained single for the rest of her life. The guy she went off with after the divorce didn't stick around for long. She lived in Jerusalem until the twins were sixteen, then moved to Jaffa and became quite a successful artist. She wove and painted and drew . . . and people actually paid her for her work. We met infrequently at first, then more and more rarely still until we were finally strangers incapable of disappointing each other, let alone of awakening the kind of anger in each other's breasts that we were once world champions at producing. The last time I ran into her, I actually didn't recognize her at first. Eventually, she vanished entirely from my life and from the boys'. Probably, she died.

Compared with Deborah, Avital was like a visitor from some distant star. For one thing, she was the most non-judgmental woman I've ever met. She knew all sorts of things about all sorts of people, but she didn't seem to care that much about whether people did or didn't meet the standards she set for herself. Nor did she have Deborah's innate hostility to the world, basically taking our planet merely as the stage upon which to live her life, rather than as a living, breathing enemy against which to rage and battle for as long as she could possibly hold out. We met at a party given by Yaddua ben Korcha—Avital was some sort of distant cousin of Yaddua's wife, Ruchama—and it was, at least for me, lust at first sight.

Avital was beautiful in a way few women I've known are: not merely in the sense that her face was pretty and her breasts large and her hips wide, but in the sense that she somehow managed to put it all together in a way that made her entire body an extension of her inner self. The breasts you couldn't quite stop staring at, for example, weren't merely round and soft and alluring, but were somehow suggestive all by themselves of the kind of passion that dwelt beneath the surface, of the quality of the heart that beat in the chest they adorned, even of the intelligence of the woman attached to them. Making love to her was like burrowing into her consciousness, like traveling (briefly, but absolutely really) into the inmost chambers of her beating heart. This, I understood early on, was an exceptional woman I had met.

The first evening we encountered each other, she was wearing a floor-length gold robe with turquoise trim and looked, I thought, like the Queen of Sheba must have looked when she came a-calling on King Sol. She had her thick black hair pulled back into a long braid and pinned up in a coil on the top of her head and she was wearing just enough blue eye shadow to make her look mysterious and incredibly sexy, not cheap or—as so many Jerusalem women do when they wear far too much—like those painted statues of Greek goddesses the Cretans are always trying to hawk to tourists in the *shuk*. I was smitten, then amazed to realize that she was flirting with me instead of demurely waiting for me to make the first move. That did it. I was done with Deborah, ready for something good to happen in my life and, suddenly, there she was. I felt I should at least wait until the *karpas* to ask her out, but I ended up lasting just until the waiters began mixing the wine.

"Would you like to have a walk with me along the walls after we're done here," I asked hesitantly.

"I'd like it just fine," she answered, her Hebrew so totally suffused with the accent of Jerusalem that I didn't need to ask if she was a visitor or a resident in town.

And that was that. We somehow lasted without bolting until the post-prandial wines were served, then headed out for our walk. When it ended, she invited me to escort her home. She lived alone. Her husband, the late and apparently truly lamented Elzavad ben Shimri, had been a semi-wealthy man who had been prescient enough to give most of his estate to his wife before succumbing to his final heart attack. As a result, she lived in a fine house about halfway between the Sheep Gate and the Tower of the Hundred all by herself. She didn't appear nervous or shy. She couldn't have seemed *less* unsure of herself, actually. Nor was she bashful about admitting that she liked living alone. I wasn't entirely sure whether to take that as an invitation or a warning (or, possibly, as a little bit of both), but there wasn't time to ponder the situation in too much detail. When we got to the front gate of her home, she simply took my hand and led me inside.

As things do with men and women truly attracted to each other, one thing led to another. I spent the night in her bed, then another and then a third. I was getting tired—staying home to feed the boys and get them off to bed, then (at least from the second night on) installing a woman I knew from the neighborhood to watch over things before heading over to Avital's for a night of very little rest, then making sure I was back home (and my night-watch woman paid and dispatched) before the boys woke up and wanted some breakfast—and I knew I couldn't keep that kind of routine up indefinitely. I considered various options, then came to the only one I wasn't ashamed of saying out loud.

"Will you become betrothed to me according to the law of Moses and the people Israel?" I asked somewhere towards the end of our fourth night in a row together. I suppose I could have said it more elegantly (although hardly any more formally), but there didn't seem to be any good reason not to get things totally out into the open.

"Yes," she said, reaching placing her hand on my chest directly over my heart, "I will."

And so she did. It took a week and a half to get everything organized, but the days flew by and we were married the following Tuesday. The boys appeared fine with the idea. Joseph and Yemima hosted the wedding feast at their own home, then moved the boys into their place for a week so Avital and I could be alone at mine. That was some week! But, when it ended and we moved Avital's things into my place and put hers on the market (figuring that we hardly needed to own two homes and it only made sense to rid ourselves of the one that would fetch the far higher price *and* the sale of which wouldn't require uprooting the boys from the only home they'd ever known), I knew we had made the right decision.

We were happy. The boys appeared to be at peace with my decision. I found, to my slight surprise, that what Deborah did or didn't think of my new marital arrangement was of no concern to me in the slightest. What did matter to me was the opinion of my brother and Yemima—and they were, it seemed, entirely pleased with these new developments in my life. Even the troubles that seemed perennially to plague the brethren appeared to have died down, at least temporarily. I was young—well, not *that* young, but still under forty . . . which sounds young to me now even if it probably didn't back then—and I was married to the sexiest woman in Jerusalem. My boys were thriving. My career was taking off. We weren't exactly wealthy, but the sale of Avital's house, which sold in less than a week to a couple of sheep ranchers from Gischala who wanted a place in Jerusalem and who apparently didn't have to care about the price they paid for it, left us very comfortably fixed for cash. Everything was going along swimmingly . . . until Buki's body, naked and decapitated, was found in the Wadi Kerith with thirteen copper double-drachmas stuffed into his mouth and the watchword of our particular version of the faith of Israel carved into his cold, stiff chest.

TEN

I'VE ALREADY DESCRIBED THE days that followed the discovery of Buki's body and the funeral itself. But I haven't explained my particular reason for telling about it in such detail. I was, of course, incredibly upset. We all were. That one of us was the victim of abduction and murder would have made the situation serious enough all by itself even without any extra horrifying details, after all. But the fact that that single word had been carved by his murderers into his chest—that word that encapsulated in three syllables who we were and what we strove to achieve with our endless midnight sneaking around in the sacred precincts of the Temple we guarded and served—the fact that he had been *mutilated* with the single word that all by itself represented the totality of our spiritual aspirations, that made things dramatically and incrementally worse in all our minds. So it was a weird witch's brew of emotions that were roiling and churning around in all our breasts as we readied ourselves for Buki's funeral. That all these details could have been put in place specifically to mislead us by prompting us to embrace an entirely false theory regarding Buki's death occurred to no one at all. We were outraged, but also terrified. Worried, but also shocked . . . and incredibly angry to boot. He had been kidnapped and killed on purpose by people who wanted him dead—of that we had no doubt at all—but it was we whom his murderers had been addressing with their foul deed. Of that, we were all certain. And the message was as entirely transparent as it was gruesome: clear out, give up, and get lost . . . or risk sharing your fat friend's horrific fate. And believe you me, we all got the message in all its awful simplicity.

Buki's funeral was on a Sunday, and the following evening Joseph and I headed down to the Street of the Lambs to hear the latest gossip and feel the security that I hoped would come from the company of peers and friends.

I was not the only Levite in Jerusalem who had thought to seek comfort in familiar surroundings, however, and the place was jammed to the rafters with worried men of all ages seeking solace in each other's company. We had been there most nights since Buki was taken—and I've already described the scene that first night after he disappeared—but the night after the funeral had a different feel to it. We were upset, all of us. But we were also eager to find a path forward, to figure out how to make ourselves and our families safe. And we were pretty much united in the conviction that we needed to see Buki's death more as a challenge than a threat.

Joseph and I arrived towards the end of the first watch, then washed up quickly and joined the others in the steam. It felt good to be among brothers, to be vulnerable among people from whom I knew with absolute certainty I had nothing at all to fear.

It must have been after shortly after midnight that the Great One signaled to me to follow him. I remember looking around, almost as though it didn't seem possible that it could have been me he wished to lead out of the steam. But when I looked around again, his eyes were staring straight into mine, his stare unambiguously inviting me to follow him. What he wanted, I had no idea. But that he wanted it from me, whatever it was, felt undeniable. I got up, told Joseph with a sideways chuck of my head to stay where he was—in that special way brothers can communicate in gesture far more simply than in word—and left the steam. Those of my readers familiar with the way the bath on the Street of the Lambs was laid out will recall that there was a series of small rooms on the south side of the building just off the cold pool. I followed at a distance, seeing easily that Eli was headed either into the cold pool itself or else into one of those smaller adjacent rooms.

The room that contained the cold pool was totally deserted. Had he known there would be no one there to observe us? Or had he simply not cared? Or would he have simply circled the room as though he were merely stretching his legs and then returned directly to the steam had there actually been anyone there? I didn't know then and I don't really know now, but the bottom line is that there was no one there and so he headed directly into the first of the side rooms and sat down on one of the cedar benches. I followed him in, then sat on the opposite bench. He said nothing. I waited. I think I can say with absolute honestly that I hadn't even the faintest inkling what he was about to say. Or what he might have been waiting for me to say.

We sat there facing each other for quite some time. I put my hands on my knees, mimicking his position. He looked at me, but I could tell he was somewhere else . . . present and not present in the way very intense people sometimes can manage to wander afar off mentally without losing touch even slightly with their surroundings.

The Great One was a bald, older man, but he exuded more power in old age than most men are able to project even in their youths. The hair on his chest was totally white, as was his beard, yet all that white hair failed to suggest even the slightest jovial avuncularity. He was sweating freely. (The cold pool featured very cold water, but the air overhead and in the adjacent rooms was as warm as anywhere else in the building.) I can't explain precisely why, but it felt peculiar seeing him sweat so profusely, almost as though he were inadvertently sharing some unearned intimacy with me even before he got around to saying a single word. I felt unnerved. But I said nothing, hoping my silence would seem, if not eloquent, than at least respectful.

In the end, we sat together for four or five minutes before he spoke. But when he finally did deign to speak, my life changed. And it did so permanently, although at the time I obviously had no way to know that.

"You understand that Buki was murdered?" he began.

"*Meivin*," I said simply. I understand.

"You understand the significance of the word carved into him."

"I think so."

He leaned towards me, our knees almost touching. "What is it you think?"

"That it's a threat."

"A threat against whom?"

"Against us."

"Against *all* of us?"

"Against all of us, yes."

"Including against yourself?"

What was he getting at? "Yes, of course, including against myself."

"Who do you think issued that threat?"

"I don't know. Someone who has it in for us."

"No ideas at all?" He shifted slightly forward now so that our knees actually were touching.

"*Them*, I guess."

"You guess?"

"I don't know."

"Can you think of another possibility?"

"No, not really."

"So you're sure."

"Can't I not have another set of suspects ready and also not be sure I'm right."

"I don't think so."

"Then I guess I'm sure."

"And what do we do now?"

"You're asking me?" *He* was asking *me*?

"Apparently."

"We keep our noses clean and hope for the best?"

"No." His simple answer sent a shiver through me to the base of my spine.

"We lodge a complaint with the police?"

"And do they listen?"

"No, of course not."

"Do they care?"

"No, not even slightly."

"So we're on our own?"

"I guess we are."

"And where does that leave us?"

"On our own?"

"As always . . . ." Eli's voice tapered off as though he were deciding how best to continue. But when he spoke again, his voice was clear and calm. "I need you to do something for me. For us."

"What?" I recall feeling flattered but also completely unnerved.

Eli ben Heman smiled at me and leaned back onto the wall behind the bench. He scratched under his left arm, then under his right, then put his hands back on his knees. "I want you to find out who murdered Buki."

"Me?" I wonder if I sounded as stupid then as the retelling of it makes me sound now. Probably, I did.

"Yes, you. Take as much time as you need. But find this out for me. Find out who took Bukiyahu's life."

"And what am I do to when I find the man . . . "

"Or the men."

"Or the men. And when I find the man *or the men* who murdered Buki, what am I to do?"

"How do you know it wasn't a woman?"

"A woman? Could it have been a woman?"

"Why couldn't it have been a woman? Wasn't Jezebel a woman? Wasn't Queen Athaliah?"

"Of course, they were women."

"Because you asked what you are to do when you find the man or the men who killed Buki, but you didn't mention that it could also have been a woman."

I couldn't decide if I was being patronized or guided along to seize the full implications of accepting an assignment I had no idea how even correctly to frame, let alone successfully to complete. "Well, then, let me rephrase. What am I to do with the man or men or woman or women, or with the man *and* the woman, or with the mixed group of men and women, that I come to learn killed Buki ben Yerimoth?"

"God will guide you."

"And if I hear not the voice of God?" I was trying to sound like I had some idea what I was talking about.

The Great One leaned forward and stared directly into my eyes. "In that case," he said quietly, "you'll just have to listen more attentively." He fell silent for a long few minutes before speaking again. "I won't hurt your chances of success by not allowing you to chart your own course forward," he said.

"Buki wasn't executed by some girlfriend's enraged husband, was he?"

The Great One looked away for a moment, then turned back to face me directly. "No," he said slowly and deliberately, "he wasn't. Or maybe he was—but that's not what I think."

I knew better than to press the matter. The point wasn't what he thought but what I was going to think. He didn't want to ruin my work by orienting me in some specific direction before I found my sea legs in all of this and decided how to move forward. I knew the Great One would always support me and help me if I got in trouble. But I was basically on my own. And, needless to say, I had no idea at all how or where to begin.

ELEVEN

EVENTUALLY, WE WENT BACK into the *caldarium*. The crowd had thinned out slightly while we were gone, but I didn't stay for long. I noticed Joseph fast asleep on one of the marble benches in the anteroom just outside the steam room and decided on the spot not to wake him even though I would normally have roused him so that one of us could walk the other one home. But I didn't want to tell him about my meeting with the Great One, which had been somehow conducted privately and publicly at the same time, so his being asleep was my good fortune (or that's how it struck me at the time) and I seized it. And so, after dressing hurriedly—and alone—in the apodyterium, I walked out into the cool nighttime air and headed home.

The house was dark and quiet. I felt grateful for the privacy, but also just a touch disappointed not to be able to tell my story—in detail and at length—to Avital. (Is it strange that I avoided telling any part of my story to Joseph but couldn't wait to tell it all to Avital? In the retelling, it seems that way even to me. But it felt reasonable at the time and, in fact, I don't recall at the time even having noticed the paradox.) At any rate, she *was* asleep and, since I hardly needed to wash up after having spent the entire evening in a bathhouse, I simply undressed in the dark and crawled into bed next to her. She was snoring gently, but not entirely inaudibly. I backed up against her and felt her breasts pressed into my back. In her sleep, she embraced me. But sleep itself refused to embrace me . . . and I lay there in bed for the longest time, relaxed and at peace, but somehow also ill at ease about what the dawn might or could bring.

The Great One had been clear enough. Our fellowship—our sacred brotherhood—had suffered an act of merciless aggression. That Buki's mur-der was meant at the very least to intimidate us was beyond obvious—the fact that he was seized on his way home from work, that he was stripped and made to watch his outer clothing burn *precisely* in the way *they* regularly stripped Levites found sleeping on their posts and burnt their burnooses on the spot, that his body was desecrated with the watchword of *our* faith—all of it together made the point as clear as it needed to be. Was Buki's murder merely the opening salvo in a war the other side meant to win decisively? We would find out, I recall supposing, more than soon enough. And, no, I don't recall having even the slightest intimation that there was—or even could be—any part of the story that the Great One knew but had made a conscious decision not to share.

What the coins were all about was still a matter of public debate. Some citizens thought the point lay in their number, others in their Egyptian origin. Still another school of thought considered it likely that the actual murderers, shocked by the unspeakable grotesquerie of their foul deed, had simply returned the money they had been paid to kill Buki as a way of atoning on the spot for their loathsome crime. But was the sum high enough for that theory to have cogency? I myself thought not, but there were plenty who disagreed.

There were other theories out there too, some of them slightly reasonable and others wholly outlandish. But within our circles, the point was more than clear and the message had most certainly been delivered. And it was a message not for poor Buki, who was clearly dead when it was finally delivered, but for the rest of us. *We*, after all, were the ones seeking always to have the name of God—the personal, effable/ineffable name that even the priests themselves stopped using in public at a certain point—we were the ones seeking at least daily to have that most sacred of names on our lips and in our mouths.

And we were also the ones whose songs and hymns were riddled with numerological references to the number twenty-six, the numerological value of that name. When David ben Levi, one of the greatest poets of my grandfather's generation, wrote his famous line about the pleasure involved in finally tasting "God," we all knew he wasn't talking nonsense about nonsense, merely making a discreet point about the sensation of feeling the divine name filling up our mouths. (That he was widely ridiculed and derided in *their* circles as a blasphemer and a dolt didn't make his lesson less meaningful, only his brief story more tragic. He died at the peak of his powers too, felled by his own heart at what ought to have been the middle of his life. You probably know the line "God, take me not at the midpoint of my life, You whose existence is endless." He wrote that too—it's in the great hymn called "The Prayer of an Indigent"—but whether that was an instance of prophetic insight or a mere coincidence, none of us was ever able to say.)

The whole concept of knowing God in the world by filling one's mouth with God's holy name was one of the pillars of our system. Indeed, when Assaf—that would be Assaf ben Yedutun, the son of Buki's mother's brother—had a vision in which he was commanded to open wide his mouth so that God might fill it up, we all understood that the point was that it be wide enough to accommodate the ethereal, but fully real, presence of the divine name. And so, at least to us, the meaning of the coins was transparent: thirteen double drachmas in his mouth clearly alluded to our notion of a mouth filled with the number twenty-six . . . or, rather, with the presence of the living God as symbolized on earth by the numerological value of the holiest of divine names. Like I said, the message was clear. And it was truly chilling. That it could possibly have been sent specifically to mislead us occurred, as far as I know, to no one at all . . . and least of all to me.

As I lay naked in Avital's slumbering embrace, all sorts of ideas raced through my mind. What, I asked myself, had changed so dramatically just recently? What would have moved those among the priests who truly did loathe us to move from insult and petty malevolence to murder at this precise juncture in history? Was it the fact that some line had been crossed, some line visible solely to them? Or was it simply that Buki himself had stepped on the wrong person's sandals, that he himself was the victim not randomly or symbolically, but specifically and intentionally? Or was this about something else entirely?

I had no answers to offer to even the simplest of my own questions. But my mind went on, considering other issues as they presented themselves to me at random. Why, I now asked myself, did the Great One choose me for this specific assignment? Was his selection of myself a random choice based on nothing at all or had he intended to speak to me all along and had simply been waiting patiently all evening until just the right moment presented itself to take me aside for a private talk? Was it possible that something I said in the course of the evening inspired him to charge me with finding and bringing Buki's murderer or murderers to justice . . . or had he come to the Street of the Lambs in the first place in the hope I would be present and available for the specific conversation we ended up having? And why me? I was neither the most nor the least senior among the brethren, not especially strong, not possessed of a reputation for exceptional bravery. Nor did I come from a family of special fame or renown. Although it was very appealing to imagine that he had noticed me—that he had *chosen* me—as the precisely right candidate for a dangerous but crucial mission because of my merit and my incisive intelligence, it was far more likely that he had simply needed someone he felt he could count on and picked me on the spot as the right man for the job. Or, it struck me to wonder in a somewhat less self-complimentary vein, did he merely need to ask someone whose loss, should that person get himself killed, would be entirely bearable to the larger enterprise? I lay there for a long while considering these various options and possibilities, then finally drifted off to sleep.

Morning seemed to come almost immediately, but Avital was gone when I opened my eyes and I was alone in our bed. The gentle noises of early morning wafted in through the window in our bedroom—the clatter of pots and pans in the neighbors' courtyards, the soft footfalls of my own boys as they attempted to get themselves ready for school without waking me, the distinctive sound the neighbor's donkey made when it drank water from the bucket hanging from the fence that separated their back garden from ours. I lay in bed for a while and felt overwhelmed by the events of the previous evening. It had, after all, been one thing to bow deferentially to the Great One's wishes and agree to undertake whatever task he felt it appropriate to ask of me and another thing actually to have even the faintest idea where to begin.

As I've already written, I knew Buki in that peculiar way that pertains when you've known someone casually for so long that the longevity of the relationship itself comes to feel like some version of sustained intimacy. But it was one thing to know what kind of jokes he favored and to admire his custom-made sandals, and something else entirely to have even the most remote concept of where exactly to begin searching for his murderer. Or for his murderers.

I wasn't completely at sea. I knew where he lived. I hadn't ever met Buki's late father, but I knew his mother slightly and had seen her last at Buki's funeral. And Buki himself had a married sister—the mother of his nephews—and a brother-in-law I knew vaguely. But there wasn't the slightest reason to connect any of them, most certainly including his mother, in my investigation. I didn't want to waste time. I resolved to start elsewhere, then to turn to his immediately family only if I failed to turn up any other leads.

I felt certain Buki hadn't ever been married to any of the women with whom he had maintained long- or short-term liaisons over the years. But I had no idea whether there was anyone special in his life when he was murdered. Still, something about the specific way he was killed kept me from feeling it even slightly likely that his death had been at the hand of a spurned lover. And, furthermore, how possible was it really that Buki could have been dating a woman *that* seriously without any of us knowing about it? Jerusalem, for those of you reading from afar, is a very small town. And it was even smaller back in the days I'm describing to you than it is now.

I had heard the circumstances of Buki's murder described to me so many times that I felt certain I knew precisely where he had been found. I used to go hiking in the Wadi Kerith all the time when I first came to Jerusalem. I liked it there—it was out of the way, usually deserted, always sunny (one learned soon enough not to walk in wadis in the rainy season) and eerily, strikingly beautiful—and I went many dozens of times to hike or simply to stroll for a few hours along its narrow riverbed. But what the point of that specific location was, or if it even had a point, I had no idea. Surely, it was an unusual choice. And an inconvenient one as well: luring Buki to a wadi closer to Jericho than Jerusalem, let alone transporting a man of his size there against his will, didn't strike me as though it could possibly have been an arbitrary decision. The common wisdom, as I've already mentioned, was that the site itself was meant as a kind of not-that-cryptic warning. Elijah, after all, heard the word of God clearly and unambiguously when he was hiding out from King Ahab there. But you're no Elijahs, the warning was imagined to be saying, just amateurs and charlatans mimicking his techniques with no real hope of attaining his successes. But whether that was the correct interpretation or just something we were self-absorbedly reading into it, I obviously had no way to know.

I had neither any experience at all in this kind of inquiry nor the slightest expertise in any of the skills someone undertaking an investigation like this would naturally want to have. I had never fought another man, had no special contacts in the criminal world *or* in the world of the priests, no pre-existent entrée into the presence of the High Priest. I had no real idea which of the stories of physical aggression against our circle were true and which were made up . . . and which ones were slightly true *and* slightly made up at the same time. Later on, of course, I was involved in many criminal investigations and acquired a reasonable level of expertise in the kind of sleuthing I first undertook in the weeks that followed Buki's death. In fact, it is probably precisely because Buki's was my first case that its details remain so finely etched in my memory. Or maybe it's just because I became so personally involved in the investigation, something I tried to avoid later on as I grew into my eventual calling. At the time, of course, I could not possibly have known that my work on Buki's murder would herald a sea change in my own career path. Nor could I have imagined the future I was eventually going to build on the details of my inquiry into Buki's death.

But let's return to that first morning after the Great One charged me with finding out what had happened to Buki. I had given him my word. And I felt wholly committed to following through. I had to start somewhere. The only flaw in my plan was that I had no plan. And no idea how even to begin to develop the kind of one that could conceivably catch a murderer.

TWELVE

It was a Tuesday. Two of the three courses I had been taking—one in the ritual purity of fruits and vegetables, and the other, which every Levite had to retake every second year, in hand-to-hand combat—were over, and the final lecture in the third course—the one devoted to issues in large mammal viscera—was only scheduled for the following evening. And then there would be a ten-day hiatus before the next round of lectures and classes was scheduled to begin. I was, of course, already working in the Temple—I had been elevated to permanent staff more than six years earlier as part of the general series of elevations and promotions connected with the Great One's eightieth birthday—but we had adopted a very Levite-friendly four-on, three-off schedule. So I had just finished my four days on duty and had three days off, but then we were *all* going to have a ten-day break from our studies when all we'd have to do was actually work at our jobs. But I had been freed of that now . . . and the Great One had specifically not put any limit at all on how much time I could take to complete my investigation into Buki's murder. I remember hoping I could wrap things up quickly and have a few free days before classes recommenced.

Buki's funeral was all anyone was talking about. But although the funeral service and the subsequent burial had both passed uneventfully, the atmosphere in Jerusalem was still tense and unsettled as I set myself to figuring out how to deal with this secret commission from the Great One to locate Buki's murderer. Whether the Jerusalem district police were also pursuing an investigation, I had no idea. It seemed impossible to imagine they weren't. Were Onias's men also on the job? I had no idea, but it seemed likely that the High Priest of Israel would mount an investigation, if only to *appear* interested in finding and punishing the murderer of one of his

Temple personnel. (Readers will want to recall that this was all *years* before Choni—which is how Onias II High Priest of all Israel, the Anointed Priest of the Ancient Order of Aaron and Zadok was known to all—readers will need to remember that this all happened *years* before Four kicked Choni out and elevated his brother Jason—Choni's own brother, I mean—to the position in his stead.) But whether they would declare the case unsolvable or frame some poor hoodlum and make *him* pay for a crime they themselves had commissioned, I had no idea. If they *had* actually had anything to do with the crime, that was.

Was I crazy even to suspect that the priests had their hand in this somewhere? I don't want to tell you the rest of the story before I'm ready to tell it in detail, but I can say with whatever precision my memory can still afford me that I was actually *certain* they played some role in Buki's murder from the first moment I heard of it. Was I wrong to develop a theory about the identity of the perpetrators even before I gathered a single shred of evidence? I suppose that, at least in retrospect, I was. (And even that admission is phrased far too kindly.) But unsubstantiated, unproven theories aren't necessarily false either. And I knew that too!

Enter the Witch of Ein Dor. She wasn't the *real* witch, of course—or, at least, not the one that helped King Saul conjure up the ghost of the dead Samuel about a thousand years prior to Buki's murder—and she also wasn't really from Ein Dor, or at least I've never heard that she was. How old she really was, I had no idea. She claimed to have been ninety the year of Paneas, which would have made her ninety-nine the year Buki was murdered. As far as I was concerned, she certainly could have been that old. She was a tiny woman. Her skin, nut brown and wrinkled almost beyond description, had the texture of cured deerskin. And she had almost a full set of yellowish-brownish teeth that had somehow become as pointy as a fox's over the years. Did she actually file them down to make them as sharp as they looked? It seemed unlikely, but between her teeth and her tiny black eyes, she couldn't have had more vulpine an air about her if she actually did sharpen her teeth with a file.

The witch spoke a peculiar patois of Hebrew, Aramaic, Greek, and Egyptian that was challenging for most to understand, yet her inscrutability somehow only added to her charm. And she was indeed charming, or at least to me she was. She spoke her own language. She was incredibly old. Her sharp, pointy teeth were the color of mustard. She was, it was commonly believed, possessed of no fixed residence and lived instead like some sort of urban version of the desert nomad. She exuded a peculiar odor that wasn't at all unpleasant—something like a mixture of aloes, jasmine, pepper and violets—and she always dressed in huge mud-brown garments that invariably appeared to be on the verge of swallowing her up entirely. And, on top of all of that, the mysterious dialect she used in her daily discourse was not her sole language: the oracles that were her stock in trade were delivered to her public in the pristine Jerusalem Hebrew of King Josiah's day, a dialect known to most of us today through the oracles of the prophet Jeremiah.

I knew her personally because she appeared regularly in the Temple compound late at night to participate as a guest in our midnight rituals. That was more or less common knowledge, at least among our people. But far less well known was that it was occasionally she, rather than one of us, to whom the oracle was formally vouchsafed. The whole "Moab is my washing pot" business was hers, for example. And the very famous "Be thou neither horse nor mule" psalm that everyone knows from Yom Kippur was hers as well. (They're both in the book, of course . . . but without any hint that it was she who first seized the words out of the ether and spoke them in God's name to the rest of us. But that, of course, is how things had to be. What the reaction would have been if it had been known that we were admitting women further into the sacred precincts than priestly law allowed, I can't even begin to imagine. But it would have been intense . . . and "intense" isn't even close to being the right word for the firestorm that would have ensued if we had made the enfranchisement of women part of our public platform.)

Where she is now, I have no idea. I suppose she must have died somewhere along the way, but I never actually heard anything of her demise: she simply came by less and less frequently, then finally not at all. Perhaps she died in the desert somewhere and was buried by nomads before anyone here could take note of her absence. Or maybe she's still alive—she's be a scant 155 now—somewhere still out there, still speaking divine oracles for a living, still sharpening her incisors with a flint in her spare time. It's not likely. But neither would I be all that amazed if she were to knock on the door of my home tonight to deliver some divine oracle for my personal delectation.

I think I was still lying in bed that first morning when it struck me that I could begin my investigation into Buki's murder by talking to the witch. (I should mention that there was a name she occasionally said was her own—Ketziya—but whether that was the name her parents gave her or one she herself had chosen somewhere along the way—that much, I never found out. In any event, it was the name I used both to address her to her face and to refer to her to others.)

The idea appealed to me. In fact, the more I thought about it, the more reasonable it felt at least to begin by interviewing Ketziya. For one thing, she knew Buki personally. I hadn't ever thought much of it, but now that

I was totally focused on the little I knew with certainty about Buki and his habits and friends, I realized that I had seen the two of them together on several different occasions . . . and not only within the Temple precincts. I had, for example, once come across them huddled in deep conversation just outside the eastern gate leading into the Upper Shuk, just a few steps from the booth of Idbash the Onion Seller. Of course, at the time seeing them together hadn't felt especially ominous. Nor was it even that surprising, really. As noted, Ketziya had many contacts in our ranks. So why shouldn't Buki have been among them? And if they knew each other, so why shouldn't they have enjoyed the occasional private conversation? And as far as patronizing the same onion stall, what did that mean? I shopped there myself!

And starting with Ketziya appealed to me as well because I knew that she was not above using her psychic powers to solve mysteries in need of solutions. People went to her when they lost things and more times than not she was able to tell them where to begin looking for whatever they had misplaced. I personally knew of two or three times that she had also helped people find missing children. She had even been summoned to the Temple on several occasions when some ritual appurtenance of the highest sanctity had somehow gone missing and the service could not continue in its absence. And she had helped the police solve crimes, including at least one murder, in the past on several occasions merely by summoning up the holy spirit and offering obscure, but ultimately decipherable, tips to the police regarding where to look for the body or the right way to interpret whatever clues the police had to work with.

How that all worked—if she could truly turn her gift of prophetic insight on and off at will, or if she had simply developed her mystic persona because she knew perfectly well that there was no other way a police officer would ever bother listening to a woman's insights—I had no idea. Nor did I need to know. Indeed, regardless of whether she was accessing her information from some divine source of prophetic insight or whether she had solved the cases in which she had become involved merely by focusing her intelligent gaze where only less bright people had previously looked, all that really mattered to me was the possibility that she might help me come just a step or two closer to finding Buki's murderer. Now all I needed was to find her!

THIRTEEN

IN THE END, FINDING Ketziya turned out to be the easy part. Since I had no idea where she lived, or even if she had a fixed domicile, all I could think to do was to keep to my regular schedule and wait for our paths to cross.

As it turned out, I didn't end up having to wait very long at all. Having no other plan to pursue, I did what I would normally do on a free day. I slept late, headed to the Street of the Lambs for a scrub-up, then to Upper King Hezekiah Road for a haircut and a massage, then to my brother-in-law's shop to drink tea with him before things got too busy for him to sit idly and chat about nothing in particular with someone who wasn't there to buy anything. Uriel Gedalia, Avital's brother, is five or six years younger than me, but we've always gotten along—I still see him from time to time and we still like each other even now that we're both old men. Back then, of course, we were both young fellows . . . and, at least most of the time, extremely busy young fellows at that: I had the Temple to keep me occupied night and day and he was permanently busy with his extremely successful spice business in the Upper Shuk, an enterprise that he had inherited from his father and expanded dramatically to include all sorts of products that he alone made available to the buying public in Jerusalem.

It was a very good business. Uri was the first to bring Lydian myrrh to Jerusalem, for example. And I believe he was the first to market dried sumac powder in the city at all, and certainly the first to offer it in bulk quantities. He had a knack for guessing what the next big thing was going to be—and he was more or less *always* right—but, for all his success, he never developed a swollen head and never felt above sitting in the back of his shop or upstairs in his personal lair and drinking mint tea with his brother-in-law. And I repaid him the favor by welcoming him to the Temple when he came and giving him pride of place among the faithful when he came forward to watch the priests disembowel some poor ox to the glory of God Almighty, which he seemed to enjoy more than I ever would have expected him to. Or anybody to, for that matter.

The late morning is the busiest time in any marketplace and Jerusalem's Upper Shuk is no exception. So it was long before midday that I left Uriel Gedalia to his customers and began to wonder what exactly I should do to come across Ketziya (or, to posit the more likely scenario, to let her come across me). I walked around for a while in the market, then walked slowly around the Old Palace, then around the Temple, then along the eastern and southern walls of the city. I was getting tired and, what's worse, I wasn't getting anywhere. And I was feeling a little foolish too, especially given the fact that I didn't actually have any truly honest reason to think that Ketziya was going to be able to help me at all. But I had no other ideas, so I pursued the one I did have.

By mid-afternoon, I was tired and frustrated. For all I knew, Ketziya might not even have heard about Buki's death. (That sounded unlikely, but who knew?) At any rate, the day had almost passed and so, when they sounded the *magreifa* to announce the slaughter of the afternoon sacrifice, I decided to call it a day. And, of course, it was just as I was giving up and heading home that I finally found her.

I was turning the corner into Potters' Lane. On some level, I suppose I was still hoping to catch a glimpse of Ketziya somewhere and that's exactly what I got—a momentary glimpse of someone her size decked out in the kind of brown burlap outfit she always wore turning the corner just a street past ours. I didn't want to start running, so I walked with long, even strides to the corner instead and tried to affect the demeanor of a man of leisure out for a brisk afternoon stroll. Of course, she was long gone when I got to the corner. But I headed down the lane anyway—it was called Rose Garden Lane, a name left over from when the largest shop in town selling rose plants and the gardening implements necessary to coax them into blossom was located right in that narrow street (which was really not more than a long alley leading into the Lower Shuk)—and from there into the market.

Unlike the genteel upper marketplace where Uriel Gedalia had his spice shop and which featured merchants who were all basically middlemen and retailers, the Lower Shuk was basically a free-for-all open to anyone who had something to sell and needed a place to sell it in. People from everywhere set themselves up in these rickety wooden stalls provided by the municipality on a first-come-first-served basis, then sold whatever they had brought to market and vacated the space to someone else as soon as their wares were gone—and woe betide them if they didn't vacate fast enough for whomever was waiting. As you would expect, the din was incredible. Sheep bleating, cows lowing, salesmen aggressively hawking their wares, chickens squawking, donkeys braying, armies of cats screeching as they raced in and out between the legs of buyers and sellers alike, people calling out to the customers in other stalls to inquire about the prices they were being offered—the Lower Shuk was not a place for a quiet chat. But reasonable or not, it was there that Ketziya appeared to have led me. Or was she only headed there to do some shopping? I had no idea, but I followed her as best I could to see where the chase would lead.

We circled the outer edge of the market, then crossed the Street of the Lambs about three blocks east of the bathhouse. I thought she was going to walk towards the bath, but she kept walking north and didn't appear to hesitate even slightly on her, now our, journey.

I had no idea where we were going. When we reached the northern wall of the city, about a furlong west of the Temple, she slowed her pace. I watched with great interest as she stopped at a spice dealer's shop I don't believe I had ever noticed before. She paused for a moment, then walked inside. Perhaps, I told myself, she was only there to buy something. But I didn't believe it, not for a minute.

Unsure what to expect, I followed her into the shop. There were sacks and barrels of spice all around, but the aroma was quite different from Uriel's place—more pungent and far stronger. My eyes began to tear lightly, but I wiped them dry and then, not really knowing what to do, I sat down on a low stool in the middle of the shop and waited for something to happen.

The shop was dusky, the light inside dim. I felt a peculiar kind of shiver working its way down my spine and settling unpleasantly into the cleft between my buttocks. For a long moment, it felt as though an insect of some sort had lodged itself there and I was just thinking of trying to *dis*lodge it manually when I remembered I was not alone in the room.

Where exactly Ketziya was standing, I couldn't tell. She was tiny, though, so she could have been almost anywhere—behind a sack of oleander or a tub of morningtooth or even inside one of the larger barrels. She could even have been standing out in the open directly behind me, but I somehow knew intuitively not to turn my head or to seek her out with my eyes. Instead, I remained seated and looked straight forward as I waited for something to happen. And then she spoke. I've never forgotten what she said. Nor have her words lost any of their power to unnerve, not even after all this time.

Skipping any words of introduction or welcome, Ketziya spoke with a kind of throaty intensity I knew all too well from the times I had witnessed Levites successfully receiving divine oracles in the Temple. But whether she actually was receiving a divine oracle, or if she was merely expressing herself in the manner of those through whom the Almighty chooses to speak to the world, I obviously had no way to find out.

An unexpected gust of cold air whistled by my feet. I felt a sudden pang in my stomach almost as though my bowels were becoming loose, but the feeling passed quickly and was replaced with something entirely different. It was somewhat like the initial stages of sexual arousal—minus the sense of pleasure anticipated, of course—in that I felt my pulse quickening and my skin becoming ultra-sensitive to the weight of my clothing as Ketziya managed with a few words to shove me over a threshold I myself had walked up to and which I was suddenly not at all certain I wanted to cross. It was, however, far too late now to turn back. And so I chose instead to sit as calmly as possible and to listen to whatever it was tiny Ketziya had brought me to this place to tell me.

"Hear my words, Doeg of Edom," she said, apparently either addressing some ghostly presence she alone could see or else addressing me indirectly by speaking to that specter. "How dare you take pride in your evil ways, you who are known as a hero?" she continued. "How dare you spend all day long doing abominable deeds? Your tongue thinks of naught but evil schemes; it is like a polished razor that does ill to whomever it touches. You love evil more than good, the telling of a lie more than speaking justly. You love the muttered lie and you admire the speech of swindlers. But this too must you know: God will demolish you forever, annihilating you and sweeping you out of the tent, uprooting you from the land of the living. The righteous will look on and be stupefied. They will laugh at such a one and say, 'Here is a fellow who did not make God his refuge, who trusted in his great wealth, who schemed mightily.'"

And, with that, she was gone. Did her words constitute some sort of message? And, if so, then from *whom* was it a message? And how had that person known to send me a message through Ketziya, given that I hadn't mentioned her name to a soul in connection with this investigation the Great One had laid on my head not twenty-four hours earlier? Was it an oracle? I balked at the obvious implications of *that* thought, then forced myself to reconsider. I was, after all, someone who had devoted his life to the cultivation of precisely the kind of message I had just received. But what it meant, I had absolutely no idea.

I wrote it down immediately, hoping I was remembering her words correctly. It *felt* as though I had. I did my best. (How *her* words ended up part of *our* book is also a good story, but one I'll have to tell some other time.) But what *was* she trying to tell me? I studied her words intently, trying to wring every last scintilla of meaning out of each syllable. Why I believed them to have any importance at all is another question entirely, of course. But I did. And not only did I think they had some importance, I was somehow sure she possessed information absolutely crucial to my nascent—actually, not *even* nascent—investigation.

I began by considering the obvious. She had called the person she was addressing—not me, surely, but *somebody*—she had called that person Doeg of Edom and she had pronounced his name exceedingly carefully and with far more emphasis than you'd expect from someone who just wanted to be understood easily. It's a good story, actually. When David was fleeing from the increasingly demented King Saul, he needed a weapon to use to defend himself and so he headed to Nob, where the sword of Goliath—the very sword David had previously used to behead his Philistine enemy— where Goliath's sword was stored for safekeeping. He gets it from the priests there—and takes provisions for his men as well—then leaves, but he makes one enormous error of judgment before being on his way. There was a man there who didn't belong, a guy named Doeg of Edom. What Doeg was doing there, no one has ever explained too cogently. Maybe he was dating one of the priests' daughters . . . or maybe he was just present by coincidence to purchase something or to deliver something. Whatever . . . he is there and he is someone loyal—and totally so—to Saul, even in the latter's semideranged dotage. David sees him there, but somehow fails to realize that Doeg is going to tell Saul how the priests have aided someone whom the king had personally marked for death. And that is exactly what actually does happen. Of course, all Saul needs to hear is that the priests of Nob have aided David and the next thing we hear is Doeg being commissioned to execute the entire priesthood of the Nob sanctuary. Which he accomplishes expertly, inadvertently allowing only one single priest to escape.

Later on, David owns up to his error and admits that it was precisely because of his failure to comprehend the obvious that all those many of God's creatures—scores of priests plus their wives, children, oxen, asses and sheep—were killed. So that's the story we all learned in school. But what was Ketziya speaking about here? Surely, it now seemed to me, she hadn't really been communing with Doeg's ghost, but referring to someone in my world—someone in Buki's world too, perhaps—as Doeg, as *a* Doeg. But whom could she have meant? I tried to remember if tradition has anything to say about Doeg's physical appearance, but I couldn't think of a thing. He's called an Edomite, but what exactly did that mean? That he really was from Edom? Or that he had red hair? (The name Edom sounds vaguely like the standard Hebrew word for "red" and it was entirely normal back in those days to poke fun at guys with red hair by calling them Edomites.) Or maybe the reference was merely meant to imply that he was a man consumed with anger and rage, as the prophet said in the name of God: "For three trans-gressions of Edom I will turn away its punishment, but for the fourth I will not turn it away: because he pursued his brother with the sword, refusing him all pity, and also ever stoking his own anger so as to keep the flame of wrath alive forever." That phrase "pursued his brother with a sword" nestled into my consciousness and stayed there. Was that some sort of allusion to Buki's fate? Surely the prophet Amos wasn't speaking from his grave to me directly . . . but what if Ketziya's words were intended all along to remind me of Amos's? I played with the Hebrew and wondered if she had possibly been speaking in anagrams. But I came back to reality soon enough and found myself feeling semi-certain that Ketziya had called Buki's murderer a Doeg because he had killed one of his brothers with a sword and denied him all mercy, allowing himself instead to be consumed with rage. And maybe because he had red hair.

One of his brothers? I made a note to myself to check in Amos as soon as I got home to see if I was remembering the verse correctly. Did the prophet really indict Edom for the murder of a brother? Was Buki's murderer one of us, we who surreptitiously (but not all *that* surreptitiously) called ourselves each other's brethren? And if it *was* one of us and that per-son *was* someone of whom it could reasonably be said that he was given to the perpetual stoking of his own flames of anger and rage . . . then who could that possibly be? Or was I off the deep end before I had even started? I reminded myself that the priests were also our brethren, that we were all members of the tribe of Levi. (Is that a confusing concept? We *all* belonged to the tribe of Levi theoretically, but only we were ever called "Levites" in daily discourse, which term was *never* used to reference the Temple priests.) And I reminded myself as well that Ketziya had made no real allusion to Amos and had merely called the person she was addressing—the person whom I was surmising was Buki's murderer—as Doeg. Perhaps, I thought dejectedly, she had meant something entirely different, something I had yet even to think of.

Stepping out into the street and making my way south in the narrow alley, I returned to Ketziya's words and began to analyze them as best I could.

FOURTEEN

A RED-HEADED BROTHER. AN enemy given over wholly to anger. Someone whose tongue was a polished razor, thus someone known for an unusual level of eloquence. And someone whose misdeeds might possibly trigger eviction from the tent. Now *that*, at least, anyone would understand. There wasn't a Jew in Jerusalem who didn't know David's hymn—for unschooled readers, that's David ben Zakur the Levite, not King D.—that began by asking rhetorically who might hope to sojourn in God's holy tent on God's holy mountain. It was entirely normal to refer to the Temple as "the tent" . . . so a picture was beginning to emerge in my mind as I wandered rather aimlessly through the narrowest alleyways of the quarter of Jerusalem I knew least well of all, the section just to the west of the Temple mount along the city's northern wall.

Eloquence. Possibly red hair. A quick temper. Lives in the Temple or at least might have to face expulsion from the Temple for his misdeeds, so at least spends enough time there for banishment to be a serious punishment. Is a Levite or a priest, and is somebody given over to abominable deeds. For a long while, I walked slowly forward cataloguing abominations. Ketziya hadn't used the usual word to denote a deed so repulsive and abominable that it fell naturally into its own category of lexicographical badness, but one far more rare . . . and, it suddenly struck me, far more significant. *Chesed eil kol hayom*, she had said—you spend all day long doing deeds abominable unto God—but she had called those deeds by one of those so-called contronyms—a word that has two meanings which are each other's opposites. There aren't that many of them in Hebrew—there are way more, as most readers will know, in Greek—but there are some. And *chesed* is most certainly among them. Mostly, it refers to acts of lovingkindness and grace. But sometimes it refers to truly abominable deeds, to crimes so bleak and bad that merely to label them as criminal is hardly to damn them at all.

I began to ransack my somewhat meager memory banks to remember what specific acts are called *chesed* in the Torah of the priests. (And lest you think I'm anticipating my own conclusions—yes, of course, I was thinking priests by this time. Live in the Temple, quick tempered, eloquent, angry . . . who else can she possibly have had in mind? And the priests, who constituted a kind of sub-clan within the larger tribe of Levi, were at least genealogically our brethren.) I was hardly an expert, but the only verse that jumped out at me was one of the ones we had to memorize for our initial entrance exam. And *that* verse I knew by heart: "If a man should take his sister—regardless of whether she is his father's daughter or his mother's—and see her nakedness, while also letting her see his own, then this is a *chesed* and they shall both be cut off from their people."

Now this was getting interesting. Mind you, I kept reminding myself, I had no real reason to believe that Ketziya knew anything at all about Buki's murder. But I didn't think that, not really, not for a minute—she had to have understood what it was I wanted to know, she led me to that spice shop, she allowed me to hear when she was visited by the spirit of the living God (if that's what it was, I mean—and neither a simple, clever way to get someone she was irritated with into trouble nor some delusional fantasy to which she had momentarily succumbed). And then something else struck me, something I had somehow—and this was interesting in its own right, now that I thought of it—something I had somehow skipped over. Hadn't she made reference to Doeg being a man of great wealth? The real Doeg—the one in the Bible—is hardly there at all . . . and we, the readers, are certainly not told how much wealth he did or didn't possess. But she had said something about wealth, I felt certain. I reviewed the text again, using the hand copy I had made of her oracle so as not to have to trust my own memory. And there it was, the very last line of her speech: "They will laugh at such a one and say, 'Here is a fellow who did not make God his refuge, who trusted in his great wealth, who schemed mightily.'"

And with that, the pieces of the puzzle fell into place one after another like dumplings into hot oil. Red hair, after all, was one thing. And red hair combined with a sharp tongue and a hot temper, was also something. But red hair combined with eloquence *and* easy rage *and* great wealth, however, could only point in one specific direction. And, yes, he had a sister.

FIFTEEN

THERE WASN'T A JEW in Jerusalem who didn't either know or know of Benjamin Ginnethon ben Baruch Hakohen. I hadn't ever been introduced to him personally, but he was the priest who had presided at my own investiture ceremony and at Joseph's, and I surmised that he could certainly have served in that capacity at Buki's as well. Whether he and Buki had that or any other relationship, I had no idea. But I was going to find out.

In a world of difficult, stubborn, imperious, condescending, self-important priests, Benjamin Ginnethon was in a class all by himself. At least four cubits tall and possessed of more fiery red hair than any man I had ever seen—or, for that matter, any woman—he was not easily missed in a crowd. And he had a reputation to match his appearance. He served in the Temple as its second in command, the so-called Vice High Priest, but it was widely assumed that this was not a position he intended to fill for long. Mind you, his position was far more important—and far more powerful—than its formal title, with its inherent intimation of second-fiddlehood, would necessarily suggest to the reader unacquainted with the ins and outs of Temple politics. But, for all his power and influence, he was still Number Two . . . and no one who knew Benjamin Ginnethon could imagine he intended to tolerate that kind of secondary status for any longer than absolutely necessary no matter how much power he actually wielded.

We called him the Firebrand or, using the Hebrew term even when we spoke Aramaic or Greek, the Ood. He was the one who invariably ordered our people to strip down when he found them asleep at their posts—and he was one of the very few senior Temple officials who ever personally patrolled at night—so he could burn their robes to ash, then make them wait, freezing in just their underbreeches and (he must surely have hoped) deeply and permanently humiliated, until morning came and they could race home to dress. And, of course, he looked like a firebrand too—a tall, lean stick of a man with red and orange hair leaping off his head in all directions at once. So to us he was the Ood, the Firebrand. He was a horror. And his sister was worse. But I'm getting ahead of myself. As usual!

Was it the Ood that Ketziya was trying to implicate in Buki's murder? As I wandered semi-aimlessly through the streets of the city, I considered the evidence. I had to admit that he fit the bill nicely. He had a sharp tongue and was famous for his temper. He was a priest of the tribe of Levi. He had red hair (and was, indeed, sneered at by our people regularly because of it and called the Oodomite or the Ood of Edom, or sometimes just Esau) and he was eloquent to boot. He also had a very nice singing voice—as nice, I have to admit, as the best of our people—and he occasionally sang some songs of his own composition in one or another of the wine bars near the Fish Gate. This part, I knew from personal experience because I myself had been present once when he was giving forth in song. I obviously had no way to say for certain whether or not he was telling the truth about having personally composed the songs he was performing, but I remember thinking that the songs themselves were exceptional pieces of work both in terms of their melodic structure (which was somehow complex without being so complicated as to be off-putting) and their rich use of internal rhyme. I remember that evening well, actually. I had gone there alone for some reason—where Joseph (my usual partner in crime) was, I can't recall—but I went by myself and ended up sitting with one or two people I recognized from class, but whom I hardly really knew at all. And thus, freed from the obligation to talk too much to anybody, was I also free to focus on the music, which I enjoyed immensely.

His sister, Meirav Serach bat Baruch Hakohen, was another story entirely. As a young woman, she had married a very successful man, an importer of gold and semi-precious stones, especially turquoise, from Arabia, Persia and Hindustan, but he died as a young man. That much, everybody knew. As did we also all know that they had a single son, Tola, who had duly inherited the entirety of his father's estate. But, in that Tola was all of five years old when his father died, the estate that was formally his had been entrusted to his mother, who was duly named as the court-appointed guardian charged with protecting the value of its assets and spending only what she deemed necessary to support little Tola appropriately until he attained his majority.

That much was common knowledge, but there was a good deal more here to consider. For one thing, Ikkesh's body—Ikkesh ben Tovim was the late husband—his body was found one spring day in an alley just inside the

Dung Gate barefoot, but without any marks of any sort on it. The authorities presumed he must have had a lethal heart attack, but the populace wasn't buying it. He was young, he was in excellent health, he had no history of heart pain (or of any kind of internal distress) and he was lean and strong—not at all your candidate for a fatal heart attack in what should have been the prime of his life. Instead, the common wisdom had it that he was poisoned . . . and it wasn't necessary to go too far to find a suspect: little Tola's right to inherit the totality of his father's estate effectively guaranteed that control of his father's wealth would pass directly, if not permanently, into his mother's hands, which it was generally assumed was precisely where she wished it to be for as long as possible. Why Ikkesh ben Tovim was barefoot when he died, or at least why he wasn't wearing shoes when his body was discovered, no one knew. But the detail faded quickly. Even I barely recalled it until Asa Gad, whom I haven't even introduced into this story yet, recalled it to me. But what it meant I too had no way even to guess at until much later on.

That Meirav Serach's lifestyle took a sudden, very public turn for the more luxurious was one thing. (She was, after all, in full charge of her late husband's fortune.) But that her brother—you see what I'm getting at, I suppose—but that her brother Benjamin Ginnethon *also* started living dramatically better than he had previously been able to manage on his priest's income, that *too* escaped the attention of . . . no one at all. Benjamin G. was married, but—in the opinion of the masses—neither too devotedly nor too happily. His wife, a long drip of water named Esther Malka, used to spend so much time at her parents' estate in the Sharon that she was only rarely seen in Jerusalem, which arrangement appeared to suit both herself and her husband perfectly. It certainly also appeared to suit her grieving sister-in-law, Meirav Serach, and thus was it only a matter of time before Meirav Serach sold her home and moved herself and Tola into the Ood's house. What everybody said out loud was how nice Benjamin was to take in his poor widowed sister and her boy. What everybody thought privately, on the other hand, was far less printable in a work that children might conceivably read some day. Or *was* it just about money? Many were of that opinion as well. To say the very least, though, the arrangement struck any number of Jerusalemites as so peculiar so as to be bordering on the bizarre. Benjamin's wife now came home . . . never. Meirav Serach comported herself more and more like the lady of the house. The boy, who knows what he thought? The situation was so odd that it was actually considered beyond the boundaries of normal gossip for the wags of Jerusalem. And, believe me, anyone who knows Jerusalem at all will know just how far beyond the pale of acceptability something has to be to land in *that* category.

So maybe Meirav Serach arranged her husband's death so she and her son could move in with her brother or maybe she didn't. Or maybe she just had the courage to make the best of things when Ikkesh died naturally and her brother's estrangement from his wife presented itself to her as a situation only a fool would refuse to exploit. For all I myself knew, it could well *just* have been about the money! But the bottom line is that Ikkesh wasn't dead for a month before Meirav Serach and her boy moved in with her brother and set up housekeeping as his . . . as his something.

Could Benjamin Ginnethon have had a hand in Buki's murder? It was, at best, a long shot. I knew of no connection between the two of them, nor had I ever heard of anything linking Meirav Serach and Buki. Whether the late Buki knew or had any relationship of any sort with Meirav Serach's late husband, I also didn't know. It wasn't inconceivable that Buki could have been one of Ikkesh's customers, but even if I could prove that—which I ab-solutely had no idea how in the world I ever could prove it anyway—but even if I *could* prove it, what would that information mean? That a dead man once owned a business and that another dead man bought something there once or twice . . . or a thousand times! So what?

But Ketziya's oracle had to mean something, didn't it? Or did it? How exactly I knew she wasn't spouting gibberish, I can't say. How I knew she wasn't purposefully trying to mislead me, I also can't say. But since I had no other ideas, I suppose I figured it couldn't hurt to start by asking the simplest of questions, one that I thought I probably *could* answer simply enough. Did the Ood know Buki? Finding out wouldn't be that hard. For one thing, I could ask him.

I mentioned before that Jerusalem was a small town in those days, but it's probably going to be hard for readers today to understand just how small it really was. It's not such a big place now either, of course, but then it was truly a one-donkey town. The Temple was the focus of everything and the rest of the town basically existed to service, house, and feed the people who lived or worked there. We all knew each other. There were times when I would walk through the Fish Gate and make it all the way to the Temple without encountering a single person I didn't know by name. We didn't all get along—that much totally *is* true. But not getting along doesn't mean not knowing the names of the people you aren't getting along with . . . and the truth is that we did all know each other, if not intimately, than at least by name. So finding BG wasn't going to be a huge problem. And approaching him wasn't going to be all that complicated either—all I was going to have to do was locate him and ask for a moment of his time. His reputation was fierce, but I didn't think I'd set him off just by asking to talk for a minute. After all, I reminded myself, don't self-absorbed people like it when others ask for their counsel or solicit their help? Isn't the whole *point* of being self-absorbed precisely that it never feels unnatural for strangers to turn to you for information or assistance? You are the greatest and brightest person who ever lived, after all! So what could be more normal than less great people asking for your help? What I was actually going to say to the man, of course, was another question entirely and one I hadn't even begun to work out in my mind. But my first job was to find him.

When I got home, I found Avital in the courtyard boiling a pot of leeks on the garden hearth. This, in and of itself, wasn't so unexpected—Avital makes excellent potato and leek soup—but that we both had come home earlier than expected *and* that there weren't any children around *and* that neither of us had any place to go before she was due at her sister's for supper (that was whom the soup was for) and I had to show up for a final lecture on the art of eviscerating large animals—that, we both interpreted as a highly unexpected and highly desirable concatenation of events well worth the trouble of exploiting maximally.

For those of you who have never had the pleasure, there is absolutely nothing to compare with the experience of making love to a beautiful woman on a good carpet in a warm room in a cold house in the dead of winter with a pot of purple leeks boiling on an outdoor hearth and filling the house with the delicate aroma of God's best vegetable. I don't know why I was so overwhelmed with desire—although I can assure you that it was way more than just opportunity that was filling me with desire and drawing me forward—but I can hardly recall ever making love with more abandon, with more passion, or with more emotional involvement than I experienced that wintery afternoon half a century ago. Avital, for her part, was equally in-volved—it felt like I could almost feel my whole soul, my whole life, entering into her sphere of being. I know that sounds idiotic when you see it written out, but there really are two kinds of sexual involvement in the world: the kind that leads to the penetration of body parts and the kind that leads to the admixture of souls. This was the latter—and when we finally finished, I felt like I might never stand up again. And, indeed, for a long while, we just lay there on the rug, trying not to focus on the fact that that same rug had once adorned the *traklin* of my first set of in-laws' vacation house in the up-per Galilee and was only left here by my first wife because she had developed the peculiar sense that it was haunted by her mother's stepmother—from whose estate my former in-laws had inherited it—whom she loathed more even than she disliked me. But I digress yet again!

As we lay on the rug, I felt winded, tired, and totally and utterly spent, and I could tell Avital felt the same way. And so, for a long time, we just lay there side by side, warm and cozy . . . and I told Avital about all the things that I've been writing about in these last few chapters. I told her in detail about my interview in the bathhouse with the Great One and about my visit to Uriel Gedalia's shop, then I described the scene in the spice shop—the other spice shop, not Uriel's—with Ketziya and I declaimed the oracle, which I continued (slightly amazingly) to be able to recall by heart. Avital snuggled up close to me and pressed her back up against my chest as I told her what I thought the oracle meant. She listened carefully. And she didn't much like what she was hearing.

"You're not thinking of taking Benjamin Ginnethon on all by yourself are you?"

"Maybe."

"He'll have you arrested and no one will ever hear from you again."

"Arrested? On what charge?"

"He won't need one." Avital turned her head so she could see my face. "He won't need one and you won't hear one, but you'll disappear just the same and I'll never see you again."

"If he's not guilty, he won't need to be so touchy."

"Who says he's not guilty? But it won't matter. If he is guilty, he'll kill you. If he's not guilty, he'll kill you anyway . . . and tell himself he was only defending his honor."

"I won't go alone."

Avital sighed and I could feel her breasts heave. "Yes," she said entirely correctly, "you will."

"I don't have to."

"Yes, you do."

"I thought you'd be pleased if I didn't go alone."

"I would be. But we both know you are going to do this alone. Taking someone along makes it look like you want a witness to hear his confession. He'll have his back up anyway, but bringing your own backup will make it impossible for you to get anywhere. Of course, you'll go alone."

"Well," I countered, "I'll confront him in a public place."

"Confront him? Confront him how? Are you going to ask politely if he murdered Buki ben Yerimoth? Is he just going to tell you he did?"

Avital had come across a serious weakness in my plan: I had no plan. I suppose if I had to say what my fondest hope was, it would have to have been that I come away from my encounter with Benjamin Ginnethon certain that he was Buki's murderer, or the employer of Buki's murderer or murderers, which information I could then relay to the Great One and be done with the whole business. But the chances of him telling me that were less than zero. And if that was the case, which it certainly was, then what exactly *was* the point of confronting him? I was sure I had had a reason. But, for the life of me, I couldn't quite recall what it was. In the meantime, however, Avital's question was hanging on the air and demanding an answer of some sort.

"No, of course not. Not in so many words, at any rate."

"Well, what then?"

"I'm going to ask him about Buki and he'll tell me nothing at all, whereupon my tiny role in this great adventure will be over.

"And you expect it to be that simple just to walk away?"

"Even simpler than simple. I ask, he answers, then I tell the Great One what happened. Or else I ask, he *doesn't* answer, and then I still tell the Great One what happened. I'm done either way."

Avital said nothing, For a long moment, she just lay there lost in thought. But then she didn't say anything at all, just got up and went out into the garden to add some previously boiled potatoes to the simmering pot. Knowing that the last thing Avital needed from me was advice on how to make soup, I got dressed, sat down to review the material we had gone over the previous week in class, and tried to put the whole matter out of my mind.

Twenty minutes later, the whole afternoon felt like a dream. Meeting the Great One, encountering Ketziya, Avital, the rug, the soup . . . it all felt like it had happened over weeks, not in the course of the previous twenty-four hours. I read for a while, then it was time for us both to leave. Zakur, Yehoram and the twins were already at Avital's sister's place, having gone there directly from school to spend the afternoon. She finished up making the soup, then transferred the pot into a large wicker carrier box designed to hold cauldrons of hot food and, almost before I had time to look up from my scroll, she was gone. I was alone in the house. Class started in forty minutes. I had, I thought, plenty of time . . . but I was also feeling antsy and slightly ill at ease. And so, instead of waiting for the last minute like I ordinarily would have, I gathered up my things, locked the door behind me, and stepped out into the street.

SIXTEEN

UNLIKE THE WITCH, THE Ood was not going to complicated or difficult to find. In fact, if anything, he was going to be difficult to avoid. As Vice High Priest, the *segan* (as he was popularly called by everyone) was almost always present in the Temple during the morning and late afternoon sacrifices. On Sabbath days and on festivals, he was invariably front and center. Even when the High Priest himself showed up to participate in the service, which was an increasingly rare occurrence in those days, Benjamin Ginnethon rarely stepped too far back. So locating the *segan* was not going to be a big challenge. But knowing what to say to him was a different question entirely.

I went to class, glad to have something else to focus on for a while. The lecture was actually more interesting than I had expected it was going to be, but I didn't stay for the question and answer period that always follows the formal presentation and instead went straight home. When I got there, the house was still. Everything appeared to be in order. From the fact that the soup tureen Avital had brought to her sister's was in its place, I knew they had all come home safely. From the fact that the door to the boys' rooms were closed, I could surmise easily enough that they had all gone right to bed. Of Avital herself, there was no sign. I might normally have stayed up for a little while to review some of what we had learned in class that evening, or even just to read a bit as a way of unwinding, but it had been an exceptionally long day and all I really want to do was to get to sleep. I locked the front door, checked the latches on the downstairs window shutters (which I almost never bothered to do before turning in), and then climbed the stairs up to our bedroom. As I had predicted, Avital was fast asleep. I undressed, replicating almost precisely the scene that had unfolded when I had come home from my interview with the Great One the previous evening. I slipped into bed, pulled Avital's left arm up over my side, then backed up against her slumbering form so I could feel the warmth of her body pressed up against my back. But now that the day had finally ended and I was safely tucked into bed, sleep refused to come.

And so, instead of giving myself over to the rest I had more than earned, I lay awake in my bed and tried to come up with a plan. I had promised Eli ben Heman I would do what I could to solve the mystery of Buki's murder. I had, even despite having no real idea how to go about doing such a thing, made some progress in the single day I had been at it. True, that progress consisted almost exclusively of listening to a woman whom I had no specific reason to suppose had any relevant information about the matter at hand, but it was—at the very least—something. And something, as my subsequent adventures in the field of crime detection proved over and over, is always better than nothing.

I tried to approach the issue first by considering the players themselves and trying to get them and their relationships to one another entirely straight in my head. That led nowhere, or at least nowhere useful, and so I decided to take another tack entirely and instead to attempt to list the questions I would like to have answered before getting even indirectly involved with the Ood. This actually turned out to be an interesting, potentially useful exercise. And, indeed, looking back from the vantage point of so many intervening years, I can see that the day on which I finally knew the answers to all the questions I innocently listed while lying in Avital's unwitting embrace was also the day on which I was truly done with this whole sorry affair of Buki's murder and mutilation.

The first questions had to do with Buki himself. Benjamin Ginnethon had (at least according to the rumor mill) banished his wife to the Upper Galilee, then moved his widowed sister and her son into his home after the death of his brother-in-law, Ikkesh ben Tovim Hakohen. From that series of events arose several interesting questions. What did the possibly-sordid-possibly-innocent story of the Ood and his sister have to do with Buki's murder? Had there been a relationship between Buki and Benjamin Ginnethon? Did Buki have a relationship of any sort with Ikkesh ben Tovim? Or with Meirav Serach herself? Or, for that matter, with Esther Malka, BG's absent wife whose position as lady of the house had now apparently been usurped totally by her own sister-in-law?

From those few questions came others. What actually had happened to Ikkesh ben Tovim? Had he had a heart attack, as everybody said was so unlikely? Surely the laws of probability allow for the occasional improbable event—and it is certainly so that people who appear to be in perfect health occasionally do keel over and die entirely unexpectedly, thus provoking all sorts of sinister, yet completely groundless, theorizing. Or *had* Ikkesh been murdered . . . and, if so, then by whom? Asking who stood to profit from his death was a reasonable first step when considering as untimely a death as his, but not, it struck me, an inevitably useful one: surely there are all sorts of people who benefit in different ways every single day of the year when death unexpectedly touches some specific citizen without the beneficiaries themselves having played some role in that person's demise!

Layered on top of all this, of course, remained the original set of questions that all Jerusalem was debating. What, precisely, did the way in which Buki was murdered have to do with any of this? Why was he decapitated posthumously or, for that matter, at all? Were we right about what the coins meant? And why was Buki (or his body) brought to the Kerith when it would have involved so much less effort *just* to ambush and murder him in Jerusalem in the dark of night, then leave him in some dark alley to be discovered by passers-by as soon as the sun came up the following morning? Did the murderer choose the Kerith because it was there that the ravens fed our hero Elijah, prince of the prophets of Israel? Or was the location in which Buki's body was found ultimately unrelated to the reason for which he was murdered?

The house was perfectly still. Avital's body was warm and soft as I pressed up against her and felt myself relax almost completely. And then, just as I was finally letting go of what had been a singularly long day, a single thought came to me . . . and, rather like a good night kiss somehow arriving from the deepest recesses of my own psyche, it was that thought that permitted me finally to drift off into a deep, restful sleep from which I only awoke when Avital herself was already busy preparing the boys' breakfast and the sun was climbing ever higher in the eastern sky as a new day dawned over the Holy City.

SEVENTEEN

As a young person, I almost never remembered my dreams. Most of the time, I couldn't even remember the details of the conversations that Avital and I used to have just before falling asleep at night. Indeed, there are times when I have to reread all of what I just read the night before in bed, so totally does the onset of sleep erase the mental activity that precedes its nightly arrival. I suppose other people may be different. But that's how it is with me, and that's why, even after all these years, I can still remember being pleasantly surprised when I awoke and knew exactly what I had been thinking about as I had drifted off to sleep the night before. Now that I'm about to tell you the rest of the story, the initial idea—the one that came to me as I lay awake in bed and worked through the whole story yet again from the very beginning—will sound obvious. It even sounds that way to me, even though at the time it felt stupendous.

How I got through the whole day that then ensued, I have no idea. I didn't have to go to work, so I devoted myself to having the kind of day I associated with men of leisure. I helped get the boys off to school, then spent a long hour at the bath on the Street of the Lambs, then did some shopping in the Upper Shuk. I ran some errands for Avital, devoted an hour or so to helping Joseph and Yemima coax a dove out of their eaves, kept what I hoped was a low profile. I tried not to think about Buki, not about his life *or* his death, and I tried even not to focus overly on what I had learned from Ketziya, if in fact I had actually learned anything meaningful from her at all. I was obliged to take an examination on the material I had learned in that class in large mammal viscera, and I wanted to get that out of the way before too much of what I had learned managed to evaporate from my all-too-porous memory. (In those days, brethren didn't sit for examinations all together as became the standard practice later on. Instead, you simply showed up at the *archayon* whenever you felt ready, solicited a list of questions from the archivist on duty, then wrote out the answers on the set of parchments that were used and endlessly re-used for this kind of test.) To my amazement, the exam was simple. I knew the answers to almost all the questions, recognizing almost everything on the diagrams I was called upon to label and finding the whole experience so little onerous that I actually wondered at one point if I was taking the right examination. But, for all the exam was relatively simple, it was also so long that it took me almost two hours to be done with it. I smiled in a friendly way to the archivist as I handed him my work, signed the waiver allowing the parchment to be scraped clean after being graded. (The parchments, as noted, were endlessly re-used. That meant that once they were graded, the grades entered, and the parchment itself scraped clean, the test could neither be re-graded nor one's work re-assessed. And that was why we were obliged to sign a kind of waiver agreeing not to contest the results once they were formally entered. Now that they use bound papyrus leaves for these tests, I think the test booklets themselves are stored in the archives. But things were different in my day. Everything, it seems, was different. Except for the parts, of course, that are exactly the same.)

At any rate, I handed in my scroll, signed the waiver, and returned home to find the boys ready for help with homework and Avital tending to a large cauldron of peppery cabbage soup. We had a pleasant dinner together and then, while Avital and I cleaned up, Yehoram gave an *ad hoc* concert on the *gittit* to show how far he had come along in his music lessons since the last time he had played for us. He was only eleven then, still very much a boy, his voice still sweet and untroubled by any intimation of adolescence. He played for a while without singing, then accompanied himself while he sang two songs he had learned in school. Readers my age will know the success he had later in life with his music, but this was far too soon for us to seize just how talented he actually was. Nonetheless, Avital and I were mesmerized. Even the twins were sufficiently captivated by their older brother's songs to sit quietly during the performance, which is not something ten-year-old boys, or at least *our* ten-year-old boys, did too often at all! When Yehoram was finished playing, Avital sent Zakur and Yehoram to wash up and prepare for bed while I myself gave Nathaniel and Asarela a scrub-down, then told them a story. Eventually, all the children were asleep and the time had come for me to put my plan into action. Within a few minutes of kissing the boys goodnight, I was mumbling something to Avital about sharing a late-night narghile with Joseph as I made my way out the door and into the night.

Later on, things became a lot more fossilized, if that's the right word, in terms of who was permitted to serve on which watch and how often one could apply for night duty. But in an earlier day things were far less complicated for all of us. There was a duty roster, of course, but signing on to a work detail to which one hadn't formally been assigned wasn't a big deal: there was almost always extra work available and enough money in the fund to compensate volunteers looking for it. As a result, the late-night shift was never really closed to any who wished to participate. Partially, this was due to the fact that it was generally freezing on the hill late at night. And partially it was due to the fact that slackers ran the ever-present risk of being stripped and beaten if they were found sleeping at their posts. And, of course, it was also partially due to the reason—unspoken and formally unacknowledged, but totally real—that a Levite might wish to appear at midnight in the Temple courtyard for his own personal reasons. I wasn't looking for extra work. I wasn't even looking for extra money. But I needed to appear in the courtyard. And I had a very real reason for wanting, for needing, for *having* to do so.

EIGHTEEN

I WENT DIRECTLY TO the Temple. As I felt certain would be the case, they were short a few men on the midnight shift and I was able to sign on easily. I put my outfit on, laced up my felt boots, stood in line with the rest of everyone to receive a specific assignment. No one, not even myself, had the slightest way to know if anyone else present had an ulterior motive for signing up for work that evening. For a moment, it struck me that I also had no way to know if the Great One had charged anyone other than myself with the task of unraveling the details surrounding Buki's murder. It stood to reason that he could have. Wouldn't two people working on the same mystery be twice as likely to succeed in solving it? And yet I somehow didn't think it had come to that, couldn't quite bring myself to think that his confidence in me had been so slight that it would have seemed to him only prudent to lay the same task on someone else's shoulders as well as on my own. I put the matter out of my mind. The evening shift began.

As usual, *they* were bedded down for the night in Hearth House, their on-site dormitory. It was a handsome structure and a well-guarded one—the priests were supposed personally to man the guard post by its front door, but that guard—if there even was one assigned to duty that night—was nowhere to be seen and, as far as I could see, it was just us in that cold, windy, sacred place. If there were priests stationed that night at either of their other guard posts, I had no idea. But I've already mentioned that one of the mysteries I only eventually solved was just how it was that priestly guards patrolling the site somehow *never* showed up at just the wrong moment. Even Benjamin Ginnethon himself, who so loved finding our people asleep at their posts, never seemed to appear at the wrong moment.

The moon rose, a slender crescent in the sky. Our patrols returned. The night was dark. The stars twinkled attractively above, but without casting much light on the world. I felt a certain ill ease seize me, an emotion I knew all too well. My lower back became damp with sweat. The night suddenly became colder, the air heavy with expectation. The moon was fully visible in the dark sapphire sky. I felt ready. I *was* ready. Or at least I thought I was.

The ritual began. The prayer. The hands. The shoulders. The cauldron. Then, just slightly at first and then more and more strongly, the light. As we stood and shivered in the frigid air of a Jerusalem winter, the light rose. I felt the muscles in my legs tightening, those in my neck growing taut. My heart began to pound within my chest. I could feel the blood coursing through my veins, something like the way one feels with one's wife when the invisible line is crossed and there is simply no turning back.

The soundless thunder. The blasts of the silent shofar growing, somehow, louder and louder within me. The combined forces of desire and selflessness, of hope and fear, of trembling so violent as to be almost uncontrollable . . . all this happened just as I knew and expected it would. And then, as the world fell away, I heard what I had come to hear. A word. Then another. Then a third. Words in our ancient language, but also in no language at all. But this language that was no language wasn't exactly a language that I simply hadn't ever learned and therefore couldn't speak as much as it was a language outside of language, a kind of communicative reality that existed beneath and beyond and behind the world of words and their mundane meaning. To say the same thing in other words, the experience was framed in words yet was *also* wholly and absolutely inexpressible. And yet . . . somehow . . . despite everything I knew and ever would learn about the way God exists in the world . . . *somehow* I felt the words taking shape within my brain, within my psyche, within the least accessible chamber of my beating heart. It was like love, like coupling with a woman, like dread so deep that it can barely be expressed at all in words let alone adequately described. I had come to ask a question, but my question remained unasked, thus also unanswered. And yet . . . somehow . . . the light that shone from underneath the threshold leading into the sanctum came to meet me and, in a way I will never manage to describe, turned at first into *just* sound and then into actual language.

Mah betza bedami, the voice asked, plaintively in the cold night air. "What profit be there in my blood?" *Mah betza berideti el shachat*? "What profit be there in my journey to the netherworld?" *Hayodcha afar*? "Can dust confess the truth?" *Hayagid amitecha*? "Can it speak the truth, *your* truth, the truth *you* need to learn?"

Do you know those words? You might! In the course of my lifetime, I had this experience, I believe, seventeen times. Each time, I tried to write it down, to preserve its meaning for future generations. But, in the end, my sole contribution to the edition of the psalms you probably own was the one in which those words were permanently enshrined as permanent testimony to my experience of the divine realm at this level of communicative intimacy. Of course, I didn't quite understand them at the moment. (They say that no one ever fully understands the words spoken until enough time passes to make it possible to consider them fully dispassionately.) But I have never forgotten those words I heard, nor have I forgotten the moment they insinuated themselves into my heart, into my brain. They constitute my estate, the only thing of real value I will leave behind when the hour comes for me to draw my last breath and leave the world behind for the living. They are my testimony and my treasure. They are my own proof—my indelible, undeniable, and unimpeachable testimony—to the fact that our *torah* was rooted, not in theory or fantasy, but in stone-cold reality. (And yes, "our *torah*" is exactly what we called the Psalms when we spoke privately and out of anyone else's earshot.)

The evening concluded quickly enough after that. Because I had signed on for the full shift, I couldn't leave. Nor, speaking honestly, did I really want to. I felt exhausted but also exhilarated. The patrols moved on. The moon finished rising, then began to sink. The stars twinkled on for a while, then became fainter and less distinct. Eventually, the second watch ended, then the third. The first rays of sunlight became visible over the eastern horizon. The day people arrived; the night people were logged out, then dismissed. Uniforms were returned. Weaponry was checked back in. We were free to go.

I walked home. It was a Thursday, the seventh of Kislev. I had the day free. I needed to sleep. But more than that I needed to decipher the experience I had had. It seemed to be pointing me in a specific direction, only I hadn't quite figured out which one. Was Buki himself speaking to me from the beyond? Was he challenging me to find meaning in his death, to solve the mystery *surrounding* his death by figuring out who had profited from his demise, to let his dust speak the truth? Was Buki telling me to seek the truth in the story—or perhaps even in the setting—of his murder? Or was it in someone else's dust that he was encouraging me to seek the truth? Or was I going off the deep end by imagining that the words I had somehow heard were related even tangentially to Buki's death? That certainly seemed possible, but I found myself nonetheless unable to shake the feeling—rooted though I knew it to be in my experience in the Temple the previous evening—that Buki's death was not about money or about women. It was about us. About who we were. About what we did. About whom we irritated. And about how far our foes would go to make us stop. Later on, I learned to be less sure of myself, to find in my own uncertainty the road to the true explanation of whatever it was I was investigating. To say the same thing in different words, I learned to find wisdom in insecurity, in uncertainty. And I learned that, although the most obvious explanation is almost always the correct one, that isn't *always* the case.

NINETEEN

WHEN I GOT HOME, the house was empty. The boys were in school. Avital must have gone out shopping after walking them there, which she often did. I went up to our bedroom and lay down on our bed. The sunlight streaming in through the window over our bed was yellow and bright, but the room itself was still cool with night air. The faint scent of eucalyptus permeated the room—the neighbors had a eucalyptus tree that bent over so far as almost to touch the side of our house—and there was a kind of peace in that room that was almost palpable. I felt good. I hadn't slept all night, but I no longer felt exhausted or even that tired. I felt, if anything energized. But I knew I had to sleep, at least a little. I lay back on the silk cover—Avital always made the bed in the morning even before she got dressed—and reviewed the situation yet again. Who, I asked myself, stood to benefit from Buki's death? And who from Ikkesh's death? Could there possibly be one person who stood to benefit from both? That thought, simple though it sounds in the retelling, electrified me. I felt focused, drawn to working this through as carefully as possible before giving myself over to sleep.

Ikkesh, I had learned merely by asking around, had had a brother, a man named Asa Gad whom I hadn't ever met. Like Ikkesh, he was a *kohen*, a priest, but not a working one who ever participated in the Temple cult. Had Ikkesh not had a son, Asa Gad would have been his brother's heir. But Ikkesh did have a son, the little boy I've already mentioned named Tola. So Asa Gad specifically did *not* benefit from his brother's death. Just the contrary—once Ikkesh had a son, Asa Gad was unlikely ever to inherit any of his brother's considerable wealth. Benjamin Ginnethon ben Baruch, on the other hand, only stood to gain a lot—or anything, really—from Ikkesh's death if he was conspiring with Meirav Serach to defraud her own child out of his rightful inheritance. Was that the point? *Could* that have been the point? But, I re-minded myself, if that actually had been the concept—that Ikkesh be mur-dered so that his widow and his murderer could conspire successfully to steal his fortune from his only child—would he then have moved Meirav Serach into his house so openly and brazenly, thus inviting speculation of the most untoward (and surely also the most unwanted) kind? Or was the idea to be-have that openly precisely so as to suggest that they had nothing to hide, that there was no reason in the world for him *not* to take in his widowed sister? That thought, I found as arresting as it was upsetting. I resolved to set it aside, at least for the time being, and return to it later.

Buki, I felt certain, could not have been *that* wealthy a man at the time of his death. He did own a home, which certainly had some serious value. And, judging from the way I had heard that home was furnished and the way he traveled freely whenever the spirit moved him, he must have had some money tucked away somewhere. I hadn't ever heard that Yerimoth, his father, was especially wealthy, but Buki was his father's only son and would have inherited the entirety of his estate. Added to this thought was the detail that Buki had no children and no wife. True, he did have a sister and a mother, but was his estate large enough—could it possibly have been large enough—for them to consider taking a human life to gain access to it? Judging from the way they both were carrying on at his funeral, I could hardly believe their grief to have been feigned. Still, I reminded myself, couldn't the whole point of their public misery have been to mislead the misleadable public?

And yet, this whole line of thinking didn't really make much sense. For one thing, it was not at all clear to me that his mother or his sister would be his heir now that he was dead—as far as I know, the only way a female can inherit the totality of any man's estate is if she is his only child or if she is the daughter of his only child. Otherwise, the estate will always pass to the closest male relative . . . which would probably have been one of Buki's great-uncles or one of their sons. And on top of all that, I didn't *really* think that Buki was anywhere near wealthy enough for anyone to kill him to gain access to his money. The more I thought about the whole matter, the less I felt I understood. And the more perplexed I became.

And then, just as I was attempting to formulate the exact words I was going to use to admit to the Great One that I had failed him completely, a single idea somehow popped into my head that drew me off into a slightly new direction. The words I had heard in the Temple, in the style of all true oracles, had been almost fully obscure. I had thought it through as best I could more than just a few times, obviously. But now the second part, the part featuring the rhetorical question "Can the dust of the dead confess the truth?," insinuated itself in my brain and refused to budge. Rather in the way one might let a large dog cuddle up into one's lap and simply sit there until it grows tired of being there and moves on of its own accord, I stopped struggling and let the oracle talk to me in its own mysterious way. *Can* the dust of the dead speak? I considered the question seriously. Surely, I told myself, it cannot. I continued my reverie. But let's imagine, I proposed to myself, let's imagine just for a moment, that it could, that the dust of the dead *could* somehow come back to life just for a single moment to say something, to reveal something, to confess something. And let's imagine, just for a moment, that Buki's enormous frame were actually to rise from its earthen tomb to share a single secret with the living rather in the style of the prophet Samuel when posthumously summoned back to the land of the living by the original Witch of Ein Dor. What would Buki want to tell me if he somehow returned to reveal one single secret? Would he tell me who had murdered him and why? Or would he leave such a tedious piece of information for me to figure out on my own? He wasn't the most forthcoming of men, I remembered. I closed my eyes again and conjured up an image of the last time I had seen Buki before he died. And, almost to my complete amazement, there he was!

It had been in the bath house on the Street of the Lambs, just a few days before he disappeared. How many days? It certainly wasn't the day before. Was it a week earlier? Less than that, I thought. Maybe three days before. Maybe four. He bathed there all the time, after all. So did I. So did all of us, really. As a result, his presence was hardly the kind of thing that would have struck me as memorable at the time, much less as being charged with any particularly profound significance. I shut my eyes tighter and, to my amazement, I found I could see the scene clearly.

We were in the caldarium. The vapors were rising from the belly stones in every corner of the room rather in the manor of ghosts rising from their earthen tombs. This felt right to me . . . and when I focused just a little more intently I found that I could see Buki before my closed eyes almost as though they were open and I were merely looking out from my own stone at the scene unfolding around me. He was slick with sweat, his enormous belly reddened by the heat. He was holding—I tried to focus my eyes more clearly—he was holding a towel of some sort, but not one of the red and white ones the owners of the establishment made available to paying patrons. That too made sense to me—the towels were meant to be wrapped around your waist when walking from one part of the building to another but a man of Buki's size could never have gotten one of the standard-sized towels around his giant waist and so, like all the largest men who frequented the establishment, he had taken to bringing along his own towel when he came to bathe, one big enough to do the job amply even for a man of his girth. The towel itself, I could now see clearly, was a deep shade of blue. I shut my eyes even more tightly and, as I did, I could see Buki rising from his place. Slowly, almost ponderously, he approached the stone on which I myself was lying. He had a sad look about him, almost as though he somehow understood that his life was to end in only a few short days. He looked pensive, even bleak, but then he appeared to pull himself together and came even closer to where I was lying.

I forgot that I was lying on my bed in my house and was wholly in the scene now as Buki came closer and closer. From my supine position on a heated stone table in the caldarium, I watched as he approached. Sweat was dripping off his chin onto his stomach. The scant hair on his chest was matted with perspiration. His penis, shaded beneath the swell of his belly, was bobbing up and down as he walked. I ought to have sat up to meet him at eye level, but I didn't and perhaps even couldn't have. Instead, I lay where I was and watched as he came closer, then crouched down apparently to whisper something into my ear, something that he clearly did not wish the others to hear, something private. I felt myself sinking into a state of intense calm and wholly focused anticipation. And then, as I lay totally still, I felt his lips pressing up onto my right ear.

"You can do this," he said. And then he was gone.

I fell into a deep sleep after that, awakening when it was already mid-afternoon. For a few minutes, I lay still on my bed. I was covered by a green blanket that Avital must have thrown over my sleeping form when she came home and found me asleep on our bed. But even without the incontrovertible evidence of the blanket, I knew Avital had come home while I slept because I could hear her puttering around in the courtyard, presumably getting things ready so that she would be able to prepare our evening meal upon returning home with the boys after retrieving them from school.

I got up, washed my face and neck at the washing stand, then put on a pair of tan linen breeches and, slightly bizarrely, one of Avital's very loose-fitting blue silk tunic-tops. Thus peculiarly yet comfortably attired, I went downstairs to see what there was to eat. Avital had just set the kettle to boil on the garden hearth when I kissed her, then forced myself to banish the incipient desire that I could already feel beginning to assert itself. We had business to conduct, she and I . . . and it wasn't going to be *that* kind of business, at least not until the conversation I needed to have with her was concluded.

I told her everything, then fell silent. For the briefest of moments, I felt Buki's ghost flit by. But he didn't linger and then it was just us living folks present in the room.

TWENTY

TWILIGHT ALWAYS MAKES JERUSALEM look spooky—the honeystone takes on a slightly sinister grayish tinge in the dying sunlight and the air turns cold so quickly that it almost feels like the ghosts of a thousand generations have seized the city and are chilling its lanes and alleyways with their spectral presence. I've never been especially sensitive to the cold, but I do remember feeling distinctly chilly as I stepped out into the street and headed towards the Street of the Cheesemakers (which, by the time Avital and I were living there, did not have a single cheese shop left anywhere along its entire length). I absolutely do remember feeling a certain premonition of danger. And I also recall telling myself I was just being silly, that it was the evening chill combined with the fact that I had somehow gotten myself involved in a murder investigation that was unnerving me and making me feel a tad insecure. I reminded myself that I was more than capable of defending myself if necessary, that I had nothing to feel insecure *about*, that I was going to take a long walk and then end up on the Street of the Lambs and sweat for as long as it was going to take for me to evolve a cogent plan forward.

I was walking down the Street of the Cheesemakers lost in thought when I noticed a boy walking just a few paces in front of me. I recall thinking that he wasn't especially remarkable, just a little boy of eight or nine wearing an ordinary white cloak and a pair of sandals. Why I even noticed what the boy was wearing, I can't say. I suppose it was odd to see an unaccompanied child wandering around the city at dusk, but I don't think that was what attracted my attention. Nor was it anything about him physically—not his gait or the way he had his hair pulled back (as was fashionable for kids back then) or anything like that: he was just a boy walking alone in the street a few paces in front of me. What *was* odd—although ominous only in retrospect—was the degree to which he seemed somehow to be anticipating my route as he, then I, turned right on the Lane of Roses, then right again on Pottery Market Street, then left on Upper King Hezekiah Road. We were about a block north of the Street of the Lambs, when the boy turned to face me. I remember looking down at his round, unremarkable face and expecting him to ask me for some coins or to ask if I'd like to meet his big sister or something like that, but he said nothing at all and, just a moment later (or so it seemed at the time), I woke up somewhere else entirely.

I didn't wake up all that easily either. As consciousness came back to me slowly, I was able to gather some information almost without moving merely by running my hand over the contours of my body. I didn't think any of my limbs was broken. I was lying on some sort of mat. My brain was aching. My head had a huge bump on it that hurt even when I grazed it gently with my hand. And I was very cold.

I had no recollection at all of what had happened after that little boy had turned to face me nor was I sure how much time had passed. I could see some light filtering in from a window at the very top of the wall next to the mat, which led me to guess that it was early morning. I could hear muffled voices, perhaps from an adjacent room, but I couldn't make out anything they were saying. It's a sign of how long it took me to seize the seriousness of my situation that I remember being slightly buoyed by the sound of those voices. But when I let my arm reach out along the ground to the side of the mat and felt a bone-button on the ground in a pile of ash, I realized that my cloak had been burnt in a make-shift campfire that had been kindled on the earthen floor of the room in which I was being confined. It was not an encouraging discovery.

For a while, I just lay there on my side waiting for something to happen. I needed the privy. I was hungry and cold. I had no idea where I was. Finally, I found the strength to stand up and survey my surroundings on foot. I was in a locked room. The door had no inside handle. It did, however, have a peg with a bucket hanging from it. And there was something else about the door that I now noticed: that it had its own much smaller door built into it. I turned my attention to the window and thought it must have either been covered over with some sort of fabric or smeared with some kind of gunk. Or was it just filthy with grime? It was hard to say. The other two walls had neither windows nor doors. Nor did they have any pegs. The room itself was the size of a smallish bedroom in a modest house not unlike my own.

I filled the bucket, then set it in front of the little door in the big door. The smell was acrid, but not overpowering. I considered my options, which didn't take long at all because I didn't actually have any. I could scream, but I supposed they wouldn't be holding me in a place where my screams could be heard. I could lie down and wait, but that seemed so passive as almost to be cowardly. I could devote myself to battering down the door, but I doubted I could do it . . . and the fact that they had burnt my robe meant I could hardly hope to go home unnoticed even if I did somehow escape. I could pray, but it seemed early on to seek divine aid. I'd wait, then. And if things got truly desperate, then I'd call on the Holy One of Israel to make things right. But prayer felt like a last resort kind of gesture, the kind of thing it would be wiser to hold back until I was truly desperate. Which I wasn't. Yet.

I lay down, then stood up, then lay down again and allowed my mind to wander. Had Buki been held in this same place? Did the fact that I had apparently been abducted have anything to do with the fact that the Great One had asked me to investigate Buki's murder? Was I possibly *just* the next Levite scheduled for harassment? Or was this *just* another example of urban mayhem—a citizen abducted and held for ransom by ordinary criminals who had nothing at all to do with Buki's abduction or with the spiritual politics of the day?

After what felt like hours, the little door in the big door opened for just long enough for someone to remove the bucket and shove two loaves of bread and two empty buckets into the room, and also to leave me a pitcher of warm, brackish water. And then, just as I was carrying the food and the buckets into different corners, the big door itself opened just long enough to shove someone new into what had just previously been my private suite. My new roommate, unfortunately, was clearly unconscious. I don't know how he avoided breaking his head open when they shoved him in, but he somehow landed, I thought, safely and was lying in the dark on the ground without moving. I touched his face and felt his beard, then found a pulse so I knew he was alive. Other than that he was alive, however, I could not tell a single thing about him nor did I recognize him in the dim light. Was he one of us, perhaps a new arrival from out of town? It seemed plausible. Whether he was being held for the same reason I had been seized depended on why, specifically, I had been seized in the first place. Could he *also* have been involved in investigating Buki's murder for the Great One? It seemed unlikely, but not impossible. And, of course, it was also entirely reasonable to imagine that this new, silent friend of mine had been investigating Buki's death for some other reason, possibly even for his own private one. Or somebody else's death. Or nobody's death at all.

The faint sunlight became slightly less faint towards midday, then diminished in the course of what I took to be the afternoon hours and finally vanished entirely. Towards dusk, the little door within the big door opened again and the two buckets I had left in front of it were removed. A few minutes later, it opened again and two new buckets were flung back empty into the room. A pitcher of cold water and a plate of stale *pita* and olives was shoved in too, whereupon the little door was shut tight. It was nighttime. It was silent. My roommate continued to breathe, but not to awaken. I ate the olives, drank the water, then filled the bottom half of the bucket and replaced it by the door. I lay down to sleep on the mat and somehow fell asleep. When I awoke, it was still pitch dark in the room. I checked on the other guy. He was still there, still breathing, still either asleep or unconscious. If I had had a blanket, I would have covered him up. Or maybe I would have covered myself up . . . but there was no blanket, only a single mat, an empty plate, an empty dish, an empty bucket, and a not empty bucket. I filled the not empty one, then put it back by the door and sat as far away from the stench as I could.

Dawn came, then breakfast—a few more *pitot* and more water—then a clean bucket or, at least, an empty one. An hour or so after that, the other guy began to stir and then tried to sit up. He looked towards me, but I wasn't sure if he could see me in the dim light. In any event, he said nothing.

"Are you hurt?"

No answer.

"Did they drug you?"

No answer.

"Do you know why you are here?

No answer.

"Can you understand me?

In the gloom, I could see, I thought, a flicker of a smile. "Yes."

Contact had been made. Now all I had to do was to make something of it. "I am David. David ben Simon Halevi. A Levite."

"Asa Gad Ben Tovim Hakohen. A priest. From Beth Tzur."

Whatever I expected he might say, that wasn't it. Was it possible that Ikkesh ben Tovim's brother was lying on the floor of the same cell in which I was being held? Could this be a trick? Surely, it could have been. But he had been beaten seriously and quite violently. Could my captors have gone to that extreme to fool me into taking another into my confidence? Would Asa Gad ever have agreed to participate in a scheme that involved subjecting himself to a hiding like that? I resolved, at least for the moment, not to let on that his name meant anything to me. We'd see later on what this was all about. But, I figured, why not leave at least a card or two up my sleeve? Then I remembered that I had no sleeves, that my entire outfit consisted of a pair of threadbare linen underbreeches. This was not really an outfit that lent itself to hiding anything . . . but I resolved to do my best anyway. "A priest?" I asked, almost as though I hadn't heard him clearly. "You don't say!"

A slight widening of the eyes, followed by an equally slight nod of what was clearly a very bruised head. "Not a working specimen. But yes, by genealogy and family status, a member of the House of Aaron ben Amram, High Priest of all Israel."

"Do you know why you are here?"

"Where do you piss?"

"There's a bucket."

"Where?"

I brought him the second bucket, then stepped back as he filled it. "You can put it by the door. Over here." I pointed towards the door.

He hung the bucket up. "Sorry it doesn't smell great."

"Just wait."

He laughed a little. I laughed a little. The ice was breaking. Were we on our way to becoming friends? Maybe! But I was still highly suspicious.

"I'm David," I began again.

"Asa Gad."

"Do you know why you're here?"

"Not really. I thought the whole idea was to kill me."

"Why would anyone want to do that?"

"Because I know something I'm not supposed to know."

I tried to keep the excitement out of my voice. "And what's that?"

"If I tell you, they'll kill you too."

"Too? You're not dead."

"Not yet."

"Not yet," I agreed.

"But I am locked in a dark room with a disgusting bucket and no way out."

"So am I, actually. And we have two buckets."

A long pause. "I'm glad you're here. I'm not sure I could take this alone."

"I'm glad for the company too."

In retrospect, I realize that I ought to have been highly suspicious that I suddenly found myself in a locked room with someone claiming to be Ikkesh ben Tovim's brother. But I suppose I was feeling desperate for a friend, for an ally, for someone to talk to. He sounded genuine. He sounded friendly. He sounded guileless, like someone with nothing to hide. But even if he *was* a plant sent in solely to lull me into revealing how close I was to finding Buki's murderer—if that's what this was all about—I was still grateful for the company.

Within the hour, we had abandoned any need to nod to propriety and we were sitting as close as we could in the hope of deriving some extra body warmth from each other. When evening fell, there was a new feature: when the buckets were replaced, the new ones were accompanied by two rancid-smelling blankets. The old pitcher and plate were taken and a new one, this time with spelt bread and chickpeas was shoved inside. There was, I noted with grim satisfaction, twice as much food. Amazingly, I felt more grateful for the blankets than I felt enraged at being confined against my will in the first place. I knew Avital must have been hysterical with worry by that third evening and imagined, incorrectly as it turned out, that the entire community of brethren—if not the entire city—must have known I was missing. In my mind's eye, in fact, I could just see them all gathered in the steam on the Street of the Lambs discussing my disappearance. Would the Great One tell them that I had been asked to investigate Buki's murder? I had no idea. Would he send someone out to find me? I didn't know that either. Or would he just wait for my body to be found and then send someone out to investigate my murder just as he had sent me out to investigate Buki's? I found these questions intensely troubling and chose consciously not to dwell on them. Once the room was entirely dark, Asa Gad and I both fell asleep and, as far as I could tell, we both slept until some faint sunlight was coming in through the grimy window at the top of the wall facing the door.

TWENTY-ONE

ANOTHER DAY PASSED. UNLESS I had lost track of the days entirely, it was Saturday. I was just imagining the scene at home and wondering if Avital had set a place for me at the Sabbath table the previous evening when suddenly, unexpectedly, some sort of door opened up in my mind and a plan suggested itself to me.

Asa Gad and I had adopted the courteous custom of retreating to the furthest corner of the room when the other one needed to squat on one of the buckets. And so, on the fourth day of confinement in my semi-private dungeon, I found myself standing in the far corner of the room, the one furthest from the door, while Asa Gad rather noisily voided his bowels into a bucket that, as I recall, was already quite full enough. I tried to think of pleasant things while I stood patiently in my self-assigned corner and listened with only half an ear to his malodorous grunting. He was taking his time about it too, but I was hardly in a position to complain. But then, just as I stood there, something happened.

As I stood in the corner, I noticed a piece of plaster right in front of my face that appeared to be discolored. The light was faint, but the grimy window was just over the corner to which I had retreated and even in the dimness I could see that there was a discolored patch of plaster right in front of my nose. I reached up and touched it. It was damp. I pressed on the spot with my finger and the plaster gave way just slightly. I could smell the acrid odor of mold as my finger poked into the plaster and that smell plus the ones Asa Gad was generating—I can actually conjure up that particular acidulous reek even now—those smells combined to generate in me, of all things, a sense of slight hope. And, yes, I know how unlikely that must sound. But somehow discovering that small patch of mold somehow reminded me that

we weren't being held on the moon, only in a room somewhere in Jerusalem. I had obviously known that all along, but I was suddenly energized
by the thought that our captors had probably not known about that patch
of mold and that it was possible, therefore, that there were surely other
things—maybe even lots of other things—that they *also* hadn't known about
or considered seriously. I really do realize how ridiculous—and ridiculously
naïve—this must all sound now, but somehow that simple fact that the wall
was just plaster and that our guards were just men filled me with some faint
optimism. When Asa Gad was done in his corner, I called him over to show
him my discovery.

"Big deal. So the wall is damp."

"It *is* a big deal. This wall is not that solid. If moisture can get in, then
we can get out."

"How?"

"I'll . . . I'm not sure. But just wait, let's try to change something."

"To change something."

"Let's start working with what we have instead of doing nothing at all."

Asa Gad began to sound vaguely intrigued. "What do we have?"

"Well," I almost laughed, "not much. Almost nothing at all."

"But something?" I could hear cautious hope in his voice alongside the
skepticism.

"Well, we have some things."

"We have two disgusting donkey blankets and a bucket of our own
feculence." He used the Jerusalemite's most vulgar term for it too. I smiled
for the first time in days.

"We have two buckets' worth, actually. And we have each other."

"I guess, but so what?"

I thought for a second. "Well, why don't we start by using each other's
shoulders. Climb up on me and look out the window and tell me what you
see."

Had it really taken that much time for me to think seriously about that
window? It sounds silly in retrospect, but it was quite high up and much too
small for either of us even to imagine shimmying through to freedom. And
it was filthy, or at least that's how it appeared from ground level.

"You're too weak."

"To support you, you mean? I'm fine."

"I weigh a lot."

"Half of what you used to weigh is in one of those buckets, so it's actually the perfect moment."

Asa Gad laughed, as only someone who has gotten used to squatting
on a bucket in front of a perfect stranger ever could. "Okay then, I'll try."

Now it was my turn to squat down. Asa Gad sat on my shoulders, his thighs wrapped around my head. I remembered suddenly how it had felt carrying my boys around on my shoulders in just the same way. Nathaniel and Asarela used to love being held aloft like that more than anything—and their bitterest fights as younger children had been when one felt that the other one—they were twins, remember—when one felt that the other had been awarded more time up there than he himself had. Asa Gad was considerably bigger even than Zakur, my eldest. But he was a skinny guy and he didn't weigh all that much. I found myself quite able to stand up with him on my shoulders, but he still wasn't anywhere nearly high up enough to look out the window. I remember wishing pointlessly that he had used a corner of his donkey blanket to clean himself, then decided to think happier thoughts. After all, I myself had been keeping my own blanket clean too.

Then, taking care not to lose his balance, Asa Gad attempted to stand up. Leaning forward to place his hands on the wall, he managed to lift one leg, then the other, until he was kneeling, rather than sitting on my shoulders. Neither of us had eaten a decent meal in days. We were both disoriented and dizzy. But a lot seemed to be riding on this. He knelt there, hands pressed on the wall, his shins perpendicular to my shoulders.

And then he stood up. I could tell he was feeling dizzy, but neither of us said a word. First one foot, then the other. Then a long pause while he regained his balance and leaned forward to hug the wall. I reached up and held his feet in place on my shoulders. I could hear Asa Gad scraping at the window with his fingers, trying, I supposed, to rub some of the grime away so he could see more clearly. A long few moments passed. For some reason, I was hesitant to ask any questions. He said nothing. I waited. More moments passed. And then, in a husky, raspy voice, Asa Gad finally spoke.

"I can see the walls."

"The walls? Of the city, you mean?"

"Yes, of course, the city walls."

"We're not inside the city?"

"We are inside. I can see the guards on top facing out."

"Where do you think we are?"

"It's hard to . . . wait, I think . . . do you know those white stone buildings next to the Fish Gate?"

"The Three Angels, you mean?" There were three very narrow buildings made of white sandstone standing just to the south of the Fish Gate. I believe they had once been the headquarters of some prefect back under the PTs, but local legend said they were built by Nehemiah back in the days of old Artachshasta the Unpronounceable—Good King Artaxerxes to you now that everything worth even *trying* to pronounce has to be Greek—the

legend was that they were built by Nehemiah as his headquarters in Jerusalem, then taken over by Alexander the Briefly Great when he passed
through town a century later. Whatever, they were well-known landmarks
and everybody called them the Three Angels. Why that was, who knew?
Was it because the three angels who came to visit Abraham were popularly
depicted as tall, slender men dressed in robes as white as snow? Or were the
building named after some other angels? I had no idea. But I certainly knew
the three buildings Asa Gad could see.

I began to figure things out. It seemed unlikely that I was too far from
where I had been abducted. I conjured up a mental image of Upper Hezekiah Street. It had been almost dark when they seized me, but there had been
plenty of pedestrians and peddlers still out and about. Had anyone seen
them take me off? I felt sure someone must have. But if the way they had
explained things to onlookers was that I had apparently fainted or suffered a
stroke of some sort and they were going to take me somewhere to rest until
someone could figure out who I was and how to contact my family—in that
scenario, they obviously would have had to take me to the nearest house, not
load me into a waiting donkey cart and head off with me to some distant
pre-planned destination. Suddenly that all made sense. But now that Asa
Gad was telling me that he could actually see the Three Angels through the
grimy window, I resolved to think things through even more carefully.

Asa Gad was apparently going to keep looking out the window for
as long as I could hold him in place, so I had time to think. I felt his feet
on my shoulders, felt them—this will sound silly, I know, but I remember
feeling that they were grounding me, holding me in place, allowing me to
think clearly for the first time in days. I had followed the Lane of the Roses,
then turned on Pottery Market, then again onto Upper King Hezekiah. I
had been only a single street north of the Street of the Lambs when they
seized me, but at the end of the road with all those fancy homes and private
rose gardens, not the end behind the bathhouse. If the Three Angels were
visible from the window in our cell, then the window almost definitely had
to be facing north—which accorded well with the fact that I hadn't seen any
direct sunlight since arriving And then, suddenly, I had an idea.

"Asa Gad, you still up there?"

"Apparently."

"Look to the right as far as you can."

"I'm doing it."

"What do you see?"

"Nothing."

"Nothing at all?"

"No, not nothing at all. Just buildings, Lots of them."

"Can you see the edge of the Temple?"

A long pause. Then, he spoke. "Maybe."

"What do you see?"

"It's hard to say. But maybe . . . maybe I can see the place the Fortress meets the northwest corner of the outer wall around the Temple Mount."

Excellent, I thought. I knew exactly what he meant. That corner was unmistakable—no corner of the outermost wall that ran around the Temple Mount connected with anything like the great fortress built in the days when Solomon's Temple was still under construction and which now served as the northernmost boundary of the Holy City. We were therefore somewhere to the west of the Temple in a room with a window facing north and probably not far at all from the site of my abduction. Who the man standing on my shoulders really was, I had no real way of knowing. Was he truly Ikkesh's brother? I had no idea. But he hadn't been anything but friendly towards me since being pitched into the room in which we were both being confined and I was intent on exploiting his presence to get us both out of there. I'd worry about who he really was some other time, I told myself. And, who knew, maybe he really was Asa Gad ben Tovim and the people holding us had no idea at all that I had already managed to make some sort of connection between Ikkesh's murder and Buki's. Or, I recalled yet again, maybe this has nothing at all to do with Buki.

The time had clearly come to find out what Asa Gad knew. I squeezed his ankles slightly. "Asa Gad, you still up there?"

"Who wants to know?"

"Why are you being confined here?"

"I told you, I know things I'm not supposed to know."

"Do you want to tell me what they are?"

"I told you that already too—no!"

"What if I told you why I'm here?"

"You mean, you tell me and I'll tell you?"

"Well," I pretended to consider the situation. "Okay."

"No."

"We certainly aren't hiding much else from each other."

A guffaw. "No, we aren't."

"And it might be . . . it might be helpful if we knew if we were here for the same reason."

"Helpful?"

"In figuring out how to get out of here."

"How could knowing why we're here possibly help us get free?"

"I don't know. But I certainly won't be able to say it won't help us at all unless I know what it is."

Asa Gad appeared to be considering this line of thinking. "You under-stand that you're going to get yourself killed for your trouble."

"If I know your story?"

"Yes."

"But you yourself weren't killed. You're here, aren't you?"

"I'll be killed next time. This is just to show they mean business."

"So you think they'll eventually release you?"

"Eventually."

"And you think they'll release me too?"

"I have no idea. I don't even know why you're here."

I thought carefully, then took a huge chance. "Come down and I'll tell you."

"Really?"

"Without me having to promise to tell you why I'm here first?"

"Yes."

"Promise?"

"On the honor of the High Priest of Israel."

A snort, followed by a long pause. "Okay."

"So come down."

He came down, gingerly lowering himself to a kneeling position on my shoulders, then hopping down to the floor as though he were some sort of Spartan gymnast. He was a skinny man, possessed of not much body hair, narrow shoulders, a slim waist and a peculiarly long neck. He wasn't a bad looking fellow, but he had a certain haggard, slightly desperate look to him, a look I recall thinking that probably wasn't solely a result of his incarceration.

He reached for the donkey blanket, folded it up neatly into quarters, then placed it carefully on the ground and sat down on it. He drew his knees up to his chest and held them with both arms. I stood my ground, then succumbed to what was apparently some sort of invitation and, folding my blanket as he had his, sat down on it.

The room was damp and, by now, fairly dark. The reek of the bucket permeated air that would have been stale and musty anyway. The tempera-ture was dropping, but I wasn't too uncomfortable. I suppose I could have just started talking, but I was suddenly unsure of myself. I had just agreed to tell my story to a man I didn't know . . . and who was either in cahoots with my captors or else in trouble with them himself. On the other hand, I needed to do *something*. And so I inhaled sharply, drew my own knees up towards my chest, and then, thinking of my children for a long moment and of Avital, I pulled myself together and told Asa Gad why I thought I was being held.

TWENTY-TWO

FIGURING THAT I HAD no real reason to hold anything back at all, I didn't hold back anything at all. Asa Gad listened intently as I told him about Buki, about what we *all* knew—or thought we did—and about what I personally thought. I told him about my meeting with the Great One and about my sundry adventures since then. I told him about that incredible scene with Ketziya in that spice shop under the city's northern wall and about what I had made of it. I mentioned everybody by name—not just the Great One and Buki and everybody connected, even tangentially, with that story, but also Benjamin Ginnethon and Meirav Serach. I told him where I had been going on the evening I was seized. I even told him the precise words of encouragement Buki's ghost had whispered into my ear. And it was then, when I mentioned the words Buki's ghost had said to me—it was precisely then that Asa Gad finally lost his composure.

Had I hit pay dirt? It was hard to tell. Asa Gad wasn't actually doing anything at all, but I could feel his gaze intensify and I noticed, or I thought I did, that he was grasping his shins with such force that he was having trouble breathing normally. I wasn't quite sure what to make of it, so I decided to probe just a touch more gently.

"Bukiyahu ben Yerimoth is someone to you?"

Silence.

I decided to take a different tack entirely. "So tell me about your brother."

"Did you know him?" Asa Gad's voice was strained, almost hoarse.

"I had been living here for six or seven years when he died, so we could have met. But I don't believe we ever did."

More silence. Ill ease was emanating almost palpably from Asa Gad's side of the cell. I waited, then finally asked the obvious question. "Do you know what happened to him?"

Asa Gad waited a long time before saying anything. But finally he did speak. "Yes," he said, "I do."

Now it was my turn to speak, but I couldn't think of anything to say. Instead, I tried to catalogue what I knew about Ikkesh ben Tovim—about his life *and* about his death—and concluded that I didn't really know all that much about him at all. I had heard his name here and there over the years, of course, but the gossip—or at least the posthumous gossip—had been all about his wife and the boy . . . and their relationship to Benjamin Ginnethon, especially after Benjamin's shadowy wife Esther Malka vanished from the scene completely and the rest of everybody moved in together. Still, I did know some things. I knew that Ikkesh had been an importer of gold and precious stones, especially turquoise. I remembered hearing that he himself had been to Hindustan several times and that, more than anything else, had made him a kind of a celebrity in town.

You have to remember that international travel beyond the perimeter states wasn't just a novelty in those days—it was almost unheard of. Or at least for regular citizens it was. Of course, people went to Syria and Egypt on business all the time—that wasn't considered at all exotic. And some people, although not very many, had been to north to Ionia or south to Arabia on trading missions of differing sorts. But no one other than Ikkesh—and I really do mean no one at all, at least no one of whom I myself had ever heard—had ever traveled past Bactria into the land of Hind. And it had been that trip, or more specifically the combination of new spices and new kinds of precious stones that he brought home *from* that trip, that had catapulted Ikkesh into the big leagues. As Asa Gad sat still and said nothing, I found myself wondering just how big those leagues actually were. Was Ikkesh famous and rich, or just famous? Had he turned his travels into real money or only into the kind of make-believe money featured in stories one listens to for as long as one is lying on a warm belly-stone and then forgets entirely? And then a new thought suddenly struck me. What, I wondered, exactly *had* Ikkesh brought back from the land of Hind, from Hindustan? Stones and spices, to be sure. But what else might have come with him? That, I suddenly realized, was the real question, the important question. But there were also others worth asking. Was Ikkesh really rich enough to be murdered for his money? There wasn't any proof, as far as I had heard, that he had been murdered at all . . . but if he *had* been murdered, then what would his murderer have stood to gain? Money, obviously . . . but his wealth went to his son and the son was a minor, so the only person who could logically have orchestrated his murder for his money would have been Meirav Serach. But was there *that* much money? And why would she have complicated her life so dramatically for almost nothing—her access to his wealth was fully open to public scrutiny because of Ikkesh's death, whereas her access to her husband's money was probably total—and totally invisible to the public—while he was alive.

Could Ikkesh have brought back something else from the east, some treasures of inestimable value that . . . that what? I was stymied, unable to finish my thought. If Ikkesh had been killed, then there had to have been a motive. But what could it have been? And what connection—if there was any connection at all, that was—what connection could there possibly have been between Ikkesh's death and Buki's? Ketziya had pointed me towards the Ood . . . and I had somehow ended up incarcerated in a cell with the brother of Benjamin Ginnethon's sister's late husband. Was that a coincidence? It felt almost impossible to imagine that it was. And yet . . . if it didn't mean nothing, then what *did* it all mean? I had no real idea, but the time had clearly come for me to say something back to Asa Gad, who was still sitting on the ground with his knees pressed up under his chin and his arms wrapped around the outside of his shins.

In the end, I decided to keep it simple. "Will you tell me?"

Asa Gad looked at me like he couldn't quite believe what he was about to say. "Yes," he said simply. "I will."

I expected him to start speaking, but he said nothing. "Ikkesh was your older brother?" I finally asked.

A wan smile. "Yes."

"His death must have been a terrible blow."

A cloud passed over Asa Gad's face. "It was terrible."

"I remember hearing about it."

"What did you hear?"

I saw no reason to dissemble, so I simply answered the question. "Just that he died. I remember when it happened. He died so unexpectedly. A heart attack, right?"

"That's what everybody said."

"But you think differently?"

"I know differently."

"So how did he die?"

"He was killed. Murdered."

"Are you sure?"

"Yes. Would I say such a thing if I wasn't sure?"

"Do you know who killed him?"

Asa Gad released his legs, stood up and took a few steps towards the southern wall of the cell. We were in almost total darkness, but a few beams of faint light were illuminating some small section of the cell and it was there, in that dim illumination, that Asa Gad now stood facing away from me. "Do you really want me to tell you that?" he asked without turning around.

"Am I going to regret having asked?"

"Probably."

"But you want to tell me?"

He turned to face me and squatted down so I could see him more clearly. "In some ways, I do. But I can keep my secret. You don't have to take this any further if you don't want."

"I want you to tell me what you think."

"What I know."

"What you know."

Asa Gad stood up. I began to stand up too, but he motioned for me not to. He stood directly in front of me and looked down. I looked up. Our eyes met. We had reached a crossroads and we both knew it. In a moment, if I let him proceed, we were going to both be on the same side of a fence that might conceivably separate us from a lot of things that neither of us was going to want much to be separated from. True, we'd have each other . . . but was that going to be enough? Defecating into matching buckets is one thing, after all . . . but we were strangers on every other level of normal intimacy. Still, there was a certain urgency to the moment, a conclusion to the conversation that felt—to me, at any rate—that felt fated to occur. I couldn't see Asa Gad's face clearly, but there was a distinct tone of kindness in his voice that I found both encouraging and slightly unnerving. But the truth, I think, is that I would have been no more able to walk away from hearing Asa Gad's answer to my question than I would have been able just to walk away from the cell in which we were both being held and just leave the whole adventure I was having behind.

"My brother was killed by . . . by Dan Iddo ben Uziel. From Shephem."

"By . . . who?" I had been so ready for him to say that his brother was murdered by Benjamin Ginnethon ben Baruch Hakohen that I did a kind of double-take when he spoke the name of someone completely unknown to me.

"Do you know Dan Iddo?"

"Dan Iddo?" I repeated. I must have sounded like an idiot.

"Dan Iddo ben Uziel. From Shephem."

"No," I stammered, "I don't know him. I don't even believe I've ever even heard his name."

"Well then," Asa Gad responded, this time crouching down so that our faces were at the same level, "I'll have to tell you the whole story, won't I?"

TWENTY-THREE

"IKKESH WASN'T JUST MY brother," he began, a catch in his voice that I hadn't noticed earlier when he spoke his brother's name now easily audible. "He was my friend. And my teacher. Our father was away for most of my childhood, so it was almost always just the three of us at home: Ikkesh, our mother and myself. Our mother was a sickly woman who spent most of her time in bed. And so with our father endlessly travelling and our mother just as endlessly ailing, we kids were basically on our own most of the time. School was over by noon—you must know all this, I suppose—regular school ends by noon so that the future priests of Jerusalem can take the kinds of courses they run in the Temple for youngsters in line eventually to serve at the altar. The only thing is that we were never actually enrolled in those classes . . . and so we were on our own from noon until after dark and that was when Ikkesh took me under his wing and taught me how to live in the world. He wasn't that much older than me, you know, only six years. But six years is a lifetime for children. And it seemed to me that Ikkesh knew everything about everything. He knew how to steal fruit from the orchards on the road to Bethlehem without getting caught. And he knew how to get there and back without being seen. He knew which lenders in the city would employ us to run cash around town for a few *zuz* a pop, no questions asked. And, of course, he knew all about girls. I was too young even to begin to know what that was all about, but I saw clearly that there was a whole secret world Ikkesh had somehow been initiated into that was closed—if not forever, then certainly for the foreseeable future—to boys my age. And even if he can't really have known everything there is to know, he certainly knew a lot more than I did—which was nothing at all.

"I worshiped my brother. I loved him and envied him and I wanted to be just like him . . . but, most of all, I knew I was safe when we were together. He wasn't just handsome, either—although he really was very good-looking—but he was confident and sure of himself in a way that only a thirteen-year-old in a city like this one can be. Even as a little boy, I knew he was a risk taker. We were well off, but Ikkesh always wanted to have his own money, never wanted to be dependent on anyone else, not even on our parents. I guess all children harbor some anxiety about the world, but that wasn't how things were when I was with Ikkesh. Not when he and I were running some sack of copper drachmas from one lender to another and then sneaking back through the alleyways only Ikkesh seemed to know with a much smaller bag of silver shekels. Not when he and I were sitting in the middle of some pomegranate orchard in the hills gorging ourselves on stolen fruit or swimming together in a lake in the woods on the way back home. Not when . . . not when I had a fever when Father was away and Mother was too sick to notice and Ikkesh stayed home for three solid days, washing me down with cold water and telling me stories that were so incredibly long and boring that I'd eventually fall asleep despite how sick I felt. And then, when I'd wake up, he'd be sitting right there in the same chair he had been in when I drifted off . . . just waiting for me to awaken so he could sponge my forehead or give me some more of Mother's lime wine laced with so much honey you could almost stand up a knife in it."

Asa Gad paused in his story and looked directly at me. I wasn't quite sure what he wanted, but he appeared to be waiting for me to say something. Was he hoping I would somehow find the right words to endorse his feelings, to let him know that I know what it means to love a brother so much that the power of the emotion is almost painful to bear? I loved Joseph like that, I suppose . . . and I also lost my father at an early age. But our situations weren't really analogous. For one thing, Joseph was only two years older than me, so I never quite had the experience of feeling that he was the man of the house even when he was, briefly, the oldest male living in our home. It's true, of course, that your older brother being the man of the house because your father is always away on business is hardly the same thing as your brother being the man of the house because your father is dead. Plus our mother remarried almost immediately after our father died, choosing as her second husband a much older widower who had previously been her uncle-by-marriage. Nevertheless, I knew what he meant about his feelings for Ikkesh even if my feelings for Joseph weren't quite the same. I wasn't quite sure what to say, but I felt I had to say something. "His death must have been a terrible blow," I said, thinking how inadequate a response that was to someone who had just spoken so passionately about his love for his late brother.

"A blow?" he echoed simply. "It was one I've never really recovered from. I've gotten used to him being dead, obviously, but that's not the same as being over it. I'm not over it. I'm not ever going to be over it. He's dead and I'm not, but that's as far as I'm prepared to go in terms of accepting things. I accept that he died, obviously—I'm not totally crazy—but I am absolutely not prepared to leave his death unavenged. What true brother ever would?"

Because Asa Gad had clearly meant his question seriously, I felt I had to answer. "No one worth anything at all ever would leave a brother's death unavenged," I said calmly. "No brother worth anything even *could* leave such a crime unavenged."

"You couldn't be more right," Asa Gad said almost in the style of a teacher delighted to hear something intelligent come out of mouth of a dull student he had previously doubted would ever say anything too clever at all. "No true brother ever could."

"So what happened?"

"You realize we're at a crossroads here, David, don't you? I know all sorts of things about Ikkesh's murder, things I've found out all on my own. I don't know everything—I will, but I don't yet—but you have to understand that once I tell you, you won't be able to go back and not know them anymore. They'll be part of you and you'll be part of the picture . . . whether you like it or not. So are you really sure you want to know what only I can tell you?"

I answered immediately. "I am sure, actually."

"Really?"

"Really."

Asa Gad looked at me intently now, almost as though he were interested in seeing what I truly looked like. The light was very dim—and it was growing dimmer by the moment—but he continued to stare at me, apparently lost in thought. And then, just when I thought he wasn't going to say anything at all, he did speak. "Have you ever heard of Chandragupta?" he asked.

TWENTY-FOUR

THE LAST SYLLABLE OF King Chandragupta's name, which I'm certain I had never heard of up until that moment, was still hanging on the air when all hell broke loose. But whether it was just a coincidence or whether they had been listening at the door all along and waiting for the just the right moment to pounce, I had no idea.

At any rate, Asa Gad had just begun to tell me what he knew about his brother's murder, when the door was suddenly flung open and four men came into the room. Two of them ran over to me and shoved me down onto my stomach, while the other two set to beating Asa Gad methodically and slowly. They must have brought some sort of lash with them, because I could hear the horrifying smacks of leather on skin. And I realized he must have had something jammed into his mouth, because all I could hear was the sharp swats on his back and, I imagined, his buttocks and the backs of his legs. They gave him at least forty lashes, I think. And they were hard ones too. I thought they meant to kill him, but imagined they had chosen to do it this way so as to leave room for arguing later on that he was merely being punished for some punishable offense when he unexpectedly expired. And, I figured, I was going to be next.

When the lashes stopped, I fully expected to start feeling them on my own exposed back, but instead of beating me senseless and then leaving me either to die or not to die, they threw some sort of sheet over me carried out of the cell. I was sure I was wearing my winding-sheet and that I was now in the extremely small group of people privileged, if that's the word, to feel the scratchy fabric of their own shrouds on the way to the grave. Asa Gad, I guessed, was still laying on the floor. Was he still alive? I couldn't hear a thing, not even moans or groans. Was he dead? He could have been but it felt unlikely even *they* would have murdered someone in front of a witness, so I concluded—hopefully—that the idea of making me witness to Asa Gad's beating was probably to discourage me from telling about my confinement to anyone at all once I was eventually released.

I wasn't killed. (I suppose that much must be obvious.) But I also wasn't beaten. They, whoever *they* were, carried me into the street and threw me into a cart. The sheet came off and was replaced by what I took to be a donkey blanket. No one said a word. The cart moved forward. I could smell the donkey, but otherwise had no idea where I was or what was happening to me. An hour later, the cart stopped. The blanket was removed. I was lifted up by unseen hands—the sun had long since set and the night was totally black out in the country—and unceremoniously dumped out by the side of the road. I was cold, scared to death, and ravenously hungry. The cart moved on. I was totally, absolutely alone. And I was wearing the same linen underbreeches I had been wearing for the last week.

Where was I? Out in the country, obviously, and no more than an hour's cart-ride from Jerusalem. In fact, I could see the signal lights atop the city walls in the distance and it seemed obvious to me that I was out in the hills to west of the city. I had nothing to cover myself up with, no obvious choice but to begin to walk back to Jerusalem. I figured it would take at least four hours, which turned out to be pretty much exactly right. But they were a *long* four hours, let me tell you.

I was freezing, exposed, scared, and very apprehensive about being seen. I had no sandals on my feet and my feet started to bleed almost im-mediately once I started walking in earnest. As I walked, I warmed up. I tried to keep up a steady pace, but my feet were in such pain that it was almost impossible to walk normally at all, let alone with purpose. Still, I had no choice but to persevere. There was, after all, at least some smidgen of a possibility that this wasn't an elaborate set-up designed to make it appear that I died accidentally while hiking at night in the Jerusalem hills wearing almost nothing at all and that I could conceivably end up this evening sleep-ing in my own bed next to my own wife. That seemed almost impossible to imagine, but, because it was at least slightly plausible, I forced myself to walk forward and focused on the sight of the city walls barely illuminated in the pale moonlight about four hours ahead.

As I walked, I reviewed the situation in as much detail as I could. Since being appointed by the Great One to figure out what actually had happened to poor Buki, I had made some tiny steps forward. Possibly. Or else I hadn't made any progress and was just convincing myself that I had. I had followed Ketziya—and I reminded myself that I hadn't actually had any specific reason to follow her, as there was nothing at all connecting her even tangentially to Buki's disappearance—and been vouchsafed an oracle of some sort for my efforts, an oracle that pointed me directly at the Ood, at Benjamin Ginnethon ben Baruch Hakohen. But, I reminded myself, even that had possibly been nothing more than a fantasy on my part—she hadn't spoken his name aloud and it had been I myself who had deduced that it was the Ood to whom she was making oblique reference. He still struck me as the most viable candidate for the position—he had the red hair, the wealth, the eloquence, the proclivity for abominable deeds, and he did live—or at least sojourn at length—in the Temple. But, of course, I had no proof that Ketziya had meant any of that. Plus, we only called each other—our fellow Levites—brethren. Only an outsider would refer to priests as our brethren because they are, after all, members of the tribe of Levi. But, of course, Ketziya actually *was* such an outsider.

Had the Ood actually murdered Buki? This was all so confusing. Nothing linked him to Buki's murder, or at least nothing I had uncovered. What I *had* thought was that he was possibly responsible for the death of his own brother-in-law. But now Asa Gad, possibly with his dying breath, had indicted someone else of that murder, someone whose name I had never heard before in my life. Who was this Dan Iddo ben Uziel? Was he a priest? A Levite? Asa Gad had appended neither Hakohen nor Halevi to his name . . . but that was hardly decisive. Still, if he was a Levite, I surely would at least have heard his name before. Could he be one of the priests, one of *them*? I supposed he could well have been, but he could also have been anyone else in God's world. Of course, no one at all had ever been charged with Ikkesh ben Tovim's murder, nor had his death ever definitively been labeled a murder. But even if it had been, I still had not uncovered even the slightest shred of evidence linking the Ood *or* this Dan Iddo with Ikkesh's death, nor (as far as I knew) had anyone else other than Asa Gad himself. Still, I felt I was on to something. What it exactly was I was on *to*, however, was a whole different matter.

I continued my review, partially to keep focused and partially to keep my mind off the incredible pain I was in. My feet were in agony. I was shivering so violently from the cold that my eyes were actually tearing. I knew my only hope was to shut out the world and focus within. And so I did, continuing my review as though my life depended on getting the details entirely straight. As perhaps it did!

In partial recompense for my initial efforts, I had been abducted and dumped in a cell somewhere in Jerusalem. At first, I was entirely alone. But then, amazingly enough, I had a cellmate who turned out to be none other than the brother of the late Ikkesh and he had a clear theory about the identity of his brother's murderer. But when he revealed the name of his primary suspect, it hadn't been Benjamin Ginnethon at all, but this previously unknown Dan Iddo ben Uziel from the town of Shephem. It struck me to wonder why Asa Gad was being held in the first place. Surely, a beating like the one he received cannot have been a simple ploy to make me think he was being held against his will when all along he was merely there to coax me into revealing how far I had come in my investigation! But if the point was not to impress me with the heat of the fire with which I was playing, then what exactly *was* the point? It seemed to me—and even after all these years it still seems to me—that the point of his incarceration was to accomplish two related ends: to make it clear to *him* where the path he was wandering would eventually lead. And to make it clear to *me* that I was wandering a parallel path towards the same ugly end if I continued to pursue my investigation and let it lead me where it would.

There was only one further piece of information to consider: that a moment before our captors burst into our cell and ended our conversation, Asa Gad had mentioned the name of King Chandragupta. (He hadn't even used the royal title, only said aloud the man's name.) I found out some more details eventually, but at the moment I hadn't had the faintest idea who this Chandragupta was or where he was from, let alone what he could possibly have to do with Ikkesh ben Tovim's death or, even more extendedly, with Buki's. But his name—his mysterious multisyllabic, totally non-Hebrew name—somehow spoke to me and beckoned me along a path I still barely knew to exist.

Still, I told myself, things were falling into place at least slightly. Two men had been murdered. They hadn't been killed at the same time or in the same way. There was no reason to think that the two men knew each other—or that they had any friends or relations in common. Buki was a working Levite and Ikkesh was an import/export man. Buki was single, but Ikkesh was married. Both men lived well—Buki because of his family's money and Ikkesh because of the success of his business and his personal trading acumen—but neither, I didn't think, could be counted among the truly wealthy citizens of Jerusalem. There was nothing tying them to each other at all except, possibly, Benjamin Ginnethon, whom Ketziya had *possibly* indicted of Buki's murder and who was also the brother-in-law of the late Ikkesh, of whose murder his own brother had *unequivocally* indicted someone else entirely. Such as they were, these were the facts I was reviewing in my head over and over as I trudged forward in the frigid night air towards the Holy City.

TWENTY-FIVE

I GOT HOME. HOW I got there, I can't really remember. As I fully expected it would be, the front door was bolted from the inside. My feet were so sore that I could barely stand up as I stood at my own front door and banged loudly enough on it, I hoped, for Avital to hear. But she didn't respond to my knocking and I remember supposing that she must have been fast asleep in our bed.

Our bedroom was at the back of the house on the second floor. It overlooked a small spice garden and we used to like sleeping with the window shudders wide open almost every night of the year—it had been, in fact, Avital, who had taught me about the pleasures of sleeping snug and warm under a heavy blanket in a very cold room—and that was where I presumed she was: in a deep slumber under a heavy blanket either dreaming or not dreaming of her missing husband. I crept around to the back of the house and sat for a moment in the garden. The house was still. There was a wooden bench towards the back of the oregano patch and it was there that, finally, I rested. I think I may have fallen asleep, but after a few minutes I awoke and, standing up, tossed a few pebbles into the open window.

There was no response. I waited. I tossed some more pebbles. I called her name. And then I began to worry. I could see that the window shutters were wide open. It was almost dawn, but the sky was still far too dark for me to see anything inside the room no matter how far back I stood. The house was totally silent. The boys' bedrooms were at the front of the house. There were two—the larger one for the older boys, Zakur and Yehoram, and the smaller one for the twins—and they both had windows facing the street. When I first approached the house, I noticed that the window shutters in both rooms were closed—but that was the normal procedure: Avital liked our shutters being open onto the garden so she could fall asleep smelling the thyme and the oregano, but she liked the boys' to be shut to keep out any street sounds that might disturb their sleep.

I waited, then tried again. The back doors were bolted too. But there was a small side door that opened into a vestibule just off the main hallway connecting the front and back of the house. We hardly ever used it, but I knew it was there and as soon as I came around to the side of the house and saw the door frame in splinters and the door itself ajar, I knew that things were very wrong. I pushed the door. I can't recall what I was expecting to happen, but it merely swung silently open. I stepped into my house.

I hobbled upstairs to the twins' bedroom and, as I had somehow known was going to be the case, it was empty. The beds were made. The boys' toys and scrolls were put neatly away. Their bedroom looked like the kind of room innkeepers show perspective guests: all the comforts of home were in place, but without there being any evidence of actual people enjoying them. Everything neat and in its place. No mess. No clutter. And, of course, no boys. I went to the older boys' room and it was equally neat. And equally empty. I dragged myself down the corridor to our bedroom, although I suppose I already knew what I was going to find there. Our bed was made. The room was neat. There were three anemones in a vase by Avital's side of the bed next to a jug of water, half full. The shutters were wide open. The bed was made. But my wife was gone. And so were my sons.

TWENTY-SIX

WHEN I FINALLY WOKE up, it was already past noon. My feet were still very sore, but I took myself as best I could to the wine bar next to the Fish Gate where the Great One usually takes his lunch. He wasn't there, however, and I was told he was probably already at the Street of the Lambs. And that was precisely where I did find him: soaking in the heated tub just outside the caldarium. I hadn't found him alone, however, but had no intention of waiting. And, since his company was an Egyptian lad of about seventeen or eighteen who worked for the bathhouse and who had been engaged in massaging the Great One's shoulders while the latter perused some scroll he had brought along to read in the tub, I simply spoke without holding back for a moment.

The Great One had listened carefully, then fell into a kind of reverie. Or maybe that isn't the right word—but he fell silent and for several long moments he said nothing at all. And then he turned to the Egyptian boy and, to my amazement—and I really did think I knew most of what there was to know about Eli ben Heman—spoke to him in what I took to be fluent Egyptian. What he said, I had no idea. But the boy understood and without saying a word went to the door leading into the caldarium and, turning to face out, stood there and guarded our privacy.

When the boy was in place and facing away from us, the Great One turned to face me. "Tell me everything," he said, simply.

I sat back down. The water was cool and was making my feet feel slightly less sore. I waited a moment to gather my thoughts and then, as instructed, I told the Great One everything. I told him about Ketziya, about my theory about Benjamin Ginnethon ben Baruch Hakohen and about my abduction. I described the cell to him and I told him where in the city I thought it must have been located. And, of course, I told him about Asa Gad. And about Asa Gad's theory that his brother had been murdered. When I said the name "Ikkesh," I thought I noticed the Great One's cheeks flush slightly, but it was hard to tell—and the heat of the water in which we were both sitting made it impossible to be sure.

While I spoke, the Great One said nothing. But then, when I was done, he asked the obvious question.

"And this Asa Gad felt that his brother had been murdered by Benjamin Ginnethon, the very man you had come to suspect in Buki's murder?"

I had expected the question. I had no reason not to answer it honestly. But something seized me, some spirit of mistrust rooted in . . . in I have no idea what. "Yes," I said, almost casually. "He did."

Why didn't I tell the Great One the truth? Asa Gad hadn't said that he suspected his brother-in-law of his brother's murder at all, but specifically that he felt certain his brother had been murdered by someone named Dan Iddo ben Uziel from the town of Shephem. And then he had uttered the mystery name "Chandragupta" a moment before our captors burst into the room. Even after all these years, I can't quite explain why I didn't tell the truth. I didn't have the slightest doubt about the Great One's probity. I trusted him and I liked him and I felt honored that he had chosen me to find out what I could about Buki's murder. I didn't think for a moment that he was other than how he seemed or that there was some possibility that he was behaving in a duplicitous or deceitful way with me. Any of those would have been good reasons to hold my tongue, but none of them applied and, if truth be told, I think I was as surprised by my lie as the Great One would have been had he only known.

I suppose I was trying to enlist the Great One's assistance in bringing down Benjamin Ginnethon and didn't want to dilute his future efforts in that regard by muddying the water with alternate suspects. When I write that out, it sounds crazy. Or at least base and indefensible. But, to speak on my own behalf, I was trying to simplify, not complicate, things. There were, after all, several different crimes in need of investigation here: Buki's abduction and murder, Ikkesh ben Tovim's murder, and Avital's—and the boys'—abduction. I had no question what my order of priorities was: finding Avital and the boys trumped everything. Did I imagine that there was some chance that these various crimes—and I was not entertaining the possibility, not really even for a moment, that Avital and the children had not been abducted—that these *incidents* were unrelated? Nothing related them, of course. Except for me, that is—and that, I think, is why, when the Great One asked his entirely reasonable question, I responded with what I believe to be the only lie I ever told him. It was all about me, I suddenly realized—I had been sent to investigate Buki's murder. I had been incarcerated with the man trying to investigate the murder of Ikkesh ben Tovim. And, of course, it was my own children and my own wife who were now missing. Did I fear them dead, really? It's an interesting question. I don't think so—I myself had only been abducted, after all, so I suppose I was thinking that that was probably what had happened to them. I wasn't so naïve as to imagine that they were being held in the same place that I had been confined—they must have realized that someone who knew the city as well as I did would have at least a reasonable chance of guessing where I had been detained—but I suppose I thought they were being held under similar conditions elsewhere. I hoped they were together.

And so I lied to the one man other than my brother whom I trusted the most in all of Jerusalem. He asked me if Asa Gad suspected Benjamin Ginnethon of his brother's murder and, as though I were passing along some snippet of inconsequential gossip rather than indicting a man of murder, I simply said that, yes, he did.

I suppose the concept was to lead the Great One off in his own direction while I pursued matters in my own way. In retrospect, it was a crazy thing to do. But once it was done, it could only be undone by declaring myself a liar . . . and that, I was absolutely not prepared to do.

And then another thought came to me, rather out of the blue: there was actually another crime to consider alongside Buki's murder, Ikkesh's alleged murder, and my family's abduction: there was my own abduction to take into account. And Asa Gad's too, for that matter. And these other crimes brought along yet other questions in their unsettling wake. My abduction was obviously about me too, but what about Asa Gad's? Did my connection with Asa Gad begin when the door to my cell was open and he was flung inside? Or was I connected to Asa Gad in some other way, some way that was unknown to me but which my captors had seized all too precisely and had acted upon for reasons I had yet to learn?

Had Avital reported my absence to anyone? I had been gone for days. Surely she would have gone to . . . to someone! I would have expected that she would have started with Eli ben Heman, with the Great One himself. But he appeared not to know I had been missing for days and I was almost certain his ignorance wasn't feigned. Had Avital gone to the police? She surely could have, but I had no idea if she did. Was I supposed to report to the police now so that they could call off their investigation? But what if she hadn't gone and there was no investigation—did I really want to start up with the police if I didn't have to? But if Avital didn't go to the Great One and she didn't go to the police, then to whom *had* she gone? Was it conceivable that she hadn't gone to anyone? I didn't think so. It wasn't in her nature to do nothing, yet I couldn't quite guess what she had done. And then, suddenly, a new line of thinking presented itself. What if she and the boys had been taken the same evening I had been seized? They could possibly be supposing that I was crazed with worry, that I was the one home waiting for them to return. Or was the house tidy and clean because Avital herself had gone out to find me? Were the boys safe and lodged with some cousin or one of Avital's many aunties? That would explain a lot, but it still left Avital herself unaccounted for.

All this passed through my mind in a matter of seconds. And then my thoughts turned from Asa Gad and Avital to my brother Joseph. He was my closest friend in the city and my only true confident. Avital, of course, knew that . . . so if I didn't come home one evening, her immediate first thought would have been that Joseph and I were together somewhere. Would she have gone to see him? As soon as I thought of it, I realized that that was precisely what she would have done. I needed to see Joseph immediately. If he hadn't disappeared too, that was. In the meantime, the Great One was talking.

" . . . find him." I had missed the beginning of the sentence, lost in my own thoughts. Whom had he said we needed to find? Avital and the boys? Asa Gad? Benjamin Ginnethon? "After all, you will certainly recognize him when you see him again, won't you?" Asa Gad!

"Yes, of course."

"Did he say which service unit he belongs to? Or which priestly clan?"

"No."

"So he could have been a plant—someone they threw in your cell to make you feel less alone, to get you to say what you knew, to inform them about the status of your investigation."

"I can't believe that."

The Great One looked down his nose right at me. "Why not?"

"Because . . . because I . . . because you had to know Asa Gad. He was for real."

"Was?"

"Or is. I don't know. I can't bring myself to think he might be dead."

"If he wasn't a plant, I think he certainly might be dead."

"Then why him and not me?"

"That's an excellent question."

"And do you know the answer?"

"No. But if I were you, I'd find out."

"I should find out? How?"

The Great One was silent for an unnaturally long time. "Well, you could find Asa Gad alive."

"And where would I even begin looking?"

"Well, you could start by knocking on his door and seeing if he answers." The Great One appeared to mean this seriously, not sarcastically.

"And how do I find out exactly where he lives?"

The Great One took my hand and drew me back down to the step he was sitting on. We were next to each other now in the extremely hot water and I felt that odd combination of energy and lethargy the bath always produces in me. I turned my head to look right into his eyes. I knew, almost intuitively, that everything depended on whether I flinched or not . . . and, amazingly, I didn't. I stared into his eyes and waited for his answer. Eventually, it came. "His late brother's brother-in-law must know where he lives," he said quietly.

And so the die was cast. Would the Great One have sent me to confront the Ood if he had known that it wasn't he, but one Dan Iddo ben Uziel from the village of Shephem, whom Asa Gad had indicted of his brother's murder? Given that he was primarily interested in locating Buki's murderer—and that he was assuming that the same trail would lead to Avital and the boys—I suppose he might have. But, of course, there was no way to know that then and there's certainly no way to know it now. At any rate, I knew to proceed with caution.

"And I should just knock on his door?"

The Great One seemed to consider this a profound question, although I had actually meant it almost flippantly. "Only if you want anyone who might be watching to know you've come a-calling," he said.

TWENTY-SEVEN

MY BROTHER WAS AT home when I got there. He had been expecting me, he said.

"Why?"

"Because Avital told me you were gone, that she had no idea where you were."

"And how did you respond to that?"

"How I responded? I told her you'd show up eventually, that she was not to worry."

"And how exactly did you know I was going to show up eventually?"

"I can read, you know." Joseph now produced a flat envelope with what appeared to be a single vellum leaf inside. "Go ahead," he continued, handing me the envelope. "Read it."

"Why don't you read it to me?" I had no specific reason not to take the envelope from his hand and read what was inside, but I was feeling just a bit bullied and I wasn't quite ready just to do as I was told."

"Some doors you must step through yourself," Joseph said calmly.

"And you haven't stepped through this door yourself yet?" What in the world were we talking about?

"Yes, of course, I have. That's why it's your turn now, brother."

I opened the envelope and held the letter at the right reading distance for my slightly far-sighted eyes. And then, in the flickering light of my brother's living room hearth, I read the words that he had already seen and knew I had to read for myself. "Before the defiled among us can eat *teruma* this evening, Ben Simon, your wife and children will be home. We took you and you are safe. We've taken them and they too are safe. Another chose to ignore a similar warning and paid the price for his refusal to see reason.

How goodly and how pleasant it would be for brethren to dwell together in peace! But the choice is yours."

The letter was not signed. But the message itself couldn't have been clearer or more blunt: back off or pay the price of refusing to back off.

I considered the text of the letter. There was no question who the author of the letter meant when he spoke of "the defiled among us" eating *teruma*. For those unfamiliar with our laws, I'll explain. Every farmer in the Land of Israel has to pay a grain tax to the priests who serve in our holy Temple. Never mind that they're only on duty for a handful of weeks a year—they are still supported by this tax, which is formally left unfixed by law but which more or less everybody pays at a rate of 2%. That's the good news, but there's also bad news: *teruma*, as it's called, has to be eaten in a state of absolute, uncompromised ritual purity. Now, other than those who have come into even inadvertent contact with the dead, most contaminated souls can deal with their problem by visiting the *mikveh*, a kind of bath deemed able to undo most kinds of ritual contamination, and immersing oneself in its waters. But bathing isn't enough because the sun *also* has to set and the stars come out before the bather can resume eating *teruma*. So when the author of the letter talked about "the defiled among us," he can only have meant to say that he was one of the priests who were so damn arrogant in their relationship to us that Romamti-Ezer's poem about brethren dwelling together—which the letter writer had had the almost unimaginable *chutzpah* to cite almost verbatim—that Romamti-Ezer's vision of priests and Levites living together in peace has ended up sounding like sarcasm rather than idealism. So I had been nosing around in the right barn after all!

Still, there were plenty of unanswered questions. The letter seemed to be implying that Buki was similarly warned. Had the Great One sent Buki to identify Ikkesh's murderer as he had sent me to resolve Buki's? That would work, I thought, but it really was almost too simple to imagine that Buki had zeroed in on Dan Iddo ben Uziel of Shephem and that Benjamin Ginnethon, upon learning of the success of Buki's investigation, had felt obliged to stop him—to stop Buki, I mean—before he got the evidence he needed categorically to prove Dan Iddo's guilt. According to this theory, he had warned him first (so the letter said), and then, when Buki had ignored the warning, he had killed him.

The principal question was why Benjamin Ginnethon ben Baruch Hakohen would have cared about any of this at all, let alone passionately enough to risk his own life to keep Buki from revealing what he had learned. And to that question, I could only think of two reasonable answers. Either, I figured, there had to be some connection between the Ood and Dan Iddo that was not public knowledge, some link binding them together that would make it reasonable for the former to act as he had to protect the latter. Or else, I reasoned further, Dan Iddo hadn't been acting on his own at all, but had simply been hired to do a job by somebody else who stood to benefit in some way from the death of Ikkesh ben Tovim . . . and *that* person had to be someone whom Benjamin Ginnethon would put everything on the line to protect. I could even think of someone who easily fit both sides of that bill, too: someone in a position personally to benefit from Ikkesh ben Tovim's death *and* whom Benjamin Ginnethon would exert himself maximally to protect. And I knew where she lived!

TWENTY-EIGHT

AND NOW THINGS BEGAN to speed up for me, almost as though time had somehow accelerated and the minutes that used to fill up a full hour or two now only lasted for half as long. I knew that I needed to speak again, and at length, to the Great One. But I wasn't going anywhere but home first . . . to see if the letter was right about the whereabouts of my family.

As I hurried along the smooth stone streets, I considered the matter from yet another vantage point. The letter said that my family would be home this evening—and before the defiled priests could resume eating *teruma*, which is to say before the stars become visible in the nighttime sky. But how could the author of the letter have known when I would read it? As I walked, I considered the matter: I had been released yesterday late at night. I walked back to town and arrived just before dawn. I had found the house empty, but I hadn't left. Or at least I hadn't left right away. For one thing, I had been suffering from fatigue bordering on exhaustion. I was half-frozen. My feet were in almost unbearable pain. I was famished. The only reasonable thing to do was to wash my feet, try to clean the wounds, bandage them as best I could, then eat something, then sleep. In retrospect, even I can't believe I lay down to rest without knowing where my boys were, or where Avital was, but I did. And I slept like a rock for many hours.

I've already explained how I found the Great One and what we had to say to each other. And then I ran to see Joseph and he showed me the letter that had been delivered to him earlier in the day. So whoever wrote the letter obviously felt confident guessing when I would see it. Unless, of course, I was being watched and the plan was simply to release Avital and the boys on whatever day I finally got around to reading the letter Joseph was holding for me. That possibility, however, struck me as unlikely.

In the meantime, I reached my home. Dusk had enveloped the Holy City and the muted sounds of evening were everywhere. Under normal circumstances, my favorite time of day is when the clatter of the *shuk* finally dies down and the peacefulness of evening comes to Jerusalem's lanes and alleyways, when things finally begin to slow down as sunlight vanishes from the city's honeystone walls. If they were going to be sent home before the priests could eat *teruma*, they would have to be there already.

I walked briskly, or at least as briskly as possible, along the lanes that led to our street. The house was looming in the distance, about a hundred cubits in front of me. It looked still. I noticed the front door ajar, but was certain I had locked it when I left in the morning. I felt in the pocket of my outer cloak, and the key was still there. I put both hands on the wooden door and pushed it in just ever so slightly. All was still inside. I entered my home. In the faint light, I could see that the vestibule was empty. The hearth was cold. No appeared to be home.

I was amazed, actually. I had completely expected Avital and the boys to waiting to greet me. The letter said they would be. The letter had offered me a truce if I backed off, and I had certainly not *not* backed off since then. In fact, I hadn't done much of anything since reading the letter at Joseph's except talk with my brother for a few minutes, then race home. It didn't feel right, didn't figure. I went upstairs to change the bandages on my feet . . . and that was when I saw them.

Avital was gagged and tied to a chair with so much rope that she looked like a mummy. I could see she was breathing and I imagined she was more terrified than physically hurt, but I left her be and went after the boys. And I found them too—tied to each other with long ropes, gagged and blindfolded. I undid the blindfolds, pulled off the gags, then told them to wait while I freed Avital. I ran downstairs, then returned with a huge cleaver we used to use to chop sides of beef into more manageable pieces. The ropes cut away easily. She was free. I used the greatest care to cut away the gag . . . and then the two of us ran back to the boys and freed them as well.

It all sounds so dramatic, but, in the end, no one was much hurt. Slowly, the story came out. Four masked men had burst into the house the previous evening, gagged then, put burlap sacks over their heads, and dragged them to a waiting cart, then hauled them off to a room that sounded suspiciously like the one I had been kept prisoner in along with Asa Gad. The incident hadn't led to tragedy, but neither did any of us ever forget the experience. And, years later, when Zakur wrote his best psalm—and the only one of his paeans to David actually to end up in the final collection—and spoke about his enemy ambushing him, chasing him, confining him in a dark spot "as one already among the dead," I have no doubt he was thinking about what it was like for him as the oldest son to be so totally unable in his father's absence to protect his mother or his brothers from the scoundrels who took them from their homes and who could just as easily have killed them as set them free.

Avital recovered quickly. She lit the lamps and laid a fire in the hearth, then began to prepare a stew. And then she told me the story of the previous few days, stressing how she had willed herself not to panic when she realized I was missing, how she herself had gone immediately to tell Joseph that she had no idea where I was, how he had calmed her down and assured her that I was almost definitely out of town for a few days on a mission so top-secret that even he wasn't sure what precisely it was all about. I washed my feet carefully, then took the boys to the Street of the Lambs for a quick bath and scrub-up, then brought them home, dressed them in clean clothes and we all sat down to eat. No one said a word about what had happened. No one asked me where I had been. No one told me where they all had been. No one asked me anything at all, in fact, so intent were we all on creating an atmosphere of normalcy on that most unusual of evenings.

As for me, I was happy just to be home, happy not to have to decide whether or not to follow the Great One's suggestion that I try to find out from Benjamin Ginnethon how to contact Asa Gad. By midnight, the boys were fast asleep, and Avital and I were done cleaning up. We went upstairs together, but we were both asleep within seconds of lying down in our bed.

TWENTY-NINE

I WAS UP EARLY the next day. It was Monday, the eleventh of Kislev, and it was still before dawn. Long before dawn, actually. I lay in bed, though, totally awake and thinking, thinking, thinking . . . with a little wondering and worrying thrown in for good measure. I undid the bandages on my feet and, as I massaged them slowly and purposefully, I catalogued my ever-increasing collection of "if's": *if* this Dan Iddo had killed Ikkesh and *if* Dan Iddo had been working for Meirav Serach and *if* Buki had somehow found out about that . . . and *if* old Baruch Hakohen's other child, Benjamin Ginnethon, had been sufficiently exercised about the possibility of Buki publicly implicating his sister in the plot to murder her own husband—or even if he himself had chosen to get rid of Ikkesh for reasons possibly only tangentially related to his sister's future and *if* Buki had found out about it and then refused to back off his investigation . . . then maybe I was on to something. But those were, admittedly, an awful lot of if's. And, although I had managed to spin out a huge, complicated web of possibilities and plausibilities, I hadn't actually succeeded in proving too much. In point of fact, I hadn't really proven anything at all.

I was waiting at the wine bar next to the Fish Gate when the Great One arrived for his midday meal. Luckily, he was alone. I watched him enter, then be seated. In a moment, I was sitting at his table, asking him if he would mind me joining him. What could he say? He nodded, then smiled slightly. I sat down.

"Did you send Buki to investigate the murder of Ikkesh ben Tovim?"

This question appeared clearly to have surprised the Great One. "Now why would I have done that?"

"I have no idea."

To that, the Great One said nothing. But then, almost when I thought he was not going to say anything at all, he did speak. "Did you know Ikkesh ben Tovim?" he asked.

I thought for a moment, then answered honestly. "No. Did you?"

The look on the Great One's face suggested that this was a complicated question for him to answer honestly, but when he did speak his voice was clear and steady. "Yes," he said, his single syllable sounding sounded forthright and unambiguous.

Finally, we were getting somewhere. "Did you know him well?"

"I grew up together with his father."

"And you . . . you kept in touch as adults?"

The Great One leaned over the low table between us. "With his father? Of course, I kept in touch with him. He was . . . a friend. Of mine. Of ours. And so was his son, may he rest in peace."

THIRTY

IT'S NOT ALL THAT well known these days, but there was a time when the archives of our Holy Temple in Jerusalem constituted one of the finest libraries in the Levant. There were almost a quarter of a million scrolls in the collection, as well as tens of thousands of foreign-language works on parchment or leather scrolls, or on clay tablets, each one purchased, stolen, or inherited from its former owners by patrons anxious and eager to create in our capital a center of learning that could one day conceivably rival Alexandria itself. The collection was housed partially within the Temple, but there was a large honeystone building nearby that served as the collection's formal headquarters and there were also warehouses all over Jerusalem in which materials were stored and satellite storage facilities in several distant suburbs. Each one of these facilities contained wonders beyond the telling of it, but the catalogue itself was the jewel in the crown, the single achievement—and it was an almost unparalleled achievement in its day—that granted the collection its inestimable value by making it totally usable. In its day, there was almost no place in the world to which a citizen—not a king or a *strategos*, but a regular person—to which such a person could freely come and seek the information he lacked. (Regarding the "almost" in that previous sentence, see below. I'll get there.) That the library existed at all was an achievement of almost unparalleled importance. But that the library was open to the public—and that the label "public" was not restricted to the wealthy or the powerful—was itself a kind of achievement as well and, at that, one that paralleled the fact that the library existed in terms of its importance for the average citizen.

To match the wealth of the collection and the detail of its catalogue, there existed a staff of librarians trained and willing to assist the public in their efforts to use the collection. Where these librarians came from—and how they were selected and under whose auspices they were trained—to none of that would I have been privy back when the story I am attempting to tell was actually taking place. But that the library—or, as it was called by the average person in the street, the *archayon*—was available to all who wished to enter its portals in search of knowledge, *that* we all knew . . . and, of course, I knew it as well. And so I went there directly from my interview with the Great One. It was a quiet Monday afternoon at the *archayon* and the place was more or less deserted. I found a librarian, stated my mission, was told to wait. The time I spent waiting, however, turned out to be well worth the effort.

I suppose this is where I should fill in some background information for people unfamiliar with the history of this part of the world.

Almost two hundred years ago, King Seleucus went to war in the distant east to conquer the lands—the only lands, really—that had somehow eluded capture by Alexander, Seleucus' master and mentor a third of a century earlier. (Alexander had pushed so far east into Hindustan that all India must all have seemed reasonably within his grasp, but then he made the decision to return to Babylon to regroup. What led to that decision, none can say. Probably it was a spur-of-the-moment tactical determination, but it turned out to be one of those spontaneous battlefield decisions that end up altering the course of history because it was there, in Babylon, that Alexander died at age thirty-two. That he was poisoned is almost unquestioned these days, even if the identity of his murderers has never been firmly established. But it is only because of what happened to his empire that I'm mentioning Alexander in the first place: once he was gone from the scene, the empire was simply carved up by his generals into personal fiefdoms and that was how Seleucus ended up master of Persia, Babylonia, and points east.)

Seleucus was not a man to be content with what he had. Maybe it rankled him to think that he hadn't actually conquered any of the kingdom over which he ruled, that he had simply stripped his lands off the carcass of his murdered mentor's empire. Or maybe he wasn't the total dunce tradition has made him out to be and he really did have a vision for his future and his country's. Whatever the truth might be in that regard, however, what actually is beyond dispute is that the man dreamed of India. And then, almost amazingly, he actually did manage to invade a serious portion of the northwestern part of Hindustan, which was then called the Mauryan Empire after its founder and at-the-time reigning monarch, Chandragupta Maurya. The Greeks, for some obscure reason, called the man Sandrakottos. (Does that sound like Chandragupta to you?) The point, however, isn't what his name was or wasn't, but what the man was made of. And the answer to that is that he was made of iron. An emperor who (unlike his opponent) had actually conquered the lands over which he ruled, Chandragupta Maurya easily defeated the invading armies of Seleucus and concluded a peace treaty very much to his own advantage in the only way the vanquishing negotiate such things: by dictating the terms to the vanquished and then ordering them to agree to them. And that was how it came about that Chandragupta took—and "took" is, I believe, the precisely correct term—one of the Seleucus' daughters as a wife for Bindusara, the one of his sons the Greeks knew as Amitrochates (which mouthful almost makes Sandrakottos sound a little like Chandragupta). But he was also enough of a statesman to know that, when dictating terms to a defeated enemy, one must also be at least slightly magnanimous. And, precisely in order to be thought gracious in victory, Chandragupta gave Seleucus the remarkable gift of five hundred elephants. The elephants, by the way, ended up playing their own decisive role later on when Seleucus just a few years later went to war with Antigonos of Macedon, another of Alexander's greedy generals, and, by beating the pants off him at Ipsus, managed to add Syria and the Lebanon to his growing kingdom. None of that has much to do with my story, however.

In our world, Seleucus is remembered mostly as a huge blowhard who seized as much of his master's empire as he could get his hands on and then proceeded to rule as though he were somehow the legitimate master of lands he himself had conquered. But Chandragupta, whose name I had never in my life heard when Asa Gad mentioned it to me about one second before all hell broke loose, was completely unknown to me. And so, shortly after I left the Great One, I found myself ensconced in the Temple *archayon* in search of whatever traces of King Chandragupta I could find.

This mysterious Chandragupta, it turned out, not only outlived Alexander, but he outlived Seleucus too. And then, at the end of his own very long life, he managed to bequeath his kingdom to his son, the aforementioned Bindusara, whose own son is even today considered the greatest ruler Hindustan has ever known. He died just about exactly a century ago, so about forty-three years before the story I'm trying to tell . . . and his grandfather died more than a century before that. So what could this Chandragupta possibly have had to do with Buki's murder, or with Ikkesh's? I had no idea at all.

I spent hours in the *archayon* trying to ferret out at least a few useful details. I was helped by a friendly librarian, but it still took me more than four hours to uncover the few facts I did manage to learn . . . and there really weren't all that many. By the time I was done, the sun was already beginning to set. I was in a reasonably good mood. There was less of a chill in the air than one would usually expect in Jerusalem during the later afternoon hours of a day in mid-winter. And, for once, I knew what direction I needed to move in. If Asa Gad was dead, which he certainly could have been, then I was going to have to think of some new plan. But it certainly made no sense at all to start planning out new strategies while there was still some possibility, even a remote one, that Asa Gad was still alive.

I reviewed what I knew. He had been seized and whipped. I had heard the hideous smacks of the leather thongs against his sallow skin, but he hadn't screamed out. I had supposed they had jammed some sort of rag in his mouth to gag him . . . but, of course, I had no way to know if that was correct. More to the point was that I had no obvious means available to me to learn what had happened to him subsequently. They hadn't killed me, after all. So why would they have killed him? But if he was alive, then where was he? Could I go see him? I couldn't see why not. The Great One had suggested I try to locate him by asking Benjamin Ginnethon where to find him. But now that I considered the matter in more depth, I realized I had other options too. Had Asa Gad said where he lived? I thought so, but only when we had first met. Had he said he was from Beth Tzur? I thought he possibly had. Of course, this was before everybody knew all about Beth Tzur, before Judah the Maccabee won his truly stunning victory over General Lysias there about a quarter century later and within the space of one single day more or less guaranteed that the War of Independence would end precisely as it did. But this was long before that, when Beth Tzur was still just a town on a hill overlooking the Valley of Elah—where David bested Goliath, among other things—and protecting the only approach into Judah that an army of any serious size could possibly take. Could Asa Gad be there right now? There was no way to know, but, if he was alive, then there was at least some possibility that Beth Tzur was exactly where he was.

The next day was a Tuesday and, as far as I knew, I was still free to pursue my investigation into Buki's murder without having also to report for my regular duty in the Temple. My feet were feeling much better, but, free of the burden of keeping regular hours, I slept for most of the day, then spent a few after-school hours in the garden with the boys. We had a good meal, then retired early. All of us were still exhausted from our ordeal. But I was at least six parasangs away from the city heading north towards Beth Tzur by the time the boys left for school the following morning.

Because I wanted to travel as unobtrusively as possible, I had signed onto a donkey caravan of the kind that left the city for points north, west, and south a dozen times a day. This was the preferred mode of travel for no one at all who could afford any other means of transportation. It was slow. It was almost incredibly smelly. My fellow travelers were clearly people with no choice at all regarding their mode of transport. I tried to fit in. When we stopped a few miles out to drink some water, eat a few olives, and use the latrine ditch that served travelers in need, I said almost nothing to anyone, preferring to give the others the sense either that I could barely speak the language of the country or else that I was so totally hard of hearing that speaking to me was guaranteed to lead nowhere at all. All in all, we dismounted four times in the course of the journey. Off the donkey. Onto the donkey. Water in. Water out. I bought a pita at a road-side stand, then paid an extra *perutah* for the privilege of dipping it in some slightly rancid olive oil. Once or twice we had to wait for one of our fellow travelers to squat behind a bush, but the trip was otherwise uninterrupted and uneventful. By mid-afternoon, I was in Beth Tzur.

I felt hopeful that the overpowering scent of unwashed donkey would dissipate in the cool air as soon as the distance between me and my beast—a female whose leather collar gave her name as Hamutal—was more than a few parasangs. The journey, at any rate, had ended as unceremoniously as it had begun: the driver announced that we were in Beth Tzur, the caravan stopped briefly, I disembarked, the first traveler in line at the stop climbed onto Hamutal's strong back, and off they all went.

And there I was. To describe where I was standing as a depot would be to say far too much: I was standing by the side of a road just south of town between an over-used latrine ditch and an unmanned refreshment stand. For a moment, I could hardly recall why I had come to this desolate, unwelcoming place. But then I remembered what the lash had sounded like on Asa Gad's back and I resolved not to leave until I had either found him and talked to him, or else ascertained that he was dead . . . or, at least, that he had never come home.

Was anyone watching me? It didn't seem likely—no one else in the caravan had disembarked at Beth Tzur and it was hard to imagine anyone *in* Beth Tzur knowing who I was or why I had come. So I was probably safe. But I wasn't taking any chances and was therefore intent on following the Great One's advice about finding a way to talk to Asa Gad without it being obvious that we were spending time in each other's company or even, if I could manage it, that we knew each other at all.

Luckily, a plan presented itself almost instantly upon my arrival when, on my way into town, I passed what purported to be a wine bar. But the fact that it was a two-story building and was slightly outside of town made it clear to me what else probably went on in that place, an activity fueled by, but only tangentially related to, the consumption of wine. I had to be careful. But the place was tailor-made for discreet comings and goings, its front door hidden behind a hedge that shielded it from the main street and all of its upstairs and downstairs windows securely shuttered. It felt like just the kind of place I needed, a feeling more than reinforced when I went inside and found a group of men sitting by a glowing hearth in the foreground smoking *ganjha* weed and, further back in the room, a number of women looking distinctly underdressed for a drafty building on a wintery afternoon. I approached the proprietor, a nasty-looking piece of work with an unshaven face and strangely large bloodshot eyes and asked for a word in private.

He said nothing, just turned and walked through the door at the rear of the building into the backyard. I understood that I was to follow. The four or five children playing out back with a wooden hoop and a leather ball of some kind seemed oblivious to our presence.

I handed the man a purse filled with coins. He took it, weighed it in his hand for a discreet moment, then pocketed it.

"I'd like to ask your help with . . . with a project."

He seemed surprised. "A project?"

"Well," I continued, trying to reel him in slowly without allowing the line to snap, "not a project precisely, but more like a job I've come here to look after. I'd like to ask for your help."

He said nothing.

"I have a message for a . . . for a local man that I'd like to deliver privately."

"And you need me . . . what exactly are you asking of me?"

I tried to look as though I was forcing myself to smile, hoping to create the impression that this was all about some liaison I was intent on keeping from the wife, something personal and potentially embarrassing. "I'm asking of you . . . I'd like to ask you to . . . to . . ." I let my voice trail off as though I was summoning up the emotional strength to continue. "Do you know a local man named Asa Gad?"

Whatever he was expecting me to say, it apparently wasn't that. "Ben Tovim, you mean? Of course, I know him. Everybody knows him. This isn't that large a town."

I willed myself to blush, but couldn't be sure if I was succeeding. "I need to . . . to speak with him. Privately. And I'm asking you to help me."

I noticed him feel in the pocket of his cloak for the purse of coins. "How can I serve?" He sounded sincere. But, of course, this was a man whose business was all about pleasing his clients. So why would he want to sound anything but potentially helpful and friendly? Still, I felt nervous, hoping I hadn't stumbled into a trap of some sort.

"Could we . . . could Asa Gad and I . . . could we rent one of your rooms for a few hours?" Now I was sure I was blushing. Who knew I could act this well?

To his credit, my host hardly skipped a beat. "Why not?" he asked, clearly rhetorically. "Renting rooms is what we do." The unspoken words "by the hour" hung on the air for a moment, then vanished into the mist.

And then I zeroed in for the kill as I gestured vaguely towards the children in the yard. "And could one of these fine lads or lasses go find Asa Gad and ask him to meet me here later this evening?"

A broad smile now on my host's unshaven face. "Why not?" he asked again. "Friends *should* spend time together." And then he said the words I was eager to hear. "I'll set things up for this evening. Go find a room in the inn down the road and come back when the stars are all out. If he's in town, he'll be here. If he agrees to be, that is."

Now it was my turn to look relieved. "Oh, he'll agree," I said, trying somehow to sound bold and shy at the same time.

"Come to the front and ask for Migdania."

"Migdania," I echoed.

"Yes," he said pleasantly enough, "Migdania."

"And your name?"

He looked surprised, but recovered almost instantly. "Saul," he said. "My name is Saul."

And that, at least for the moment, was that.

Finding the public inn wasn't at all difficult: it was all of a five-minute walk down the road from Saul's place. I took a room, asked the innkeeper to send up some supper, and went directly to my room. They sent the food up almost immediately and, as I ate, I reviewed where things stood so as to be certain to get the most out of my conversation with Asa Gad later that evening. And then I feel into a deep sleep and only woke up when the sun had set and it was time to put my plan, such as it was, into action.

There was a water stand in the room, so I was able to wash up before putting on a fresh shirt and heading out into the cool nighttime air. Just a few minutes later, I was walking into Saul's place.

As earlier that day, there were four or five men sitting around the hearth smoking. There were, however, no women to be seen. That surprised me, although in retrospect I'm not quite sure why. But I knew my one line by heart and was eager to get things started.

I stood there for a moment, appearing to be unsure what to do next. Saul, playing his part well, approached me, clapped his hand on my back as a gesture of male-to-male solidarity and then asked politely what he could do for me.

I tried to appear nervous and unsure of myself, shy and slightly ashamed of my apparently uncontrollable libido. "Is . . . is Migdania here tonight?" I asked, my voice tremulous with feigned ill ease.

"Yes," he said warmly, "she is. I'll go fetch her."

And that's exactly what he did do, slipping into a back room and returning a moment later with a stout woman with bright orange hair and a prominent mole on her left cheek. "Migdi," he said to her in a voice loud enough for all to hear, "Migdi, this man asked for you by name."

Migdania had apparently been briefed and knew her part as well as I knew mine. "Darling!" she said aloud, clapping her hands together in delight. "I had been hoping you'd come by when you were in town. What an enchanting surprise!"

I smiled, trying my best to look overcome with desire. "I've been thinking of you since my last visit," I said warmly, the catch in my voice intended to suggest some combination of lust, guilt, and shame.

Migdania smiled back, then gestured with her head slightly towards Saul. "Settle up with the boss," she said warmly. "And then meet me upstairs. The same room at the end of the hall as last time. I'll be waiting."

I could hardly believe how well this was going. I took out my purse, then turned to face Saul. He mentioned a sum. I counted out the coins, then put them directly into his outstretched palm. And then I walked up the stairs to the second floor and into the room at the end of the hallway.

Asa Gad was sitting on a wicker mat, the room's sole appurtenance, watching me as I walked in.

"Long time, no see," he said almost playfully.

"It's so hard keeping in touch at a distance," I agreed.

Then we both smiled as I sat down too.

THIRTY-ONE

"So what's new?" Asa Gad asked, his voice playful.

I took a good look before answering. The man looked, in a word, terrible. I could see wounds and blotches of raw skin all over his neck. His face was far more sallow than the face of a man in good health should be, even in winter. More to the point, I could tell from the way he was holding himself that he was in pain. He was wearing a short cotton burnoose over loose linen trousers and, as I considered his outfit, it struck me that he was dressed in the manner of someone who could probably only barely stand the feel of anything at all on his skin. My heart went out to the guy. I hardly knew him really and yet it felt like we were in this together. As, I suppose, we truly were.

Eventually, I answered his question. "Not much," I said. "I was ambushed and kidnapped, but they let me go."

"Same here." His face darkened. "But I won't get off that easy next time."

"Did they threaten you?"

"They didn't have to."

"Does anyone know you're here?"

"I'm a man. This is the kind of establishment men frequent."

"You come here often?"

"Often enough."

"You're single?"

"A life-long bachelor. But plenty of married men shop here too."

"There's a lot for us to talk about." I had no idea how long we could remain in Migdania's room uninterrupted and was eager to move things along. But I also didn't want to rush Asa Gad, and I certainly didn't want to make him feel that all I wanted from him was information.

He nodded in apparent agreement, but said nothing aloud.

"I've done some homework since we last met."

"Homework?"

"I know who King Chandragupta was."

"Who he was? Who was he?"

I was flummoxed. How could Asa Gad not know who the man was? It had been he, after all, who had mentioned the king's name to me, not the other way 'round. But I decided simply to answer the question. "He was the king of Hind, the great Maurya who chased Seleucus back to Babylon and secured his kingdom. He was the great Ashoka's grandfather too."

Asa Gad inclined his head slightly to the right. "Is that all he was?" he inquired, smiling. "Just a great king and some other king's *sabba*?"

I thought for a long moment. I had read a several short scrolls and one very long one about Hindustan and its kings in the *archayon*. One of them, the long one, had gone into considerable detail about contact with Hind over the course of the previous century and a quarter, but I couldn't imagine what exactly Asa Gad was getting at. Chandragupta, as far as I could tell, had died exactly 109 years earlier after a long and illustrious career. He had founded a dynasty, bequeathed this throne to his son, and kept his kingdom safe against domination by Alexander's generals. Was there more? I supposed there could be, but I couldn't imagine what it could possibly be all about. "Just a great king," I echoed. "And the father of his son and the grandfather of his grandson."

"And the great-grandfather of his great-grandson too, I suppose."

"I suppose."

"And nothing else?"

I had nothing to say so I said nothing. Asa Gad looked at me with weary, almost sad eyes. For a long few minutes, he said nothing at all. And then, when he was finally, ready, he told me the story I had come to Beth Tzur to hear.

THIRTY-TWO

"The story I'm about to tell you is about what your friend paid with his life for having learned."

"My friend?"

"Ben Yerimoth. Buki."

"You knew him?"

"I knew *of* him."

"And you know what he paid for his life for having learned?"

"I do."

That certainly got my attention. "And he learned it from you?"

"From me?" An unexpected note of surprise in Asa Gad's voice. "No, not from me."

"From Benjamin Ginnethon?"

"From the Ood? No, not exactly from him either. Or at least not in the way you're probably thinking."

"I thought only we called him that."

"Everybody calls him that. Even my sister-in-law. Or at least she used to when she was trying to sound witty or clever. Mostly, though, she called him . . . well, you really don't want to know what she called him, do you?"

I did, actually. But I also knew a rhetorical question when I heard one and decided to move the discussion along in a less disturbing direction. "How did Buki come to know Benjamin Ginnethon?"

Asa Gad's eyes opened slightly wider as he turned to look at me. "How he knew him? I'm not even sure that he knew him at all before."

"Before? Before what?"

"You really know nothing of any of this, do you? I thought you were investigating your friend's death."

I felt my cheeks redden. "I'm just beginning my investigation. But you sound like you can save me a lot of leg work." I tried to sound calm, but my heart was racing.

Asa Gad looked directly at me. "This is a long, complicated story," he began. "But you really do need to know it all. I know what happened to your friend. Or at least I think I do. And, supposing I'm right, I also know how you can bring his murderer to justice. But you need to understand the larger picture here or you'll never understand the smaller one. Are you sure you want to hear this? You can't unhear it later on, you realize. What you burn remains burnt and what you learn remains learnt. And it is a very sordid story, by the way. Are you really sure you want to hear it?"

I nodded my head in assent. I felt honor-bound to listen. I *wanted* to listen. I understood that I was crossing a line. But, really, hadn't I pre-crossed it the moment I promised the Great One to do what he was asking of me? I looked deeply into Asa Gad's eyes and nodded my head. And then, slowly and now without any sort of hesitation, he began to speak.

"Chandragupta," he said, "defeated Seleucus I Nikator, just as you said, and for that he is remembered all across the world as a brave warrior. But he was more than that, David. He was scholar as well, which part of his legacy has somehow remained unknown in our lands, and he was also one of the world's great bibliophiles. The library he built for himself in his capital city of Pataliputra was of unparalleled breadth and depth. And in that he collected works representing every known language, the scope of his collection far exceeded anything in any of the lands along the Great Sea or inland from it. Our great *archayon*, for example—what percentage of *its* collection do you imagine is in neither Hebrew nor Aramaic nor Greek? Maybe, what, ten percent? Or even less than that? Well, Chandragupta's library contained twenty-eight, almost twenty-nine, thousand works in Sanskrit, the holy language of his people . . . and those represented under *three* percent of his library's holdings. A full twenty percent of the collection was in languages that no living person could decipher or understand. He collected scrolls from lands so distant from his own that no one knew how anyone had ever gotten to those place or how they had returned. Money meant nothing—when a volume surfaced that the library did not possess, King Chandragupta asked the price and then paid it. If the scroll wasn't for sale, the king's agents simply made it be for sale either by offering the owner a price he could not decline or by "arranging" for it to be given free of charge to the king as a kind of tribute offered freely out of respect for the king's love of learning . . . and the donor's wish to remain alive.

"Everybody remembers that Seleucus invaded Chandragupta's domain and was repulsed. But he wasn't the first to arrive there with conquest on his mind. Alexander himself was there years earlier . . . and he wasn't defeated at all. He decided on his own—in retrospect, surely one of history's most colossal blunders—to fall back to Babylon to regroup and it was there that he was murdered. Who killed him exactly is a mystery, as you must surely know. But the story I want to tell you takes place before all that. It was during the initial invasion, during the first of all incursions into Chandragupta's realm. Alexander's advance troops were all Macedonians, all men upon whom he knew he could count absolutely. But there were others further back in the ranks who were not Alexander's countrymen—the cooks and the medics and the scribes, but also the launderers and the mapmakers, the astronomers and the astrologers. And there were men of Judah with Alexander in India too, David. Did you know that?"

I took Asa Gad's question to be rhetorical, but he appeared to be waiting for an answer, so I quickly assured him that I had had no idea that my own countrymen—that any of *our* own countrymen—had been along for the ride when Alexander had first penetrated the border of Chandragupta's immense kingdom. "No," I said simply. "I had no idea."

"This all happened more than a century ago, but that's not *such* a long time ago," he said. "Stories remain in families, you know. And this one stayed in mine because among Alexander's Judahite cohorts was my great-great-grandfather, a man named Tovim ben Yehoseph. He had heard about Chandragupta, had heard tell of his marvelous library. Formally, he was along as an astronomer charged with directing the army's nighttime movements by reading the stars. But he was also a businessman who knew a business opportunity when he heard one . . . and along with his astronomical instruments and charts of the heavens, he *also* brought along thirteen chests of scrolls which he had every intention of selling, if the opportunity only presented itself, to King Chandragupta personally.

"And that specific opportunity actually did present itself because, when Alexander made the disastrous choice to withdraw to Babylon to spend the winter there before re-embarking on the conquest of Hindustan, he left a number of garrisons camped on the border of Chandragupta's kingdom. And it was to one of these garrisons that my great-great-grandfather was assigned.

"As you can imagine, there were endless border skirmishes. The Mauryan army commanders were no fools, though, and so they understood clearly that they had an interesting choice to make. Obviously, the combined might of their several standing armies could easily overrun a few phalanxes of Alexander's men left here and there along the border. But was that where their own best interests lay? What if there was a chance of making peace with this Alexander, a peace that would involve a huge amount of trading and a correspondingly huge amount of potential profit—was it worth losing that kind of fortune to keep their nation safe from a few hundred men who could always be annihilated anyway if they dared to cross the border? I suppose it must have been a difficult decision to make. And there must have been a serious lack of unanimity on the Mauryan side because, in the end, some of the advance camps were attacked and others weren't. My great-great-grandfather's camp, led by the then-famous General Eudemus, was one of the ones spared initially. But then the general had the bright idea of taking captive a few boys some of his men had come across in the brush, boys he formally said he wished to have trained as butlers and servants but whom he really wished to force to teach him Chandragupta's language. The boys, of whom the oldest was ten or eleven years of age, were easily seized. Their families, as you'd expect, were enraged. And so were their countrymen. By the time the dust settled, my great-great-grandfather's camp had been overrun, its structures razed, its soldiers beheaded and left to rot in the jungle heat, and its supplies destroyed or seized as booty. The little boys were all safely returned to their families. My great-great-grandfather would surely have met the same fate as his colleagues-in-arms, except that he had been bathing in a nearby river when the attack began. And by the time he returned to camp, it was already all over. Luckily, his trunks of scrolls had somehow escaped notice. And it didn't take him long to realize that he was the sole survivor of an entire camp of Alexander's soldiers.

"Old Tovim—that's how we always referred to him in our families' stories—Old Tovim knew that he had been given a golden opportunity . . . and he took it. Placing his thirteen chests of scrolls on the backs of thirteen donkeys he found tethered to their corral posts who were obviously unaware (or perhaps merely unconcerned) that their masters had all been killed, my great-great-grandfather simply walked across the border and eventually found himself in the custody of one of Chandragupta's border patrols.

"One thing led to another and he was eventually brought into the king's presence. He showed his treasures, realizing, I suppose, that he was about to become either very wealthy or very dead. But the Mauryan was an honorable man and in his culture the theft of scrolls, even from a sworn enemy, was considered a crime beneath contempt. And so the thirteen chests' worth of priceless documents passed into Chandragupta's library . . . and the thirteen chests themselves, each one now filled with golden coins, with opals and jade, and with spices the likes of which no one west of Baluchistan had ever smelled or imagined ever smelling, they were returned to my great-great-grandfather who then, taking advantage of the fact that everybody on Alexander's staff must surely have thought him dead in the attack on General Eudemus' camp, traveled home as surreptitiously as possible.

"My great-great-grandfather took the most circuitous route available to him, choosing the long road whenever the path forked in front of him, refusing even the slightest short cut. It took forever, too—more than sixteen months, according to family tradition—but he eventually resurfaced in our family's home near the foot of Mount Tabor and there he founded our family's spice business *and* our family's trading business *and* our family's currency exchange business *and* our family's gem business. We went from being average Galilean peasants to being major players in four different markets . . . and it was all due to Old Tovim's modesty, which was the reason he had been bathing by himself and at such a distance from the others in his camp in the first place. From there, things proceeded apace. Great-great-grandfather had four sons, my great-grandfather and three others. The nature of these things being that they are always fraught with all kinds of rivalries and petty insecurities, and also to avoid the possibility of his sons turning on each other after his death, my great-great-grandfather ended up leaving one of his operations to each one of his sons. Whether our great-great-grandfather determined on his own who got what or whether that was only worked out by the others after his death, I have no idea. But when the estate was finally disbursed, my great-grandfather—who, just to confuse things, was *also* named Ikkesh ben Tovim—inherited the gem business. And, with it, came not only my great-great-grandfather's contacts throughout Persia, Baluchistan, and Arabia, but also those he maintained diligently—and fully clandestinely—with the land of Hind, where Chandragupta's descendants continued to rule and where they continue to reign, as far as I know, even unto this very day.

"At first, the business centered mostly around the importation of turquoise. In a sense, it's an easy business to run—there's always a strong demand, there's never quite enough product, the price is almost always high, and the trader who has the best contacts almost always wins. And we—my great-grandfather, my grandfather, my father and, last of all, my brother—we *always* had the most product and the best prices. We traveled to the kingdom of the Mauryas so often that we ended up more often in the land of Hind than in Persia or Syria. We had friends everywhere. And we forged reliable, useful business relationships in those few places in which we didn't have true friends. We moved on from turquoise to deal in amethysts, and from there to tourmalines. From tourmalines, we moved into topaz, then into rubies, then into sapphires. There was a time about forty years ago when there was not a single sapphire in the entire land of Israel that hadn't somehow passed through my grandfather's hands or my father's. And all this too Ikkesh inherited."

Asa Gad paused for a moment so I could ask the obvious question. "Why didn't you inherit the business from your father? Why did it pass to Ikkesh instead?"

Asa Gad appeared to be considering his answer, although I knew that he must have expected the question and must surely have known how he was going to answer it without having to reflect overly. Still, I said nothing, preferring to grant him the time he seemed to need to pull his thoughts together. I had no real reason to mistrust him or to doubt his honesty, but his voice sounded just a touch strained when he finally answered my question and I found myself for the very first time wondering to what extent his answer reflected the unadulterated truth. The words that he spoke, on the other hand, were unambiguous. "I didn't wish it," he said plainly, leaving me to wonder to myself why in the world the heir to such a fabulously successful importing business would simply "not wish" to accept his due.

"So Ikkesh must have done well for himself," I said after a moment or two, eager to move the conversation back to Ikkesh's story.

"You could say that. There were whole months—and more than a few of them—in the last few years of his life during which he managed to replicate the degree to which my grandfather had dominated the market in sapphires in his day. And that's not to mention his gold business, or the tourmalines he imported directly from Mongamo, Halingyi, Shrikisetra, and Peikthanomyo. You can't imagine how successful he was. No one really could. And then, one day, he simply died. It was so unbelievable that it took us days even to begin to believe that he was gone. Do you know the story of his death?"

"I'm sure there are parts I don't know."

"You can be sure of that!" I could hear the emotion in Asa Gad's voice. "He was home for a change. He had married that hellion in the meantime, the one whose name I never say aloud, that horror of a sister to Benjamin Ginnethon. You know whom I mean?"

"I do."

"So anyway, he had married her. No one liked her. I personally couldn't stand even to be in the same room as that shrewish tart with her stuck-up ways and her overly made-up eyes. Whether she loved—or would even have been capable of loving—her husband as much as she clearly loved his fortune, I have no idea. But he fell for her and he married her and that was all there was to it. Look, the heart has its own rules. We all know that. And, for a while, things looks as though they might conceivably work out. He seemed happy. We all resolved to hope for the best. Things seemed to be working out. The smallish place in Jerusalem my brother maintained soon got traded up for a much larger place." Asa Gad fell silent for long moment, presumably contemplating the façade of his brother's Jerusalem home in his mind's eye.

"Eventually, they had a baby," he continued. "And when poor little Tola was still a lad of five, his father died. Ikkesh wasn't even forty years old. He was in excellent health. I knew him better than anyone else ever did, even our parents. I loved him better than anyone too . . . and no one, not even his wife, spent more time with him than I did. I saw him in the bathhouse almost daily. I saw his heathy skin, his healthy demeanor, his healthy, thick hair. I saw him looking better than ever, not worse, as his business thrived and his wealth increased. Whether he was happily married in the ultimate sense, I had no idea. But I knew that he was eating well, sleeping well, feeling well . . . and then, one day, while standing in some tiny little lane just inside the Dung Gate on the south side of the Temple Mount—you know the place, I'm sure, that stand where they sell fruit juice and those little plum cakes to pilgrims and *ganjha* weed to off-duty priests—so he's standing there waiting—actually, he was waiting for me, because we were going to have some lunch together before he went off to the coast on business for a few days—so he's standing there waiting for me because I was a few minutes late. And then, suddenly—and I've heard this from a dozen eye witnesses, so I know it's exactly correct—so he's standing there and waiting for me and he suddenly says to some random passer-by that he's feeling dizzy. So he sits down on the bench near the side of the stand and three minutes later he's dead. Gone and gone and gone . . . and when I finally do get there—and I don't think I was ten minutes late, if that—when I finally did show up, I find a huge crowd gathered around something, but I can't see what it is. Of course, I hear right away that someone has dropped dead and, also of course, I don't think for a minute it could be my brother they're talking about, so I start looking all over for him or some trace of him. And then, finally, someone comes over to me—I don't even remember who it was—anyway, *someone* comes over to me and tells me that he has some bad news, that it was Ikkesh who had died.

"Honestly, if they had told me that King David had come down from heaven earlier that morning only to die a second time a few hours later, I couldn't have found what they were telling me less believable. But it was true. I ran to the body, pulled back the ratty blue cloth someone had covered his face with . . . and there he was, my beloved brother, the best and only true friend I've ever had in this sad world. I didn't faint away, but I can't really explain why not. I should have. It should have been me. It should have been anyone but him. But it wasn't anyone else—it was him."

"Did you ever determine what had happened?"

"You mean why exactly my beautiful brother, a healthy, young man in the prime of his life with no history of chest pains and no signs of illness or early-onset decrepitude, why *exactly* he died completely out of the blue in what ought to still have been the first half of his time on earth . . . and by far? Is that what you mean? Or do you mean to ask why a healthy, well-dressed man walking in the street would be found barefoot after expiring unexpectedly?" Asa Gad's voice was rising throughout this last sentence along with his emotions. I wasn't sure if he wanted me to interrupt him, but I couldn't imagine not saying something in response.

"Yes to both," I said quietly.

Asa Gad began to cry. I could see the tears dripping down his sallow cheeks, but he made no noise at all, simply cried without sobbing, without groaning, without making any sounds of any sort. I sat and watched, feeling my own heart breaking for someone so devastated by loss. I imagined what it would be to live through Joseph's death. Joseph, my own brother, was a young man at forty. And he too looked well, ate well, slept well. Like Asa Gad had Ikkesh, I encountered my brother almost daily at the bath and I too could see with my own eyes that he was in the finest health, that he looked robust and strong, that his skin was lustrous and healthy. What, I asked myself, would it be like to lose him? Could I survive that kind of loss? I supposed, almost despite myself, that I could. But what it would be like to live on in the world without my brother, that I could hardly conceptualize at all, let alone imagine clearly.

Asa Gad cried quietly for a few moments, then pulled himself together and continued his story. "We're getting to the part people get killed for knowing, David," he said quietly, almost imploringly. "You've already said twice that you want to hear the story, but I feel I have to ask you a third time if you are really and truly sure you want to hear the rest of it."

I thought for a long moment. Up until that very moment, I hadn't had the slightest doubt that my answer was going to be that of course I wanted to hear the rest. But, for just one long moment, I felt the ghosts of the living—or their eidolons or specters or whatever you'd call them—I actually saw them overhead in Migdania's little *officina*. I saw Avital, of course, and our boys, Zakur, Yehoram, Nathaniel and Asarela. But I also saw Joseph and Yemima and their eldest son Ethan and his twin sisters and two little brothers. Seeing them all, ghostly but also fully present in that tiny room, gave me serious pause for thought. But I also saw Eli ben Heman too, the Great One himself, and that reminded me of the promise I had made to him. And then, just for the briefest of moments, I saw Buki's ghost hovering for a single moment just over my head. In a moment, he was gone . . . and so were my worries and anxieties about proceeding. Besides, I told myself hopefully, I was not really putting myself in danger. Just to the contrary, actually—the people whom I was going to end up indicting of Buki's murder, and Ikkesh's, *those* were the people who were about to fall into a pit out of which they would never manage to climb. I myself was the good guy, the champion, the hero. I was doing the right thing. "Tell me," I said to Asa Gad. I couldn't hear any reticence in my answer. And, judging from what happened next, neither could Asa Gad.

"So it has to with . . . it has to do with those scrolls."

Whatever I had been expecting him to say, it wasn't that. "Scrolls?" I asked. "What scrolls?"

"The thirteen donkey-loads of scrolls my great-great-grandfather delivered to the great library at Pataliputra, the library of King Chandragupta Maurya of Hind."

"Oh," I said, "*those* scrolls."

THIRTY-THREE

"To most people, the age of Alexander is already in the distant past," Asa Gad began. "But within our happy family—within *my* family, I mean—these stories were not only recalled, but treasured. The big stories about Alexander and Roxana, the ones everybody knows, we obviously told too. But the ones relating to our own family—for example, the one about how Old Tovim had been off bathing when the Maurya hordes arrived to destroy General Eudemus' camp, thus saving his own behind while simultaneously washing it—that is a story I must have heard a thousand dozen times growing up.

"Tovim's son, the first Ikkesh, was my great-grandfather, the one of his father's sons to inherit the gem trade. His son, Asahel ben Ikkesh, was my grandfather. He too was successful, but by his day what had begun as our family's normal set of business associates and suppliers had turned into a set of foreign contacts that went far beyond the links to the east that even the government maintained. You have to remember, these were the years during which the Land of Israel switched hands from the Ptolemies to the Seleucids—from the PTs, as we used to say, to the Selx—every three months. The PTs had no interest in the east. They had, truth be told, no interest in anything but their own phony pharaonic selves—and certainly none in us or in points east of here. In fact, the more completely they insulated themselves, the happier they were. But even the Selx showed no real interest in the lands beyond Bactria and Baluchistan. Or maybe there even *were* contacts of some sort—but, as far as the simple Jews of our simple land knew, the world ended at Kolachi.

"Asahel's only son, indeed, his only child—the one Asahel's wife died giving birth to—was my father Tovim. He was thus the great-grandson of his namesake, the first Tovim, and as such heir to all the family's secrets.

But he was the first one, the very first one, to focus his businessman's gaze on those scrolls—the ones deposited a century earlier in Pataliputra—and to ask himself what precisely knowing about that sale could mean for him personally and for his business.

"At first, it was just a germ of an idea, the kind of thing that flits in and out of your brain without really nestling in and settling down. He mentioned it now and then, but mostly even he forgot about it. Until . . ."

My eyes widened as it suddenly dawned on me where Asa Gad was going with this very long story.

". . . until it finally struck him that he didn't need to spend all his days wondering at all, that he could simply take himself to Pataliputra the next time he found himself crossing the boundary into Hind. By this time, Devavarman ben Salisuka was king. I don't believe anyone here other than members of my family, and now you, have ever heard of Devavarman Maurya, but he was a good guy, a friend of learning, a polyglot who, among other things, deserves to be remembered as the first, and probably the only, Mauryan ruler to learn to read Hebrew or Greek . . . and he learned to read both of them. He also had a reputation for being the very soul of hospitality. But the journey to Pataliputra was not a simple one. For one thing, who really knew where it was? The maps all had it on the great Indus River, not that far from the border. But that was completely wrong. Pataliputra is actually on the distant Ganges, which is to say at least a full thousand mils further east than where the maps said. And distance was the least daunting of my father's problems, not the most—the distance was truly immense, that much is true, but the real issue had to do with the fact that not all of the king's subjects shared their leader's penchant for welcoming guests. Not that they had much experience of foreigners at all, mind you—my father thought that he was possibly the first outsider to enter the imperial city in at least a century and certainly the first to arrive there ever on his own. He was definitely the first to apply for entry into the library. His arrival in Pataliputra was such a big deal, in fact, that Devavarman himself showed up to greet my father at the city gates—not a messenger and not a minister, but the actual emperor himself, all decked out in his imperial robes and looking, so my father told the story, like the regal embodiment of Chandragupta himself come back to life to welcome my father's great-grandfather's great-grandson to the capital of his kingdom and to escort him into the library that our family had helped make great."

Asa Gad paused, as I by now had long since realized was his regular custom, to allow me to ask the question he wished to answer. "And what did your father find there?" Even I could hear the catch in my voice as I spoke. Clearly, we had gotten to the crux of the matter.

"He found a huge room devoted solely to the materials my father's great-grandfather had sold to Chandragupta, a room so magnificent that he could hardly find the words in Hebrew to describe it. The tables were made of the finest walnut wood. The lamps that illuminated the room were made of chased gold and silver filigree. At the center of the room was a hearth made entirely of turquoise and black marble, and the hearth was kept burning constantly at precisely the right temperature to provide the kind of dry, warm atmosphere that is the most conducive to the proper preservation of parchment and leather. On the parts of the walls not covered by scroll warrens, the richest tapestries had been hung—one of which actually featured a portrait (and, at that, the only one known to exist then or now) of my great-great-grandfather arriving in Pataliputra at the head of a caravan of thirteen donkeys laden with the literary treasures he left in Pataliputra. The thing was—and, believe me, I know how difficult this must be to imagine, let alone truly to believe—the thing was that the room housing my great-great-grandfather's collection was one of over eight *hundred* similar rooms, each one devoted to the culture of a different one of the world's peoples. There were, my father reported, rooms filled to overflowing with Greek manuscripts. That much you probably think obvious—what else would Alexander's great foes have collected if not their enemy's classics of history and philosophy?—but there were also rooms filled with Egyptian scrolls, and still others featuring the literature of the Sogdians and the ancient literary treasures of Thrace. There were whole rooms filled with works in languages my father not only couldn't read, but which he hadn't ever heard of. How all of this material had been brought to a distant capital on the Ganges, as far from the far Euphrates as we ourselves are (if not even farther), my father could not even begin to imagine.

"My father knew better than to ask if the scrolls were for sale. But he did come to learn that the Mauryans were not merely collectors, but true lovers of learning. In other words, they didn't create this library of almost indescribable richness and breadth merely to enjoy the satisfaction of owning its contents, but actually to make its contents available to the world. Nor was entry restricted to scholars and brahmins, as they call their priests, but instead the entire facility, with no restrictions of any sort, was open to all. And that, as you've undoubtedly already guessed, included travelers and visitors. In that specific regard, the library at Pataliputra was similar to our own *archayon*. And, as a result, my father was not merely permitted to enter the building, but was made truly welcome there. And let me tell you, for all the villagers through whose territory my father had been obliged to pass on his way east had been wary and skeptical of his peaceful intentions, the people of the capital—clearly a more sophisticated crowd—knew a thing or two about welcoming strangers: my father was provided not merely with a card of entry, but with a suite of rooms, with a servant to help him with his needs, with a writing desk filled with a more or less endless supply of parchment and ink, and with enough time—with all the time in the world if he wished it—to sit in the room devoted to his people's treasures and to copy out as much as he wished of as many manuscripts as he wanted. No one was permitted to pester him. Nor would he be bothered at all, he was assured, unless he himself signaled an unmet need, which, he was further promised, would not be left unmet for long. He was their guest. They were, they said, therefore his servants as well as his hosts. And that was how my father was received in the kingdom of the Mauryas not quite eleven years ago."

It had been Asa Gad who had done all the talking, but I was the one who was out of breath. The sun had peaked in the sky and had now been setting for several hours. There was a chill in the room. Migdania was nowhere to be seen and I imagined she had made herself scarce specifically so as to grant me as much time with Asa Gad as we needed. Was Saul paying her to be absent at the same rate he would have paid her to be present if I had been a regular customer of his establishment? I had no idea. Nor did I ever find out. I hoped so! Wherever she is and if she is still alive, I wish her well and I pray that life has dealt with her kindly.

In the meantime, business was picking up. I heard doors opening and closing in the corridor, plus I could hear the buzz of patrons arriving after work for a quick drink or smoke on the way home or a quick trip upstairs. Saul hadn't suggested that there was as specific limit to how long we could stay—no one had appeared in the room at all since I had entered and found Asa Gad waiting for me—and I was more than prepared to pay for the time we had occupied the room. Still, I needed Asa Gad to get to the point before someone did show up and tell us our time was up.

"So what happened then? How much did he copy?"

Asa Gad looked directly through my eyes into my soul. "He copied out twenty-six full-length vellum scrolls' worth of material," he said almost prosaically.

"And what happened to those scrolls?" I asked, although I was almost sure I already knew the answer to my question.

"He gave them to Ikkesh and to me as our inheritance."

"And then he died?"

"Six years ago."

"And that was that?"

Asa Gad looked at me dolefully for the first time, almost as though he was getting tired of not being understood perfectly. "No, David," he said softly, "that was most definitely *not* that."

THIRTY-FOUR

"Twenty-six scrolls is a lot of writing," I observed, hoping to prompt Asa Gad to go into more detail.

"He was present in Pataliputra for eighteen months."

"And he had free reign of the place for as long as he was on site?"

"He was treated like an honored guest the entire length of his stay."

"And how did he know what to copy?"

Asa Gad leaned forward as though he were about to convey a secret. "He spent the first weeks there making a hand-list of the contents of all the scrolls in the room."

"A kind of catalogue, then?"

"Exactly. And he brought that scroll home with him as well. So we not only knew what he had copied, but also knew what he had decided not to copy."

"Or what he simply didn't have time to copy before he felt compelled to begin his journey home."

"I suppose. But no one was pushing him to leave. Just the contrary. My father used to tell me that he was, if anything, urged to stay on, to take as long as he wished to work in the library."

Now it was my turn to lean in. "So then what?"

"My father brought home treasures beyond belief. A full copy of Ezra's personal diary describing his work in Jerusalem, the parallel work to Nehemiah's that no one had seen in almost two centuries. A copy of the unexpurgated lamentations of Jeremiah on the destruction of Jerusalem in which was included a sixth dirge, unknown previously, in which the prophet describes a vision of his own death in such vivid detail that it was deemed too personal—and far too gory—to be included in the version released to the public. A kind of commentary on the Song of Songs—although really more of an elaborate translation into Aramaic than a real commentary—in which the identity of the Shulamith is revealed, a detail suppressed for centuries because of its political implications for the House of David. A manual, heretofore unknown in any version, of priestly practices dating back to the time of Solomon. And, to go with it, a history of the high priesthood of Israel offering biographical details regarding every single man to serve in that capacity from the days of Zadok ben Ahitub until the destruction of the Temple in the days of King Zedekiah. But, most precious of all, my father found, copied, and brought back a history of the Levitical movement that described its origins in detail . . . and in a way wholly and totally at odds with what people today think."

Now Asa Gad had my full attention. The building we were in could have burned down around us and I wouldn't have noticed. Or cared all that much.

"My father brought back proof—written proof, incontrovertible and by its very nature of unimpeachable authenticity—that demonstrated the truth of your claims. That your people were the direct descendants—intellectually and spiritually if not precisely genealogically—of the prophetic caste of ancient times. That your techniques—and, yes, I know everything about it, so there's no need to dissemble—that your techniques were not invented by yourselves, much less copied from outsiders, but were inherited from your spiritual forebears in the days of Solomon's Temple."

I opened my mouth as though I were about to say something, but no words came out. In fact, I had nothing to say, nothing to add, nothing to contribute. All I wanted to do was to hear more. And I did hear more. A lot more, actually.

"Have you ever heard of Kadmiel ben Henadad?"

I shook my head. "I'm not surprised. No one else has either. He's mentioned in Nehemiah's memoires somewhere as one of the guys who signed onto that big covenant renewal ceremony back in the day when Eliashiv ben Jehoiakim was high priest and Nehemiah came to rebuild the walls of Jerusalem. In that context, he's just another name on a list . . . but it's what he did in his spare time that really matters . . . and what he did was write a full, honest history of your people. He understood a lot of things and he also misunderstood a lot of things, but the bottom line is that he managed to prove more or less categorically that the whole movement—the techniques, the goals, the literature, the use of stimulants, all of it—travels in a direct line from the prophetic caste in the olden times when Solomon's Temple still stood to the Levites who exist in present-day Jerusalem."

I could hardly decide where to begin. "And this . . . this scroll, it actually exists?"

"As far as anyone knows, the original is precisely where my father left it in Pataliputra."

"And the copy your father made?"

"Well, that's the big question, isn't it? Where do *you* think it is?"

"Where do I think? How in the world would I know?"

"Well . . . let's say someone asked you to locate it. Where would you start your search?"

I thought for a long moment. "Well, you said it was your father who brought it here. So I'd look among his personal effects."

"But he died six years ago. I personally served as executor of his estate and I looked after the disbursement of all of his personal effects and all his funds. Everything went to the appropriate party."

"Well, if you were the executor, then you must know where the scroll went. Where all the scrolls—how many did you say there were, twenty-six?—where they all went after he died."

"Well," Asa Gad continued in a strange sing-song, "*if* I was the executor, *then* I should know where they went. "

"But you don't?"

"I don't."

"Don't know where all of them are or don't know where one of them is?"

"One of them."

"Because it was stolen?"

"After my father's death, we sat in mourning for the requisite week. We were in his own home, so there was no possibility of anyone breaking in and stealing anything. If anything, his wealth was more secure during that week when the house was constantly occupied than it was when he was still alive and the house was left empty at least a couple of months a year while my father was traveling and my mother generally moved in with her sister Leah so she wouldn't have to be alone. I didn't—you know it's our tradition not to disturb the property of the deceased until after the end of the mourning week—I didn't do anything at all until the week was up. I hadn't even really read his instructions all that carefully, preferring to embark on that sad set of tasks when we were slightly more at peace with the reality of his passing. But when I entered his study for the first time in more than a month on the day our mourning week concluded, I knew at once that things were not right.

"What was missing, I figured out easily enough. A few boxes of samples, mostly turquoise stones and some opals. A black onyx cat my father bought somewhere and liked to keep on the windowsill behind his desk. A set of tiny Sogdian warriors that someone had given him once on one of his trips and which he used to like letting us boys play with on the floor of his office while he sat at the desk and worked. And, as you've undoubtedly guessed, the scroll containing Kadmiel ben Henadad's *History of the Levites*."

I moved forward so that I could stare directly into Asa Gad's eyes. "Do you know who stole it?"

"Yes," he said quietly. "I do."

"So who was it?" I asked, realizing that this was the threshold moment that Asa Gad had promised me.

Asa Gad looked calmly at me, waited an extra beat, then spoke. "The scroll was stolen by . . . by who do you think? By my brother's larcenous brother-in-law, the brother of his horrible wife."

"And you're sure of this?"

"Of course, I'm sure. The first time it was stolen, it was stolen by Benjamin Ginnethon. He had the knowledge. He had the motive. He had the opportunity. And he had the low character necessary to steal from the dead."

"The first time it was stolen?"

THIRTY-FIVE

THE REST OF OUR conversation flew along.

How Asa Gad deduced that the Ood has stolen the scroll containing Kadmiel ben Henadad's *History* was simple enough to follow. To steal that scroll only, one would have to have known about the work it contained—absent that knowledge, why would a thief not have taken all the scrolls or at least some of them? Taking the trinkets and the stones was clearly meant to suggest that this was just a common robbery, except that no one but the police was fooled. And, of course, the police were not informed about the missing scroll, just about the other missing items. The thief, therefore, had to be someone who knew about the scroll and its contents. That limited things seriously. As far as anyone knew, Asa Gad's father had hardly told anyone at all about the literary treasures in his family's possession. Partially, this was for security reasons. But partially it was just another example of his exceptional business acumen that he wanted to wait until the exact right moment to announce even the existence, let alone the availability for purchase, of the scrolls from Pataliputra. And about Kadmiel's *History* he had been even more circumspect, revealing its existence only to members of the immediate family and a very few others. This was, after all, highly explosive material. The work did circulate outside the family, but only in extremely narrow circles. And there were absolutely no copies at all made. The priests of Jerusalem had spent years—years upon years upon years, actually—presenting the *status quo* as reflective of hoariest antiquity. That they were on top was deemed reflective of divine will. As was also the notion that we existed in the first place solely to be their servants.

So a history based on no-longer-extant documents that purported to prove, and which actually did prove, that the kind of spirituality *we* were putting forth as reasonable and rational was not our own invention, as which they regularly condescended to damn it, but something of the greatest antiquity, something as old as the people itself—you can just imagine the way *those* people would greet the discovery of such a work.

In the end, though, the path to Asa Gad's indictment of his brother's brother-in-law was a relatively straight one. Meirav Serach was greedy, but she was also simple and, when pressed, she as much as indicted her own brother of the theft, admitting (when asked forcefully by Ikkesh) that she herself had told him where in the house the scrolls from Pataliputra were kept. There was almost no one else who could have known about the scroll. But there was no one at all who could have slipped unobtrusively into Asa Gad's father's study when the house was packed with guests come to condole with the mourning family.

When called by Ikkesh into his father's study—into Ikkesh's father's study—and asked baldly if he had taken anything from the house of mourning, Benjamin Ginnethon simply said that he certainly had not and that he mightily resented the question. But his feigned outrage said otherwise to all of us . . . and especially to Ikkesh, who had stopped liking his brother-in-law almost as soon as they had met and he had seen for himself on many occasions what kind of self-important bully the Ood really was.

The second time the scroll was stolen, its theft was commissioned by a party missing from this long, complicated narrative whose absence I had somehow forgotten to notice: Bukiyahu ben Yerimoth. And this part of the story, Asa Gad too knew in detail and wanted to tell. It was, however, time to leave Migdania's place of business. For one thing, my legs were in serious need of some exercise. And, for another, I think we were both feeling hemmed in by the dimensions of that tiny room and we were both eager to breathe some fresh air. And so we rose from Migdania's mat and went downstairs. We stayed for a snack of beer and olives, then headed out into the cool air of a late winter's afternoon in Beth Tzur.

The streets were deserted. The sky above was the color of lead. It felt like it might snow. In the distance, I heard someone playing a reed flute. The sounds of a provincial town towards dusk were everywhere—pots and pans clattering, children playing for a few last minutes in the street before nightfall, women calling out to each other as they prepared supper for men just now returning from their day's work. Here and there a goat brayed in the distance. I was anxious to return to Jerusalem, but it was obvious that I could not even begin my journey home until morning. I was fine with staying in the *pundak* in which I had spent the previous night, but bringing Asa Gad up to my room would expose our relationship in precisely the way I had met him in a brothel in the first place to avoid. So we headed for the bath house, which decision suited me perfectly. For one thing, I hadn't bathed in two days. For another, I was freezing and the thought of continuing this conversation in a warm place appealed mightily. And, for a third, it was comforting to think that we could spend a little more time speaking privately in a place in which it happened all the time that men who had no prior relationship became involved in unanticipated conversation without attracting any attention at all.

THIRTY-SIX

NOT AN HOUR LATER, we were warm and cozy in the steam. No one seemed at all interested in us. It even seemed possible to imagine that no one would be able to swear that we had been there together, or even at all. For the first time in hours, I was warm. And I was feeling very eager to continue hearing the story Asa Gad has spent an entire day telling me.

This time, I opened with an obvious question. "If you knew who stole the scroll, why didn't you press the matter? You could have involved the police. You could have gone to the HP himself. You could have lodged a complaint with the Sanhedrin or even with some lower court. You could have done a lot of things."

Asa Gad looked at me for a long minute. "We thought—maybe even I still think—that he couldn't have acted alone, that his sister must have been involved."

"Even better. Have you forgotten how much you dislike her?"

"Look, Ikkesh was her husband. And he loved her. Or he thought he did. Or at least *we* thought he did. The issue was discussed a dozen times, then let go of. It wasn't the original that had been stolen, after all, just a copy. And there were no copies of the copy—of that we were completely certain. And the original, at least we all knew where *it* was: safe and sound in the library at Pataliputra. Ikkesh was convinced that his wife had facilitated the theft of Kadmiel ben Henadad's work, but he didn't really know the extent of her involvement. And he clearly did not wish to find out, something that would have almost inevitably come about as a by-product of the kind of investigation the police would have been obliged to mount if we had lodged a complaint with the authorities. We dithered for a long time, then finally did nothing. As far as we were concerned, the matter was over. We convinced ourselves that we were acting reasonably, logically, thoughtfully. We were kidding ourselves—at least a little we were—but it felt right at the moment. What can you do? Ikkesh was adamant. And I was never any good at opposing him. The matter was allowed to drop."

I thought carefully about what I had just heard, then decided to move the conversation off in a slightly different direction. "And Bukiyahu had . . . what did Buki have to do with any of this?"

"Can't you guess?"

I was totally at sea. "Did you know Buki?"

"I met him a few times."

"But Ikkesh knew him?"

"They were . . . close."

This was becoming very interesting very quickly. "How did they become . . . close?"

The color rose unexpectedly in Asa Gad's cheeks. "Ikkesh was four years older than Bukiyahu. I was two years younger than my brother, so two years older than Bukiyahu. But Bukiyahu was . . . let me ask you first, how well did you know him?"

I thought for a moment before answering. "Not that well," I said carefully. "I mean, I knew him well and not well at the same time. I saw him at the baths and in the Temple a thousand times. We were in the same room at the same time so many times I can't even begin to guess how many times that would be. I knew some of what he did with at least some of his free time. I knew he had an eye for pretty women. I knew he lived in that nice stone home by the Sheep Gate. I knew he had a sister. I knew he was survived by his mother and predeceased by his father. I knew he was immensely overweight, but that he managed to look healthy and well-fed rather than stuffed. So I suppose I can say that I knew him reasonably well."

"Did you know that he was a *shulchani*?"

"A . . . a what? A *shulchani*? You mean he converted currency for a living on the side?"

Asa Gad smiled slightly. "Not exactly like that. You want money to change hands quietly, privately, even secretly . . . but you're not sure how to arrange it. So let's say . . . let's imagine you wanted to . . . let's just think for a moment. Suppose you were . . . suppose you were someone who wanted a few moments of privacy in a public place . . . "

I think it was at that moment that I knew everything. Or maybe that's just how I'm remembering it now. But that actually *is* how I'm remembering it now. I knew. And I knew that I knew.

" . . . and let's imagine that this wasn't just a public place, but a *very* public one. Say we were talking about a courtyard in a very public building where, at midnight, someone or several someones wished briefly to be left alone to . . . to . . . ."

"To do what?"

"I know you know. And now you know that I also do."

I imagined the heat of the steam was rising. I was suddenly so hot that I wasn't sure I could stand staying seated much longer. But, paradoxically, I also felt rooted to my seat, unsure I could have left even if I truly had wanted to. But I didn't wish to leave. Not even slightly.

And now Asa Gad was taking an entirely different tack. "Did you ever . . . wonder?"

"Wonder? Wonder about what?" I knew, of course, but it felt right to ask.

"Wonder about how it works that none of our patrols *ever* finds your brethren gathered in the courtyard at midnight to take their hands from the pot, to hear the secret thunder, to see the light, to hear the voice, to experience . . . ."

My eyes were the size of saucers. "You know of all that?"

"I do. But we don't all know. In fact, only very few of us know anything. And even fewer know everything."

"You are one of them, I guess."

"One of them who knows everything? Yes, I am."

"But why you?"

"Why me? Why *not* me? I *was* my brother's brother, after all! But we're getting off track here. So let's say that contact was somehow made . . . between two great men, one great man called the Great One and another called the . . . well, you know how he's called."

For a moment, the image of the High Priest of Israel flitted across my field of vision only to vanish almost immediately. But I knew where Asa Gad was going. "And the space, it turned out, was available for . . . for what would you call it? For rent? I suppose that's exactly what you'd call it."

"Onias is one of us? A friend?"

"You give him too much credit. This was about money, not principles. But what does any of that matter? The point was that the money had to change hands surreptitiously, so that the anonymity of the soon-to-be-enriched party could remain secure."

"It was about money?" I must have sounded like an idiot, but hearing this all said so plainly and clearly was—in a word—overwhelming for me.

"People do all sorts of things for money."

"So this was just about the money?" How many times was I going to ask the same question? Even *I* knew I was repeating myself.

"As far as I know, yes. Choni—Onias—is a sick old man who won't be in office forever. Every bird feathers its nest, David, even birds of prey. And this has been going on a long time too. But you surely know that, don't you?"

I could practically feel the pieces of the puzzle falling into place.

Asa Gad was almost smiling now that he could actually see me catching on. "So let's see," he said, "how could this actually work? The money had to change hands, after all."

I heard myself speaking almost against my better judgment. "Well," I began, "one party could give someone . . . someone with a reputation for womanizing and with no connection to the mysterious goings-on to which you've just alluded, someone *no one at all* would expect to be connected with any of this . . . such a one could give that specific someone a huge amount of money."

"And that someone would take his huge wallet and his huge belly and make his way to . . . to where? To some setting in which his presence could easily be explained. Or rather explained away."

"For instance," I continued his thought, "for instance to a gem merchant, to the kind of gem merchant who might have lovely things for sale . . . just the kind of lovely things that a single man eager to please a lady friend might wish to purchase."

"Why not? Lots of men, married and single, go to gem merchants to purchase baubles to impress their women."

"And gems are so small! It would hardly be possible to frequent a camel dealer and not be seen afterwards going home with a camel, but who could tell if a man did or didn't have a sapphire tucked into his *avnet*? In fact, most people would seek to conceal the fact that they had made such a purchase precisely to prevent thieves from getting wind of it."

"So if such a man were to take himself to such a merchant with a huge amount of money, then leave with no gems at all . . . no one really would or could know what was going on. And what would happen to that money later on?"

"It would make its way into the pockets of the one man in Jerusalem who could guarantee that the privacy purchased could actually be provided. Haven't you ever wondered why a man in Choni's position would bother personally organizing the roster of night watchmen? Doesn't that strike you as seriously beneath the dignity of a man such as himself, worrying about a dull administrative detail like that?"

"But if the man needed certain specific men to be on duty on certain specific evenings, men who could be paid—or, rather, paid off—to spend the night at their guard posts without bothering to patrol at all . . . ." I let my voice trail off as yet another puzzle piece fell into place.

"And so the man with the huge belly and the gem merchant became friends?"

"Intimate friends, the kind who speak for hours about the deepest topics. They spoke about women, about God, about music, about gems, about politics. They read poetry together, and they learned the full story of each other's family. They would occasionally lie down to nap by each other's side and find themselves having shared a dream."

"I'm getting all confused here. Does this have . . . what does this . . . does this have anything to do with Ikkesh's murder?"

Asa Gad stood up and walked to the other end of the sudatorium. As I watched his bony buttocks vanishing in the steam, I tried to organize the story I was hearing in my mind. But it was too much. Details sailed in and out of my head like bats flying in and out of a deserted desert cave. I had spent hours listening to his story, but I was, if anything, more confused than ever. And then Asa Gad returned. He had only been gone for a short while, but his posture was different than it had been all day. It seemed almost as though whatever have been weighing his shoulders down had been shucked off, thus allowing him to stand up straight. He looked . . . healthier, stronger, and far more in control of himself and his destiny (and, possibly, mine as well) than he had been earlier. "It has *everything* to do with Ikkesh's murder," he said almost as though no time at all had passed since my question had been posed and left hanging on the damp, hot air.

THIRTY-SEVEN

ASA GAD DID NOT sit down. Instead, he stood before me and spoke rather in the manner of a *saneigor* giving a speech to a crowd of only mostly sympathetic judges. "Up until now," he said, "all I have told you I know to be true. Some of it, I suppose you can guess how I managed to learn. Other parts, you'll have to take my word about. But now I cross into the realm of conjecture. Part of what I am about to tell you, I think I can say with certainty is true—but without the kind of proof you'd need in a court of law. And part only might be true because it fits the details I know about the personalities of the players involved. And, believe me, at least some of what I think will shock you. It even shocks me and, as you've probably realized by now, I don't shock all that easily.

"My father returned from the east with the scrolls about eleven years ago and died six years ago at age sixty. Ikkesh only died the year before last. So what happened in the years between my father's death and Ikkesh's? Part of the story, you already know. After the mourning week ended, we realized that the *History of the Levites* scroll had been stolen. We knew who had taken it too, or we thought we did. That much you know already. But what you know nothing of . . . what you can probably not even begin to guess at . . . look, there's a part of this story that is about larceny and there's part that's about murder, but there's also another part . . . a part about the degeneracy of men . . . and women . . . and the degeneracy of men *and* women. This is a sordid story, David. But it's one that must be told. And now . . ."

I leaned forward. "Yes?"

He smiled. "And now I have to go to the latrine. When I come back, I'll tell you everything. You've earned it."

I sat back, feeling deflated. Not one man in a hundred would bother leaving the steam for the latrine (which was located in this facility on the far side of the apodyterium) when there was a perfectly good drain in the floor not twelve cubits from where we were seated which I had to imagine men used all day long without giving the matter a moment's thought. And, on top of that, there *was* no one else in the steam at the moment. After our days together sharing the use of a bucket, it seemed odd to imagine that Asa Gad was suddenly too modest to use the drain in my presence. And so, I concluded, Asa Gad had probably just wanted me to think about what he had already told me and was merely giving me some private space to think about it in.

The Ood was loathed in our circles as a bully and a self-righteous prig, but he was disliked elsewhere as well. Assaf, the son of Buki's mother's oldest brother—I mentioned him earlier when describing the dirge he composed that was sung at Buki's funeral—Assaf had written a kind of poetic indict-ment of Benjamin Ginnethon that held back at nothing, not even at calling him a *rasha*, a fiend, the worst of all terms of opprobrium in our circles.

In my mind's eye, I could see Assaf ben Yedutun clearly. He was a tall, gaunt man with sunken eyes and scant hair he preferred, fooling no one, to comb over the top of his head in a vain attempt to deflect attention from the premature hairlessness of his almost totally bald pate. He was so thin that his abdomen was almost concave, and the combination of his extreme thinness with the sallow, almost greenish, color of his skin and his almost total lack of body hair produced an air of slightly sickening emaciation. He resembled his father, but in an exaggerated way: Yedutun was lean, but Assaf was leaner. Yedutun was bald, but Assaf was balder. Yedutun had a minimal amount of body hair, but Assaf appeared to have none at all, not even in his arm pits or on the taut skin covering his bony pubis. But, odd looking or not, the man was a born poet, a gifted author, and a versifier in the ranks of the greatest we've produced. I cited the dirge he composed for his cousin's funeral earlier, but I now focused not on that great poem, but on the one Assaf had composed shortly before Buki's death.

It was a scathing indictment of a villain among us, of a *rasha* and a *reika,* of a man whom the poet permitted himself to imagine God in heaven indicting of his sins with words that were destined later to become famous, but which, at the time, were known only to those among us whom Assaf dared to trust. "Who gave you the right," Assaf imagined God rhetorically asking the dismal defendant, "who gave you the right to teach My laws or to give forth about the terms of My covenant with Israel when you hate re-proach and freely ignore My words? If you see a thief, you can hardly wait to run with him to steal—and the rest of the time, adulterers are your company.

You use your mouth to do evil; your own tongue you join to swindling. You sit with your brother and then speak evil of him, thus slandering your own mother's son. Shall I remain silent when you have done these things? If I did, you would imagine that I were just like you. Therefore I rebuke you openly and publicly evaluate your actions to your own detriment." Running with his own metaphor, Assaf then imagined the Judge of all the Earth turning to the defendant's fellow priests assembled in the divine court to attend his trial. Daring to imagine God scrupling to justify the very fact that a man invested with the sacerdotal majesty of the holy priesthood should be brought to justice at all, Assaf's words came to me forcefully and clearly. "Consider that," the poet has God saying to the assembled priests of Israel, "consider my holy words, you who so easily forget Me! Consider them lest I annihilate you and there be none to save you."

There was more too, but I was unable, at least for the moment, to remember exactly where Assaf went from there. But it was enough. I could hear the rage behind Assaf's measured words, behind the dignified strophes of his imagined indictment. Of course, Benjamin Ginnethon's name was nowhere mentioned. There were at least a dozen different ways to interpret the details and references in the poem, maybe more. But no one—and I do mean no one at all, at least not in our circles—no one had even the slightest difficulty identifying the defendant in the poet's conjured-up trial.

When Asa Gad finally returned, his bladder emptied and his posture, if anything, even more erect, I was eager to hear the end of the story and to move on to the far more difficult issue of what exactly I was to do about it other than report back to the Great One, then blissfully disengage from the whole squalid affair. For a moment, I smiled at the thought that I could walk away. I had, after all, nothing really to do with any of this. I could tell the story to the Great One as I had come to understand it, then move on to the rest of my life. But even then, even as I sat in the sudatorium of the Beth Tzur bath house and waited for Asa Gad to finish his story, I knew that that was not to be. I don't believe I could have said how I knew. But I did. Some things, I guess, you just know . . . and that's all there is to it.

In the meantime, Asa Gad was back. "Our father died six years ago," he said, "but in the years between his return from the east and his death, Ikkesh himself undertook several trips of his own. In fact, he had been gone for almost all of the year leading up to our father's death on a long, complicated trip that had taken him to distant Eudaemon at the southernmost tip of Arabia Felix, as well as to Himyar, Qataban, Azdi, Gerrha, and Tylos—all places hardly anyone around here has ever heard of, let alone actually visited. And while he was gone . . ."

I heard myself taking up the story almost against my better judgment. "And while he was gone," I said, "Benjamin Ginnethon's wife moved to her parents' ranch in the Sharon . . . and so there were left alone in the city a brother whose wife had fled, and a sister whose husband was on a very long, very arduous journey and whose return could only be hoped for, not assured."

Asa Gad's eyes opened wide. "Yes," he said, "that's exactly right. But it's not quite what you probably think . . ."

"Tell me."

Asa Gad was a strange man in many ways. He had obviously devoted the twenty-four months that had passed since his brother's demise to piecing together the story of Ikkesh's death to his own satisfaction. Was there an underlying thirst for revenge motivating him and his actions? It sounds, I admit, as though there must have been. But that's not what I thought at the moment, not even slightly.

The rest of the story was told quickly, almost cursorily. Ikkesh was away for almost the whole year that his father was ailing, returning only as his father was just days away from death. I could imagine how dramatic his return must have been. How could it have been otherwise? A son away for so long. No one certain how long he would remain away or when he might conceivably return. A father whose descent to Sheol was no longer imagined to be a week or a day off, but possibly only hours away. And then, unexpectedly—and wholly so—a whisper followed by a rumor followed by a report followed by the corroboration of that report. Ikkesh's boat had been sighted. Ikkesh had landed at Jaffa. Ikkesh was on a caravan bringing him home. Ikkesh was approaching the city gates. Ikkesh was in Jerusalem. And then, finally, the return itself. Ikkesh, dressed in his traveler's robes and followed by a dozen porters carrying his trunks and luggage making his way up the street to his father's home. And then, only moments after turning the corner, Ikkesh entering the door of his parents' home, embracing his mother, listening intently to the few words she whispers into his ear, then allowing himself to be led directly—before washing or eating, before even removing his boots or his cloak—allowing himself to be led to his father's bedchamber and there, wordlessly, kneeling by his father's silent form and resting his weary head on his father's breast, the slight rasp of his father's breathing the sole sound in the otherwise silent room until finally his father breathed no more. Surely no athlete can ever have felt more satisfaction at winning a race than must Ikkesh have as he realized that he had traveled not hundreds but thousands of mils, traveling from the most distant points on the map and somehow arriving back at his father's side in time to be present as Tovim ben Asahel abandoned life to the living and crossed the boundary that separates this sorry world of dust and mud from the world of truth that awaits us all.

The mourning week, I've already described to you just as Asa Gad described it to me half a century ago in the bath house of Beth Tzur. And it was undoubtedly in the course of that week given over to the cathartic bereavement rituals our people have so ably honed over all these many years that Benjamin Ginnethon, Ikkesh's brother-in-law, stole the one scroll that had the capacity truly to change everything in our world. And in his.

I haven't told too much about that scroll, which I eventually read carefully and in its entirely. About forty feet in length but rolled around a single roller, the scroll contained one sole work: the *History of the Levites* by Kadmiel ben Henadad. Kadmiel, who surely had readers and fans in life, faded quickly into obscurity in death. I myself had never heard of him, but when I read his book I learned that he was born about 290 years ago right here in Jerusalem. Does that sound like a long time ago? It should—it really *was* a while back. Xerxes the Great had just finished trouncing Leonidas at Thermopylae, thus enabling the Persian army to pass from Macedonia into Greece proper. That was bad news for the Greeks, but they got even worse tidings just a few days later when the Persian navy won a huge, decisive sea battle just off the coast of Artemisium. And the situation only degenerated from there. By Rosh Hashanah, the Persians were sacking Athens, whose citizens, choosing discretion over valor, lost no time decamping as best they could to higher ground. But then the Greeks came back just a few weeks later. . . and they came back with a vengeance, sinking most of the Persian fleet off the Greek coast at Salamis, thus forcing the big X to defer his land offensive to what he must have hoped would be a more auspicious moment. And it was on the *very* day that Themistocles the Once Famous was busy sinking more than two hundred Persian vessels off Salamis while losing just forty or so of his own boats—it was on that day that Kadmiel ben Henadad was born in Jerusalem. (The story of his birth, the author tells in vivid detail in the first chapter of his aforementioned work. Otherwise, who would know?)

The work itself is about far more than just the circumstances of its author's birth, however. Far more!

THIRTY-EIGHT

KADMIEL HAS BEEN TOTALLY forgotten, but that has to do with the vicissitudes of literary history far more than with the worth of his work. Setting for himself the remarkable challenge of charting the history of his own tribe (and also realizing early on that the history of the other tribes of Israel had also been willfully suppressed by generations of historians eager to serve their patron-monarchs' collective desire to think of the nation over whom they ruled as a single homogenous people), Kadmiel must have known from the outset that he had taken a hugely difficult task on himself. But he shouldered the burden well nonetheless and eventually managed to piece together an outline of the history of the Levites based on information he gathered mostly by taking seriously off-hand references in dozens upon dozens of anterior works that others had either dismissed as unimportant or else not noticed at all. Furthermore, it was he—apparently first of all— who realized that the stories passed down from generation to generation contained crucial information that no one had ever recorded in any sort of serious historical work. (He was a pioneer in the preservation of that kind of unwritten testimony too, realizing after he heard the same story a hundred different times from a hundred different people that these tales could be taken seriously as oral history.)

Starting from the mysterious detail that there are many ancient texts in which the Levites don't seem to exist at all, Kadmiel supposed that they must have entered the stream of Jewish history after those texts were written. The texts he was referencing, we all know. Moses sends out twelve spies to reconnoiter the land before embarking on its conquest, but, even though the text specifically says that one is to come from each tribe, none of the twelve is from Levi. On the day the great desert Tabernacle is inaugurated for use as a center of worship, one prince from each of the twelve tribes of Israel brings a special set of gifts in his own name as a dedication offering to the new shrine . . . but none of those twelve is from Levi either. Of course, Levi himself, the son of Jacob and Leah, is featured in a handful of stories, including (of course) in the story of his own birth, but in none of these is the man himself provided with any of the descriptive trappings of what moderns would consider normal biographical writing. It is true that the collection of Father Jacob's deathbed predictions about his sons includes an explicit reference to Levi. But even that semi-explicit reference has its equivocal side, as the text can really just as easily be read as a prediction—and none too flattering a one at that—about a different son, Simon, to which Levi's name has been added almost as an afterthought. The data, to say the least, was confusing. And even more confusing was the reality of Temple times—of Kadmiel's Temple times, I mean—in which the Levites, who had barely existed in stories relating to Solomon's Temple, clearly did exist as a well-organized, wholly self-aware group of Temple servants whose sense of themselves and of their mission was completely and utterly at odds with the party line put forward for public consumption by their priestly overlords.

Are you confused listening to this? I was too, but the bottom line—that it was Kadmiel ben Henadad who wrote the first full-length work taking the Levites' self-conception seriously and who attempted to buttress his essential argument with rational speculation about the tribe's real origins within the flow of Israelite history—wasn't all that confusing at all. Concluding that today's Levites' sense of themselves as the spiritual descendants of the prophetic caste that flourished in the days of Solomon's Temple was reasonable to the point of being the most, and surely not the least, likely theory of their origins—that single idea was the cornerstone of Kadmiel's entire work.

And it was this work, this magisterial study of levitical origins that had survived eradication by the priestly censor back home by spending precisely one full century hiding out of sight in the great library of Pataliputra, it was a single copy of this work that was brought by Asa Gad and Ikkesh's father to Jerusalem. And it was that copy that Benjamin Ginnethon ben Baruch stole with his sister's likely assistance.

I've mixed up what I learned about the book when I eventually read it and what Asa Gad told me all those years ago in Beth Tzur, but now I will go back to saying only what Asa Gad told me that day. In the meantime, he explained, Meirav Serach became even closer to her brother and then, at one point, she began to live in his home at least part of the time. Claiming that she was simply too tired to drag herself home after a late-night party she was hostessing, or insisting that it was cruel, once Tola was asleep in his uncle's bed, to wake him just to take him home and put him back to sleep, she sounded almost reasonable. Plus Ikkesh himself wasn't all that frequently there either—travelling almost compulsively in his last years, Ikkesh was away on business for more than forty of the last forty-eight months of his life. And he was ensconced in his office when he was home, counting his money or dictating letters or planning his next trip. Meirav Serach wasn't there to watch him work or to care how diligently or carelessly he pursued his affairs, however—all she cared about was that he leave her alone, which he seemed more and more willing to do. Tola, of course, lacked the experience to understand that his situation was peculiar and that most little boys only had one home and that, if they slept in anyone's bed but their own, it was in their father's that they slept and not their uncle's. Where Meirav Serach herself spent her nights, I have no idea. I know what I think, however. And, believe me, it's what you're probably thinking by now as well. Or maybe I'm just falling victim to my own depraved imagination and the truth is that she was just lonely and, when her brother invited her to be his official in-house hostess, she accepted the position and the perks that came along with it.

And then Ikkesh died. Meirav Serach no longer went home . . . ever. (Why should she have?) Little Tola now lived at his uncle's place full-time. Ikkesh's entire estate, including his house and his stock of gems and everything else, passed directly to Tola. But because he was still such a young child, his mother was appointed as his *epitropa*. Obviously, it is entirely reasonable that a child's mother be permitted to administer his estate in a case like this. And the municipal *kateigor*'s hands were tied since there was no evidence of any sort suggesting that Ikkesh had been murdered at all, let alone by those who stood to gain the most meaningfully from his death. And, as is only right, no evidence translated easily into no indictment.

Asa Gad told me this part of the story from beginning to end almost without pausing for a single breath and speaking so quietly that I could barely hear him clearly. I'm sure I haven't reported his words exactly as he spoke them, but I'm doing my best to tell you what he told me. Bear with me just a little longer. I promise there isn't much left to tell.

THIRTY-NINE

WHAT ASA GAD NOW told me stays with me still. I can only paraphrase what he said. But I can hear his voice even now as I write. And I know he meant for me to share the story not with as few, but with as many interested parties as possible. What follows, then, is my version of Asa Gad's final version of the events at hand, the last words I ever heard him speak. I speak, therefore, in my own voice, but in his name.

The first point Asa Gad made was that, when Ikkesh died and his widow became the day-to-day custodian of his wealth for as long as their son remained an underage child, the stolen scroll was more or less forgotten and its story seemed to have reached a natural conclusion.

Except for one small detail. Asa Gad then went on to point out that Ikkesh was not merely a *kohen* and a gem merchant—he was also the Levites' contact person in the ongoing, delicate balance of power that had evolved within the sacred precincts of our holy Temple. How that had come about, Asa Gad knew in detail. I believe he told me everything too, but I haven't told and won't tell it all here. But suffice it to say that there was just enough flexibility, if that's the right word, on both sides to allow the holiest of court-yards to be "available" for the odd midnight hour against a seriously gener-ous "gift" which passed almost effortlessly (and wholly discreetly) from the Great One via Bukiyahu ben Yerimoth to Ikkesh ben Tovim, and then from Ikkesh into the personal coffers of the High Priest of Israel. This part of the story, of course, no one knew. We ourselves certainly didn't know how things were arranged. Asa Gad believed that even people quite far up in the priestly hierarchy—including the *gizbarin*, the *amarkalin,* even the *ka-tikolin* themselves—knew nothing about this surreptitious agreement. And, most relevant of all, neither, as far as I have ever been able to ascertain, did

Benjamin Ginnethon. And because he didn't know that one single thing, Benjamin Ginnethon therefore had no reason to think that anyone other than his brother-in-law's intimate family would devote much thought to the circumstances of his passing.

Onias, the HP himself, may have appeared as an old man suffering from so many different varieties of palsy that he appeared to be in motion even when seated, but he had his own staff that functioned entirely independently of Benjamin Ginnethon's and whose ranks were filled with men who were wholly and fiercely loyal to him. In fact, within that detail lies the secret of their relationship: BG was left to run the part of things that fell under his jurisdiction as he wished, but the HP had his own agenda, which he was more, not less, free to pursue because of Benjamin Ginnethon's preoccupation with his own interests. And the specific way in which the few nighttime security positions reserved specifically for priests were distributed could not have been of less interest to BG. More to the point, the fact that the duty roster was administered directly by Onias must have struck him almost as a pleasant happenstance—something for the old man to look after that he himself was thus freed from having to deal with and, at that, a matter of almost no real consequence at all. But, of course, Onias—Choni—has his own reasons for wanting to control the nighttime service roster. There was, for one thing, a *lot* of money involved.

Unaware, then, of the private relationship between his nominal boss and his sister's husband, the Ood had planned his brother-in-law's murder as a way of securing at least indirect control over his money. To hear Asa Gad tell it, it was a truly diabolical plot. True, Tola would eventually grow up. Or, if Benjamin Ginnethon proved capable of an even more depraved act of violence than the murder of his own brother-in-law, then perhaps he wouldn't. But even if he did grow up, the chances of the money now under the total control of Meirav Serach still being there, or of any significant portion of it still being there, were remote indeed. I have to stress this to you, my readers: as far as I have ever been able to determine, Asa Gad was right that the Ood knew nothing at all of Ikkesh's service to our brethren. He was therefore motivated solely by the overpowering desire to enrich himself by stealing money that another man had earned.

How he did it should hardly matter, although I'll tell you the story as Asa Gad pieced it together and told it to me. To do the job for him, Benjamin Ginnethon hired a man named Dan Iddo ben Uziel from the town of Shephem, a well-known hoodlum who made his living robbing travelers along the Jerusalem-Jericho highway and then accepting promises of even great sums for the trouble of not murdering them on the spot. Benjamin Ginnethon promised him a large fee on reasonable terms: half down and half payable after the deed was done. And the deed soon actually *was* done. He did it—so Asa Gad—not with his knife but with some kind of poison he managed to get into the cup of herb tea Ikkesh ordered daily from the same tea stall in the *shuk*. (The tea-guy admitted this to Asa Gad in almost so many words, stopping just short—because the man was apparently not a complete idiot—of indicting himself as an accessory to murder.) And so must all have felt as though it had gone perfectly according to plan, and within just few months at that. Ikkesh was dead. Dan Iddo, who had been shadowing his prey, bent over the stricken Ikkesh the moment he fell, slipped his sandals off his feet, then delivered them to the Ood and received the second half of his fee. With that, his role in the story was more or less over. Or so he must have thought. And Benjamin Ginnethon must have felt no less done with the matter. His nephew was Ikkesh's heir and his sister was the *epitropa* of what was now her son's personal estate. He was apparently going to get away with the theft of the scroll that he had somehow spirited out of Ikkesh's father's home during the bereavement week the family had spent living in his home and mourning his passing. His bereaved sister was now a single woman whose kind and generous brother all would admire for taking her in under his own roof. It really did feel as though everything had gone perfectly . . . except for one detail the Ood overlooked.

Enter Buki ben Yerimoth. As I said at the beginning of this long story, he was immensely fat, but in that way that somehow suggests good rather than poor health. His skin was ruddy, not sallow. His enormous belly was firm, not flabby. When he sat in the steam on the Street of the Lambs, his entire body glistened with sweat and this, somehow, made him look virile and healthy rather than flabby or enervated. Even his almost total lack of body hair failed to make him look babyish, let alone girlish. Just to the contrary, actually: everything about Buki exuded an air of insouciant masculinity that its possessor appeared unable to keep from projecting out into whatever room he found himself at any given moment. I met him soon after I came to Jerusalem and, although we never became intimate friends, we were well acquainted with each other and—and this I do feel secure in saying unequivocally—we respected and liked each other.

Eli ben Heman, the Great One, liked him too. And it was for that reason, I believe, that he took Buki for a walk one day and asked him quietly and surreptitiously to find out what in hell had happened to Ikkesh ben Tovim. And, perhaps even more to the point, to find out whether the secret role Ikkesh played in maintaining the special relationship between the Great One and Onias, if that secret was safe . . . or whether Ikkesh's murderer had somehow wrested it from his victim before dispatching him to the next world. Buki had all the right qualifications for the job, too—intelligent enough to get it done, but also widely considered to be more than just a bit of a slacker and thus specifically not someone who would attract attention skulking around in the kind of wine bars and *ganjha* dens through which the trail to Ikkesh's killer might potentially lead. More than that, Buki had friends everywhere and not just among our people. He had dated, as noted, a thousand different women and had somehow managed to end up on good terms with most of them. He cultivated male friendships too, and with all sorts of people. And, on top of that and even despite his enormous belly, he was somehow nondescript looking—the kind of fellow who could walk through the *shuk* in front of a thousand people and then have every single one of them say the next morning that they hadn't seen a man answering his description in days. Needless to say, Buki agreed immediately to do what he could.

How he found his way to Dan Iddo, Asa Gad never found out exactly. But I suspect it was the other way 'round. This Dan Iddo was a scoundrel in the true sense of the word—not just a dishonest person or a violent criminal, but a wholly amoral human being whose sole purpose in life was to earn money by selling his ruthlessness to the highest bidder. Benjamin Ginnethon had hired him to murder his own brother-in-law and Dan Iddo had taken the commission and had been paid when the job was done. But now, I'm guessing, he somehow found out that an investigation had been opened by our side into Ikkesh's death and he saw not danger lurking but opportunity knocking. How exactly he found out that Buki was one the Great One chose, I don't know. But how hard can it have been once Buki started asking around, insinuating himself into situations where it felt likely some information might be forthcoming, and prowling around in all the wrong—or, more noticeably, all the right—places?

It can't have taken long for Buki to develop a general sense of how things were. He must have taken a good long look at the disposition of Ikkesh's estate. He surely took note of the fact that Meirav Serach and Tola had actually moved in with their brother and uncle. And then he began to question all sorts of people with ancillary roles in the story, some of whom I've written about here and others of whom I haven't bothered mentioning. More to the point, he learned about Kadmiel's history when he met with Asa Gad and the latter, who had no reason at all to withhold information, simply told him all about it.

And that, I feel certain, is how Dan Iddo found Buki and offered to tell him the full story of Ikkesh's death against a huge reward. And to sweeten the deal he probably *also* agreed to steal the scroll containing Kadmiel's book from Benjamin Ginnethon's house. I suppose Dan Iddo would have omitted the part about him *personally* having poisoned Ikkesh and laid all the blame squarely on the head of Benjamin Ginnethon. And so that would have been that: Dan Iddo would get his reward from Buki, whereupon Buki would tell the Great One what exactly had happened to Ikkesh and the Great One would then either approach the High Priest with that information or decide to let it go. But, one way or the other, it must have felt to Buki as though he had successfully concluded his mission.

Asa Gad didn't know how Dan Iddo found Kadmiel's *History of the Levites* among the many scrolls and parchments in Benjamin Ginnethon's home library. Maybe he just hoped it would be prominently displayed in that place and it actually was. Perhaps he had it out on his reading table because he was actually reading it. As I've said several times, Benjamin Ginnethon ben Baruch Hakohen was vicious and sadistic, but he wasn't stupid—and a scroll like Kadmiel's history would have been hugely interesting to him. And so must Buki have felt that he had concluded his mission successfully: he knew what happened to Ikkesh and he had even acquired Kadmiel's scroll—no doubt with the intention of returning it to its rightful owners. Which he would surely have done . . . except for one small detail that changed everything.

FORTY

BY THIS TIME, NIGHT had fallen. The Beth Tzur bath house was filling up with men finished with their winter's day's work and in need of some heat and a scrub-up and hose-down before heading home to their families and their evening meals. It was clearly time for us to go. I don't know what I wanted to happen next, not exactly. I suppose I wanted Asa Gad to take me to his home where we could finish our conversation in peace. But that was not to be. We had managed, I hoped, to avoid being noticed for almost a full day. And Asa Gad was certainly not going to risk everything by being seen with me in public, thus connecting himself to my investigation into Buki's murder. I realized that he was going to leave me and go home, and that I was going to be on my own to find my way back to Jerusalem. But there were still a few small details I needed to get straight. Or, more precisely, to confirm that I had worked out correctly.

In a few minutes, we were back in the apodyterium getting dressed. There were others around, but no one in the corner of the large room in which we had hung our street clothes. And so, as we dressed, we were able to squeeze a few more private moments of conversation out of the day.

"So what happened after that? Where exactly is Kadmiel's book right now?"

Asa Gad looked at me for a long moment as he pulled his breeches up over his boney thighs. "I don't know," he said plainly.

"Buki didn't return it to your family?"

"No," Asa Gad said softly. "He didn't."

"So it must have been in Buki's possession when he died?"

"I don't think it was."

174

"But if Dan Iddo stole it and gave it to Buki, then why wouldn't he still have had it among this things when died if he hadn't returned it to your family?"

"Because Dan Iddo went right back to Benjamin Ginnethon to tell him that Buki knew that he was responsible for Ikkesh's death."

"And not that Dan Iddo himself had been the assassin?"

"No, David, just that Benjamin Ginnethon had commissioned the murder."

"And then?"

"What do you think? Benjamin Ginnethon who had no choice but to hire him again . . . this time to take out Buki himself. And, for good measure, steal back the book."

"And did he?"

"Yes and no."

"Yes and no?"

"Yes to taking out Buki. No to stealing the scroll back."

"And the whole weirdness about Buki's death—his decapitation and the coins in his mouth, the whole business about him being stripped to his underbreeches and his outer clothing burnt—what was that all about?"

"Just a ruse meant, I suppose, to send everybody off in the wrong direction by making it look like Buki's murder was just the troubles between your people and the priests ratcheted up to its next level of badness. Which is precisely what happened, of course."

Asa Gad was exactly right: the circumstances of Buki's death had sent everybody, myself included, off in precisely the wrong direction. But now I could see clearly the reasonableness of his line of thinking.

"But he didn't manage to steal back the book. How can you know that for sure?"

"I don't."

"But you think you do?"

"I do."

Asa Gad was fully dressed now, as was I. He turned to face me and, slightly to my surprise, embraced me. I felt his thin arms reaching most of the way around my back and, as I did, I knew—or rather, I realized—that Asa Gad was a man whose respect I truly did wish to earn. "You understand that you're part of the story yourself now," he whispered into my ear.

I nodded slowly, then stepped back to ask the one important question left to be asked. "And how do you know all this?"

"I know Dan Iddo," he said.

"You know him? *How* do you know him?"

"He found me."

"He found you? Was he looking for you?"

"Dan Iddo was always looking to profit from his own crimes in as many different ways as possible. He had no conception of loyalty, no sense that he owed anything at all to the people who hired him. After he was done murdering Buki and carving that word into his chest and filling his mouth with coins, he simply showed up one day by my side and asked if I'd like to buy the story of my brother's death. Of course, he did not implicate himself, just his employer. I paid him his fee, too. And that, more or less, was that."

"That was that?"

"More or less."

"And he told you where the scroll was?"

"Not exactly. But he told me that it wasn't among Buki's possessions when he tried to steal it back for Baruch Ginnethon."

"He broke into Buki's home."

"Obviously. And he nailed that ridiculous piece of parchment to Buki's front door on the way out to suggest yet another wrong direction for the police to go off in. Or for anyone at all investigating his death to go off in."

I ignored the not-especially-subtle dig. "So where is the scroll now?"

"Well, if Buki didn't have it among his effects when he died *and* he didn't return it to its rightful owners, he must have given it to someone else, no?"

I thought for a long moment, then realized that I too knew where the scroll was. Or I thought I did.

FORTY-ONE

Asa Gad released me from his embrace, placed a dry kiss on my right cheek, turned on his heel and walked slowly through the apodyterium to the front entrance of the bath house. In a moment, he was out into the street. I finished dressing, then followed a few moments later. It was a cold wintery day at dusk. Through the windows of the homes I passed on Beth Tzur's main street, I could hear people all around. But I had no time to wallow in the loneliness I was beginning to feel descending onto my shoulders like a kind of sodden woolen cloak I knew I lacked the strength simply to shuck off at will. What kind of world did I live in? I've asked myself that question a million times in the course of my decades of work solving crimes and bringing criminals to justice. But I do believe that the first time I formulated it in so many words was that evening in Beth Tzur as I left the bath house and made my way back to the *pundak*. I left first thing the following morning and haven't ever returned.

By the time I got home around noon the following day, the boys were in school and Avital was nowhere to be seen. What I really felt like doing was crawling into bed and having a good snooze before heading out to the bath house to wash away the residue of my return donkey—a handsome creature named Azuva—and gather up some strength after my journey, but I had a huge job in front of me. And there was really no time at all to spare.

I thought through my plausible plans forward. Clearly, the path of least resistance would have been to find the Great One and, in the context of telling him what I had learned about Buki's death, ask how he can possibly have omitted mentioning to me that he personally had sent Buki to investigate the circumstances surrounding Ikkesh ben Tovim's death. Surely he can't have failed to seize the relevancy of that detail! I considered this specific issue particularly. Could the Great One have specifically wished not to prejudice me in my own investigation and chose, therefore, specifically not to send me off in any particular investigative direction at all? I guessed that, if anything, that had to be it. But I wouldn't have minded hearing it from the man's own mouth. Nor was I completely in the clear myself in that regard: I had lied to him about whom exactly Asa Gad had implicated in Ikkesh's death, so why should he not have also withheld some information from me . . . and particularly if he thought doing so would assist me in moving forward unburdened—and thus also un-misled—by extraneous, or at least unproven, theories? But I could certainly have ignored all that and just reported to the Great One what I knew and what I thought.

The flaw in this simplest of options rested in a suitably simple detail: I had no proof of anything. I couldn't prove that Ikkesh had been murdered. I couldn't prove that the scroll containing Kadmiel ben Henadad's *History of the Levites* had been stolen even once, let alone twice. (I also couldn't prove, even *in*conclusively, that it had ever even existed. I *thought*, as you may have already guessed, that Buki had turned the scroll over to the Great One. But I also wanted to avoid accusing the Great One of possessing stolen goods if at all possible.) Of course, I *also* had no proof that Benjamin Ginnethon was responsible for either crime. Nor had I ever met Dan Iddo ben Uziel of Shephem and so had no real idea if his alleged role in all this—or, for that matter, if he himself—was real or a mere figment of Asa Gad's overactive imagination. Nor could I prove that anything other than doting fraternal solicitude had prompted Benjamin Ginnethon's willingness to care for his widowed sister and orphaned nephew in the wake of their husband and father's untimely demise. For good measure, I noted that I could also not connect Benjamin Ginnethon ben Baruch with Buki's murder in anything remotely like a convincing way. And to crown my list of non-achievements with the most splendid of them all, I noted that I had also failed to demonstrate that any sort of connection at all existed or had ever existed between Ikkesh's death and Buki's. In a word, I had come up long and short at the same time: long on theory, short on proof.

I swung by the Temple to make sure I was still being left off the work roster, which I was. So the time to strike—if I could only develop a plan worth pursuing—was clearly upon me. It was already the middle of Kislev. Nowadays, of course, we would all be gearing up for the imminent onset of the Chanukah festival commemorating the day on which Judah the M. rededicated the Temple to the worship of the Almighty in the Jewish mode three decades and a year ago. But when I was involved in attempting to solve Buki's murder, those events were all still in the future. And so, having decided, at least for the time being, to reserve for the less distant future the pleasure of telling the Great One the full story of my adventures, I chose instead to focus on the plan I had evolved to bring Benjamin Ginnethon to justice.

FORTY-TWO

MAKING CONTACT WITH BENJAMIN Ginnethon was not going to be at all difficult. The Ood was always around somewhere, always skulking around the Temple forecourts, always snooping in the various vestibules and storage chambers off the three contiguous courtyards that together constituted the most sacred part of the Temple complex. He was almost universally disliked in our quarters, but I had to remind myself not to underestimate him. Indeed, it was his specific combination of ruthlessness, crudeness, arrogance, and intelligence that was going to make him the formidable foe I fully expected him to be.

Success was clearly going to lie in how clever a trap I was going to manage to lay. I was never going to be able to overpower him physically. Nor was there the slightest chance that I was going successfully to shame him into admitting his involvement in either Ikkesh's or Buki's murder. No, if I was going to succeed in bringing this man to justice, I was going to do so solely by virtue of my wily intellect . . . and by making full use of the information I had gleaned from my time spent with Asa Gad both in Jerusalem and in Beth Tzur.

As I reviewed my options yet again, a question that hadn't struck me previously presented itself. I didn't think that Benjamin Ginnethon had personally been one of my captors—a man of his height and with hair the bright color of his does not wisely let himself be seen where people are being held against their will. But if I was abducted by *his* men, then I could certainly ask how exactly the Ood knew that I was investigating Buki's murder. Certainly the Great One wouldn't have told anyone! I didn't think it possible that he and I had been overheard. But even if someone *had* somehow overheard us, the clientele on the Street of the Lambs was entirely made up of our own people. And to imagine one of us betraying the Great One by repeating his private words to me . . . and, at that, to people eager to use them to hurt us . . . it all seemed so far-fetched so as not really even to be worth thinking about all too carefully at all.

So if the Great One didn't tell a soul and I didn't, then who could have? I had told Avital everything, of course. But that she would have told anyone what I was up to was a theory not even worth the time it would take to consider even slightly seriously.

So who could it have been? There was only one person that came to mind. And the more I thought about it, the more sense it made. Ketziya had, after all, told me about Benjamin Ginnethon. So why did I think she wouldn't have told him about me? When put that way, it almost sounded reasonable. She didn't survive other than by her wits, after all, so why should she have pointed me towards Buki's murderer and not subsequently have felt justified, perhaps even virtuous, pointing Buki's murderer towards me. I was, after all, out to bring him down, out publicly to humiliate him, to shame him, to ruin his career and his life. So why would Ketziya not have wished to share an oracle with him that might vitiate, at least somewhat, the force of the oracle she shared with me? Because she occasionally participated in our nighttime rituals, we thought of her as a kind of honorary Levite. But, I reminded myself, she was also a regular in priestly circles and it was entirely possible that they thought of her as an honorary one of them just as we did.

And so I moved forward just as I had originally by deciding that I needed to find Ketziya. Readers will remember that the last time I sought her out, I ended up finding her only after I allowed her to find me. She had, please also recall, no fixed address. Or, if she did, I do not believe anyone at all knew where it was. Certainly, I didn't. But it was far more likely that she was a kind of vagabond, a woman on the move who slept where she could, ate where she could, and took the opportunity to wash out her cloak when the opportunity to do so presented itself.

It was still early afternoon, but I was already tired of waiting for something to happen. It was time, I thought, to press forward one way or the other, to be the actor instead of the endlessly acted-upon party in the drama that was apparently featuring me in a semi-starring role. But how exactly to proceed was another question entirely.

FORTY-THREE

For the first time, it struck me that I was not totally without resources. I didn't need to be reticent about finding Ketziya. Just the opposite, I realized, was the case: I would only enhance my chances of finding her quickly if I raised my profile just enough to matter.

I hadn't wandered that far from the Temple and I knew that she was often to be found in the Women's Courtyard begging for alms or offering to tell people's fortunes for a few coins at this time of day. Was she there now? I had no reason not to find out. I circled around, entered the Temple Mount through the Shushan Gate, in those days the main way in, then marched up unimpeded into the Women's Courtyard. (Non-locals will want to remember that the Women's Court was called by that name because women were permitted to congregate there, as were also men.)

It was very, very cold that particular day. Because of the wintery weather, there were almost no out-of-town visitors hanging around gawking at the splendiferous rites and, as a result, the usual throng of vendors and money changers too was, if not quite as thin as the sparse crowd of tourists, then still dramatically pared down from summertime levels. The morning service was long over, but the communal afternoon sacrifices hadn't started. There were a few women hanging around with newborns, no doubt waiting to be called to stand in attendance while sacrifices associated with the recent safe deliveries of their babies were duly offered up. Some had husbands with them, I noted, but most did not. Were the absent men huddled up together in the Israelites' Courtyard, the much smaller and dramatically narrower space just on the other side of the great Gate of Nikanor that led up into it? I supposed they probably were, then felt a pang of sadness for the poor wives left to fend for themselves and their babies while their men took advantage of the privilege offered by their gender to be slightly closer to the action.

Ketziya was nowhere to be seen. I had seen her huddled up many, many times against the western wall of the Women's Courtyard between the southern side of the rounded steps leading up to the Gate of Nikanor and the tiny door leading into the room where we stored our musical instruments (which actually extended under the Israelites' Courtyard), but although I kept turning away and then turning quickly back to see if I could somehow make her appear, she was simply not ready to show herself to me. It sounds funny to say this now, even to me myself, but I felt her presence in the Temple that day . . . and I felt it as strongly as—and, believe me, I know how ridiculous this is going to sound—I felt it as strongly as I felt my own presence in that place. I knew I was there. I knew she was there. The only difference was that I knew where I myself was and I had no idea where she was hiding.

In the meantime, a light snow began to fall. Only very rarely does it snow in Jerusalem seriously enough for there to be any sort of accumulation on the ground. But when it does snow seriously, the city is almost totally immobilized for as long as it takes for the citizens to dig themselves out. Light, inconsequential flurries, on the other hand, occur all the time in the course of most winters. Usually, they only last for a few minutes. And even when the weather really does get cold enough to sustain snow flurries for the course of an entire day, the city usually ends up looking more like it was glazed with baking sugar than coated with treacherous ice. That all being the case, I had barely noticed when it started to snow. In fact, if anything the weather appeared to be improving. True, snow was falling. But there was no wind to speak of and the temperature of the air seemed slightly warmer than even an hour or two earlier.

There is a certain feel to Jerusalem when it snows, a kind of brisk, revitalizing reminder that our capital city, even with all its walls and ramparts, is still vulnerable to forces of nature against which no city, no matter how well fortified militarily, can feel totally protected. And also of note is the way that the scents of the city seem to travel much farther than normal, and also with far greater intensity and staying power, when the temperature is cold enough to permit snow. As a result, there is a certain unique pleasure that comes from the combination of *seeing* the heavens totally white, *smelling* an unusually intense amalgam of odors—some combination of incense, manure, broiled meat, and fresh baking—that one usually encounters serially in discrete areas of the sacred complex (but which, once the temperature becomes cold enough, combine to blanket the area together as one), and *feeling* the bracing chill that raises goose bumps without really incapacitating.

I skulked around in the Women's Courtyard, then climbed the fifteen steps that led through the Gate of Nikanor into the Israelites' Courtyard to look around there for a while. There were, just as I had suspected, eight or nine men in attendance, each looking about the right age to be a new father. True, some could have been men newly cured of *tzaraat* or *ziva* eager to bring the sacrifices specified under priestly law as requisite expressions of thanksgiving. And some, even, could have been new converts to our faith waiting to bring the sacrifice that was the final step in the conversion ritual that would seal the deal with respect to their newly-acquired membership in the House of Israel. But I didn't get that sense—I personally took them all for new fathers present to witness the various sacrifices connected with their wives' successful negotiation of childbirth—and I certainly wasn't about to start asking personal questions of people I didn't know and had no reason to wish to get to know. I knew Ketziya wouldn't be there—no woman could have been—but I decided for some reason to take a look around anyway. In the meantime, it had begun to snow more vigorously than even a quarter hour earlier: the snow was falling now not in occasional flurries, but in thick white flakes that were actually coating the ground and sticking onto the cloaks of the people in attendance without melting on contact as would normally have been the case.

I spent a long moment looking at the men gathered in the Israelites' Courtyard. I wondered how much they knew about this place, to what degree they had bothered to inform themselves about the history of this Temple, about its rituals and rites, its procedures and customs. Did they even seize the difference between priests and Levites, between the *kohanim* who ran the joint and the rest of us, the slaves—to use the formally unused term as we ourselves used it all the time when speaking privately—who cleaned up, swept up, mopped up, cleaned the toilets, sang in the choir, looked after the security needs of the entire complex, and who, for the most part, remained unknown, unacknowledged, unrecognized, and unthanked. I suppose it were ever thus: when travelers dine in an inn, do any ever ask the *magister convivii* that the cook's lads be sent over so that they can be thanked personally for their service? And if we were on a slightly higher level in the Temple hierarchy than the kitchen boys would be in your average *tabernus*, it wasn't all that much higher! Or perhaps we were *formally* higher up on the ibex than the wait-staff in your average inn . . . but it certainly didn't feel that way to most of us for most of the time. I found myself wondering what the men huddling up for warmth in the snow would make of the fact that I was trying to investigate not one but two different murders, each of them somehow connected with our most sacred shrine, this place to which they had come to fulfill their own obligations under the law but which they themselves would enter and then leave without ever truly belonging *to* or becoming part *of*. Would they be shocked? I knew they would be. For a long moment, I wondered what would happen if I told them just a little about what I was doing there. It would have been cathartic, at least slightly, for me to say it all out loud to strangers. But I knew I wouldn't say a word—if I hadn't yet told the Great One what I was up to, why would I have told strangers anything at all? And yet the urge to draw these complete strangers into my confidence was almost overwhelming.

To staunch this almost irresistible urge to speak out of turn to men I didn't know about matters that could not possibly have concerned them less, I turned quickly to the east, passed back through the Nikanor, descended the fifteen steps into the Women's Courtyard and . . . and stopped in my tracks. I had somehow sensed that Ketziya was there all along, but I had had no idea how to find her. And now that I had stopped formally searching for her, there she was. This, it struck me, seemed to be her regular *modus operandi*—to appear when sought only when the seekers in question finally allowed themselves to be found. And, indeed, she was right where I had somehow expected her to be all along.

For most of the year, men and women mingled freely in the Women's Courtyard. It was an open place, there were security forces all around, and, perhaps most crucially, almost all the women present were almost always in the company of their husbands. True, the husbands were permitted to penetrate further into the complex, but they were at least somewhere around. And many—I thought, the finer ones—really did choose not to leave their wives' side in such a public place even though they technically were permitted to and could have. However, the custom that prevailed during the Water Libation Celebration was different.

I suppose you've heard of our most famous ceremony. Perhaps even some readers will have attended it. It's tamer now than it once was, but it used to be . . . it used to be an almost riotous celebration that constantly, year after year, threatened to get even more out of hand than it already had the previous year. The background is probably too complicated to explain out in detail here, but the short version is that each day of the fall festival of Sukkot features a special ceremony in which water from a local spring is ceremoniously poured out on the great bronze altar as a kind of libation intended to suggest the great value the citizens of our occasionally arid land attach to water. The original concept, of course, was that the ceremony would be a decorous and dignified expression of national sentiment, a kind of prayer in deed rather than word. And the celebration was intended to be a mere supplement, something special designed to grant some extra luster to the simple act of drawing up the water from an ancient spring and pouring it out as a libation. But even by my time that feel to the whole thing was far in the past.

Maybe things began to veer off track once they brought the acrobats in. Or the jugglers. Or maybe it was introducing the guys on stilts or the clowns, or perhaps it was when they got rid of the handful of musicians that used to provide some background entertainment and instead brought in a full-sized orchestra. In retrospect, it was definitely a mistake to provide an open bar and free buffet, which innovation ended up drawing ten times as many people as attended earlier on when attendees had to bring their own supper along or else go hungry. At any rate, one thing led to another. And, suddenly, instead of there being mostly families and the odd singleton, there were hordes of single men and women in attendance . . . and also plenty of married people who either by accident or by design became briefly (or not that briefly) separated from their respective spouses.

I've heard stories. Possibly you've also heard them too, stories about men and women behaving poorly together and separately, about couples and groups of diverse sizes taking advantage of the huge crowd to do what they would never have dared even contemplate doing in a smaller throng where they could conceivably have been caught or noticed. And that brings me to the balconies, which were installed on three sides of the Women's Courtyard for the express purpose of providing some safe place for women during the Libation Festival in which they would be safe from roving hands, unwanted pinches, inappropriate squeezes, unwished for rub-ups, and the overall bad behavior that seemed to reign in that place during those merry evenings when abandon—I should say, when Abaddon—was king and the rules were as unenforceable as they were mostly ignored.

We called them "balconies," but there were really more like bleachers with several tiers of narrow platforms on which women could stand or sit. And although they were only formally in use during Sukkot, they were permanent structures on the northern, eastern, and southern walls of the Women's Courtyard that were never dismantled. (There was no balcony on the western wall because it wouldn't have been possible for anyone standing there to see our people singing on the fifteen semi-circular steps leading up into the Israelites' Courtyard.) And, indeed, there were people, men included, who regularly climbed up there to get a bird's eye view of what was going on below.

And there, above us all, in the in the center of the top tier of the wooden balcony attached to the eastern wall of the Women's Courtyard stood Ketziya, the Witch of Ein Dor.

FORTY-FOUR

Ketziya was nothing if not dramatic.

Looking rather like a large bat that had somehow learned how to stand erect on its two tiny feet, she slowly and decorously raised her draped arms to the height of her shoulders. Affecting the look of someone entering into a state of ecstatic communion with our alternately garrulous and taciturn God, Ketziya raised her face towards the white sky and, for a few long minutes, allowed the snow to fall directly on her without brushing the flakes from her brow or her sallow, wrinkled cheeks. Then, after having gotten the attention of every single citizen in the courtyard precisely by ignoring them entirely, she lowered her eyes and focused directly on me. Even from such a distance—the Women's Courtyard was well more than a hundred cubits long and I was standing at the extreme other end of it, on top of which Ketziya's balcony was elevated at least another eight or nine cubits off the ground—I could feel her black eyes boring into me. I couldn't have looked away if I had wanted to. But, of course, the last thing I wanted was to look away. Just the opposite was the case, actually: I had come to find her, had somehow found her by letting her find me, and was now entirely eager to hear whatever it was she had to say.

"O Jerusalem," she began, her tinny, grating voice somehow matching perfectly her pteropine pose, "Sing to God, chant hymns to the One who rides upon the heavens; exult before our God, before that God who is a parent to orphans and the just judge of widows, God who dwells in the holy sanctuary, God who provides a home for the lonely, who brings forth those imprisoned in chains, who grants relief even to those brigands who dwell in the parched desert."

The witch allowed her voice to trail off as her point settled in: the same God who scruples to makes safe the Holy City is the One too who speaks to the prophets among us, to those who know how successfully to provoke divine speech. She clearly had the full attention of everybody.

In the meantime, the wind turned the falling snow into a kind of squall. I felt the flakes wet on my face, but I could not have moved from my spot even if I had wished to. The others, I noted, were equally rooted in their places. No one moved. No one spoke. There were no sounds at all in the courtyard, in fact, other than the faint whistling of the wind and the muted reverberations of Ketziya's piercing voice. She herself seemed oblivious to the temperature, however, as she looked up into the white sky to indicate that the time had come for her to speak and no longer merely to listen. "Lord, You are awe-inspiring when Your voice issues forth from Your holy places; it is the God of Israel who grants strength and power to the people. They saw Your deeds, O God—the deeds of my God, my Sovereign of the Sanctuary; the singers came along right after the musicians, all of them amidst the maiden drummers; in choirs did they bless the Lord our God, the wellspring of Israel."

And now the witch had clearly come to her point. She lowered her gaze and looked so directly at me that I could actually feel her eyes boring into me and hear her no less clearly than if she had been standing directly in front of me. I started to shiver in the cold, but I willed myself not to move, not to draw my own cloak any tighter around my shoulders than it already was, not to look away even for a moment. And I listened as though my own life depended on it. "Look," she said, speaking intensely and directly (I thought) to me, "there is young Benjamin ruling over the princes of Judah gathered together with his allies, the princes of Zebulun and the princes of Naphtali. God has bequeathed us strength; divine strength has God procured for us. From Your palace overlooking Jerusalem, that sacred residence to which the kings of the world bring You tribute, from that place, scold that beast of the reeds, the leader of that congregation of oxen willing to sell himself for a few pieces of silver. Disperse them, whose delight is war . . ."

Her voice trailed off almost as if she herself were unsure that this was all there was to the oracle. I myself was mesmerized, transfixed. I had sought her and she had appeared. I had needed her to speak and she had spoken. And then, in a moment, she was gone. How she disappeared without descending the steps that led from the courtyard up into the balcony, I have no idea. It was, however, no less good a trick than the way she disappeared from the spice shop without passing through the only door to the street. There was, however, no time for me to struggle with figuring out how she pulled off these stunning exits of hers. Nor did I want to take the time to compare notes with the others in the courtyard; she had been speaking in flawless, unaccented Jerusalem Hebrew, but I doubted if anyone present had even the slightest idea what she had been talking about. But who cared about any of that? All that mattered to me was that I figure out what it was she—or whomever or Whomever—was trying to tell me. But that she was trying to tell me something, of *that* I had not the slightest doubt.

FORTY-FIVE

THE REST OF THE day I devoted entirely to considering her words. I found that I could recall pretty much exactly what she had said and scribbled it all down as best I could on a scrap of parchment I quickly took from the storage closet where writing supplies were kept in the large room known as the Chamber of Phineas the Haberdasher. Remembering her words, however, was not quite the same as understanding them. It sounded . . . I wasn't really sure what it sounded like. I knew that she had been speaking to me, or I thought I did. And, with even more certainty than that, I knew that she was talking to me about Buki or Ikkesh, or both of them at once, and telling me how to proceed.

Once I had the oracle written down, I proceeded to read it through carefully over and over . . . and reciting it over and over only reinforced in me the sense that the answers to all my questions were embedded in its measured cadences. So all I had to do was to figure out how to mine the quarry and then haul off the ore that was apparently there for the taking.

I left the Temple through the Shushan Gate, intending to head to the Street of the Lambs for a long soak during which I was going to think all of this through. But then I changed my mind. I really did not want to run into the Great One just quite yet and I had no way to know if he was there or not. Nor, although for more obscure reasons, did I wish to go home to think through Ketziya's words. Better, I told myself, to take refuge from the snow somewhere I could be almost certain not to be disturbed. I headed for the Upper Shuk.

I've already described the spice shop owned and operated by Avital's brother, Uriel Gedalia, but I don't recall if I mentioned that he also owned the building in which it was located, including the two rooms on the top

floor that he used as the office out of which he ran his business. He and I occasionally met there to smoke *ganjha* or just to chat for an hour in a private
place away from the crowds below, but I knew that there was no chance in
the middle of a snowstorm that Uriel would have time for even a brief chat.
And I was right too. When I arrived, I found him, if anything, busier at dusk
than normally in mid-morning as he dealt with a crush of customers who
had arrived as the first few flakes began to fall to buy what they could possibly need for the next few days. I hadn't actually thought that there would
be so *many* people provoked to a state of shopping frenzy by a little snow,
but I was entirely wrong and the *shuk* was a complete madhouse with people
racing from stall to shop to store in their quest to make sure that, come what
may, they would have whatever supplies they could conceivably need for as
long as the city remained shut down. At any rate, Uriel Gedalia was not only
busy, but insanely so. He barely nodded to me as I walked through the shop
and headed for the staircase at the rear of the selling floor. I wasn't even sure
he had registered that I was going upstairs. He certainly didn't follow me. I
wouldn't really have minded if he had, but he didn't. And, in the end, that
probably turned out to be all for the best.

Settling onto the ancient *lectus* Uriel Gedalia kept up there for the occasional snooze when the opportunity presented itself, which it very rarely
did, I began to contemplate Ketziya's words.

The first part, I supposed, was simple enough. By noting that it is the
same God in heaven who effects the release of prisoners held against their
will—which I took to be a reference to Asa Gad and myself—and who looks
after orphans and brings justice to widows, the witch was making a kind of
an observation that I had somehow failed to come to on my own: that all
of us—Buki, Ikkesh, Asa Gad and myself, but also Meirav Serach and the
boy Tola—we were *all* Benjamin Ginnethon's victims. I reserved judgment
on the thrust of her comment about widows, thinking that it could bear
interpretation in two very different ways, that it could either be suggesting
that Meirav Serach was a victim in need of justice or else that she was a co-
conspirator of her wicked brother's and that God would no less surely judge
her than him. But that her opening remarks seemed to list all the involved
parties seemed certain.

And then she had moved on to describe us and our work as Temple
musicians. I tried to focus on what she had said, to decide as best I could
to whom exactly she had made reference. She had talked about the choir,
about the singers—I assumed she meant the soloists—whom the choristers
accompanied, and about the musicians. And then she had made a special
point of mentioning the Women's Drum Corps. I paused for a long moment. The WDC hasn't existed for quite a while now, but it was a feature

of Temple life from the reign of King Yehoshafat on and was in existence not for decades or for scores of years, but for centuries. Women, of course, have participated in the musical part of our levitical tasks since King David specifically permitted old Heman—a direct ancestor of the Great One's father—to train his fourteen sons and three daughters as a kind of cymbal, lyre, and harp ensemble to serve in the Temple Solomon was to build on the very spot our Temple stands now. Apparently it took a while for the concept of women drummers to catch on, but it was a big part of our musical presentation once it did. And it was a very popular part of things during the years I've been writing about.

The only problem was that none of the women involved had anything to do with the story of Buki's death or of Ikkesh's. Indeed, none of the *tofefot* had crossed my field of vision since the time I had embarked on my attempt to solve Buki's murder. I resolved to rethink the matter later on, then moved on to the rest of the oracle.

By this time, it was snowing seriously. The flakes were large and wet, and they were sticking to the ground and to the rooftops of the adjacent buildings. I could see the snow accumulating in the alleyways and, even at a height of two stories, I could hear the hubbub below as people responded to the deteriorating weather by, if anything, becoming even more obsessed with buying supplies to last for as long as the *shuk* could conceivably remain closed down.

Then there was the whole business about young Benjamin ruling over the princes of Judah, Zebulon and Naphtali—surely that had to mean something. Since we have never had a king named Benjamin, she was not talking, I didn't think about a historical personality. King Saul, true, had come from the tribe of Benjamin—but he was ancient, not young . . . and, besides, what could a mad king dead and gone for centuries possibly have to do with Buki's murder? Could she have been talking about Benjamin Ginnethon? I decided to leave that too for a moment and move along. She had also said something about a congregation of oxen selling itself for a few pieces of silver. Not sure what that meant, I focused instead on her closing admonition to "disperse them whose delight is war."

Oracular speech has gotten pretty tame in these last decades. For one thing, it's a dying art. For another, it's a dying art pitched at a dying audience. But when it does happen nowadays, it's generally *too* clear, *too* precise, *too* exactly in perfect sync with what the asker asked. And nothing says humbuggery more clearly than an oracle that simply answers the question in play in plain, unambiguous speech. Just the opposite was the case with real oracles, which were invariably puzzles with a thousand solutions and no solutions at all, mazes with a hundred entrances and no egresses you could locate easily or simply. And Ketziya's, which bore a thousand tentative interpretations but no secure or obvious ones, was definitely in that category.

I sat myself back down on Uriel's upstairs *lectus*. Did he use it also from the occasional tryst? He was Avital's brother, so his level of marital fidelity was not really any concern of mine (or, at least, not any direct concern). His wife Meshullemet was a friendly woman with a pleasant disposition. I had always gotten along with her. Avital liked her too, but we had both noticed a certain coolness between the two of them. They never touched in public, for instance, not even casually in the way that a happily married man will occasionally take his wife's hand while they walk or that a woman who loves her husband will sometimes place her hand on his shoulder just for a fleeting moment when she finds herself with a free hand while walking by his chair. True, they had produced a single child, a girl named Hephtziba who was as skinny as her mother was plump, but there had been no more children after that and Hephtziba was already a child of nine the year Buki died. Were they trying to produce more children and simply not succeeding? Or had they made a conscious decision only to raise one child? Or did the fact that Hephtziba was an only child simply reflect the fact that her parents hadn't found an evening since she was born on which they both felt it at least reasonably likely they would still be married nine months later? All these thoughts, none of them any of my business, passed idly through my mind as I plopped myself down on Uriel Gedalia's upstairs couch to think Ketziya's words through yet again.

So there I am on Uriel's ancient *lectus* in a cold room watching it snow as the sun sets in the western sky. Ketziya's words are bouncing back and forth in my consciousness, challenging me to translate them into practical wisdom . . . and, more to the point, into the kind of information I could actually use to set a trap for a murderer. And then, suddenly, I understood everything. I wouldn't go so far as to say that the gates of heaven opened up. I didn't *see* anything. Nor did I hear anything. This was one of those . . . well, I don't really know what kind of anything it was. It was just that when I finally managed to seize Ketziya's meaning, I also understood what I was meant to do.

FORTY-SIX

I RAN DOWN THE stairs, then plowed through the crowd in Uriel Gedalia's store, then tripped over a huge burlap sack of Galilean morningtooth and went flying into the street. As I flew past my brother-in-law, I said something even I myself found unintelligible. He waved slightly, wholly engrossed in some transaction with a customer. I remember thinking that he may not even have known who I was. Normally, I would have stopped to help him deal with some of the customers milling around on the selling floor, a role I occasionally played in the shop when business was too brisk for Uriel to handle easily on his own. But I didn't stop. First of all, I needed to find Joseph. I was fairly sure that my brother had the day off and that he would most likely be at the Street of the Lambs. I headed south through silent, snowy streets, then west. And as I hurried along, I thought things through yet again.

Ketziya's oracle, I now understood, was about the future, not the past: she wasn't describing something I had seen or could ever have seen, but something I was being called upon to make real. In retrospect, it sounds like a chump's observation—aren't oracles always supposed to be about the future?—but, at the time, that single insight of mine, brilliant or banal, changed everything. I knew, of course, who Zebulun and Naphtali were. I understood well enough to which of the city's many Benjamins Ketziya was making reference, or I thought I did. And, for the first time, I could imagine easily what the Women's Drum Corps was going to have to do with the scene Ketziya was challenging me to create.

This isn't the place to embark on a complicated description of the priestly hierarchy of old Jerusalem, but let me just set some basics down for readers unfamiliar with how things were. At the peak of the pyramid, of course, was the High Priest, but his was a position of ever-shifting importance. Some of our HPs were men of renown who functioned as forceful enough leaders to command respect and obedience. But that was not always the case and we've also had men at the titular helm who were wholly or partially ineffectual dullards. In those cases, however, the hierarchy has traditionally risen to the occasion and the second-in-command, the Vice High Priest (popularly called the *segan*), has been discreetly granted enough power to run the show from his titular master's side. And there are always others in the wings waiting to help out as well. There are, for example, a minimum of two *katikolin* who serve the *segan* roughly in the manner the *segan* serves the High Priest. And there are always at least seven *amarkalin* who serve beneath the *katikolin*. Beneath the *amarkalin* serve three or more *gizbarin* who function as the Temple's ultimate financial officers and through whose hands pass both the enormous volume of cash donations received on an annual basis and the vast sums of money spent each year to keep the operation running smoothly. In reality, things are far more complicated than the picture I've just drawn. The *amarkalin*, for example, had huge personal staffs who bore responsibility for distinct parts of the larger operation and who watched over the large number of daily, weekly, and monthly rituals that the *segan* himself could simply not reasonably be expected to watch over personally.

The High Priest in place when all this was unfolding wasn't mentally feeble, just a meek and sickly man whose docile nature could never have made him into the kind of leader our people desperately needed even if he hadn't suffered from palsy and the general decrepitude of ever-advancing senescence. He was, as noted, not above feathering his own nest. But he did try to provide some version of the leadership we needed. Or at least at the beginning of his time in office he did. How he ended up with Benjamin Ginnethon as his *segan*, I have no idea. Choni was greedy and mercenary, but not malevolent. Benjamin Ginnethon, on the other hand, was a viciously cruel man, someone who by the time of Buki's murder had already shown himself—and on more than one occasion—to be incapable of empathy. I've mentioned already, I think, that BG was possibly the tallest man in the city and that he was possessed of the reddest red hair any of us had ever seen. What I may not have mentioned is the degree to which he took genuine pleasure in the parts of his job that involved humiliating others. Benjamin Ginnethon hardly ever passed up the chance to administer the lash when the opportunity presented itself, for example. I myself witnessed more than a few of those beatings and I can report firsthand that the look of almost erotic pleasure that crept across his face as he wielded the whip was so disturbing as really to defy description in simple prose.

Benjamin Ginnethon's *katikolin*, both of them servile lackies, were named—I suppose you've guessed this already—Naphtali and Zebulon. These men—more formally named Naphtali ben Ahio and Zebulon ben Shashak—had worked their way up from the ranks. Neither came from an illustrious family or a wealthy one, nor was either especially blessed with any discernable gift for leadership or intellectual ability. They were, to speak clearly, two semi-competent lummoxes who did their daily work no more than adequately. And they were alike in other ways as well: both were married, both had produced two children (Naphtali had two sons and Zebulon, two daughters), both were gaunt almost the point of looking unwell, both were tall (although nowhere near as tall as their boss) and both were almost entirely bald. Seen together, they looked like fleshy scarecrows that had somehow come to life. If I were a crow, I'd have stayed away.

But Ketziya had spoken of young Benjamin ruling over "the princes of Zebulon and Naphtali" and this too I thought through as I walked, supposing Ketziya sarcastically to have been referring to the large staffs of lackeys and yes-men both *katikolin* maintained, huge teams of fawning toadies whose job it was to do their bosses' bidding without complaining and to avoid as best they could having any thoughts of their own that could conceivably impede their ability to do so.

And so, as I made my way down Upper King Hezekiah Road towards the Street of the Lambs, I suddenly realized that I had a picture in my mind's eye almost clearly drawn. At the center was Benjamin Ginnethon. (I personally had long since abandoned any doubts about his role in Buki's murder or in Ikkesh's, although I also knew that I was eventually going to have to prove his guilt, not merely assert it.) At any rate, I could actually see Benjamin Ginnethon in this mental picture I was conjuring up seated in the center of a large group of friends and supporters. To his right were Zebulon ben Shashak's people headed by Zebulon himself. And to the left were similarly arrayed Naphtali ben Ahio's people with their leader seated just to the left of Benjamin Ginnethon. Seated in front of them all were the members of the Women's Drum Corps, each holding a silver doumbek aloft for all to see. For a moment, I felt myself transfixed by the image before my eyes, but I also understood that I needed to remain focused on the more pressing question: how, exactly, I was going to proceed once I found Joseph and involved him in something I knew perfectly well I should probably leave him as totally out of as I possibly could.

I reached the bottom of Upper King Hezekiah Road just as the wind picked up. The distance to the front entrance into the bath house was no more than a few dozen cubits away. More than anything, I needed for Benjamin Ginnethon to admit his guilt, to confess to Buki's murder either in public or, at the very least, in the presence of credible witnesses. Solving that murder was, after all, the job I had accepted. And it was clearly the task I meant to accomplish. If I could also bring Benjamin Ginnethon down for having harmed Ikkesh ben Tovim, so that would be a bonus. But I was focused now on Buki . . . and I was certain that I knew exactly how to proceed.

I entered the bathhouse, paid the entrance fee, then walked into the apodyterium, undressed, and hung my street clothes on one of the unoccupied hooks. I selected a white sheet from a tall stack lying on a wooden table, wrapped it around my waist, and headed into the caldarium to see what would be waiting for me inside. It took a moment for my eyes to adjust to the steam, then another for me to grope my way through the vapory haze to the tiled bleachers at the far end of the room where my brother Joseph was seated in the center of the top row with his legs crossed and a rough, red towel lying carelessly across his lap.

I told him everything, of course. What else could I do? I was about to involve him in something that was undoubtedly going to have all sorts of repercussions I probably couldn't even begin to guess about in advance. So how could I not tell him the part I actually did know?

I started at the beginning and left nothing out. I found, slightly to my surprise, that I could recite Ketziya's oracles—both of them—effortlessly, almost as though they had entered my head and set up permanent residence there. But I told him the rest almost as accurately, including—and in full detail—the information Asa Gad had shared with me in the course of our time together in Beth Tzur. When I described Migdania to him, I blushed and he smiled. But he stopped smiling when I got up to my experiences in the Temple of earlier that day and he maintained his serious mien until I finally finished speaking.

"And?"

"And what?" I was confused. What did Joseph want me to say?

"And what is your plan?"

"My plan is to prove conclusively that Benjamin Ginnethon was responsible for Buki's murder. If I can pin Ikkesh's death on him too, so much the better. But my primary goal is to get Buki's death explained and his murderer indicted, convicted, and, if I can arrange it, executed. Or at least publicly reviled as a murderer."

"And how exactly do you plan to do this?"

I looked around the room, knowing even before I started that there was no one anywhere near us who could possibly overhear. I took a deep breath. And then I told Joseph how I planned to bring Buki's murderer to justice.

FORTY-SEVEN

I DON'T KNOW WHERE the concept came from, not even after all these years I've had to think about it. Years later, it struck me that the famous passage in Isaiah's book that mentions a "garment stained with blood and burnt with fiery flames" starts off by talking about the warrior's shoes also being burnt. I don't remember connecting the two images back then, but maybe somehow the two were stuck in my mind. Or maybe not. It is definitely true that I had taken several classes in Isaiah's oracles and prophecies, and had committed a fair amount of the material to memory. (Along with memorizing Jeremiah and learning our own hymns inside out, Isaiah's oracles were part of the core curriculum in those days and the test that followed was one of the few examinations no one was ever certified to serve without having passed.) The burnt garment stained with blood would certainly have suggested Buki's demise to me. So who knows? Maybe the prophet somehow reached across the generations to whisper the missing link in my ear to see if I was bright enough to catch on. Or maybe I just thought of it myself. At any rate, I had no other plan so I was going to run with the one I did have.

What had happened to Buki's shoes? If he was ambushed and seized on his way home from the Temple, which everybody supposed to have been the case, then he would surely have been wearing shoes. Probably, he was wearing his sandals—we were having an unusually warm autumn that year and everybody was still wearing sandals, even as late as the end of Cheshvan when the rainy season could have begun at any moment. But as far as I knew they had never been found. They couldn't have been burnt with his clothing—everybody knows that leather could never burn like that, let alone the metal studs in the sole plus the metal buckle-ring. Could the remains of Buki's sandals simply have been overlooked? I thought not. The goatherd who found Buki, and who subsequently spent days and days telling and retelling the story, had made a point of saying that the fire had turned his garment so totally to ash that he had been unable even to recognize Buki's distinctive levitical cloak in the cinders. He had been so insistent that the ash was powdery and fine, comparing it—I heard him say this myself, incidentally—comparing its appearance in the fire pit to a mixture of finely ground pepper and salt, that it seemed impossible to imagine he had simply forgotten to mention his shoes or their distinctive buckles.

But if Buki's shoes hadn't been burned and they hadn't been on his feet when he was found, then where were they? I wondered if . . . I wondered if our Benjamin Ginnethon might not have them. Could they be in his bedroom right now, silent trophies parked brazenly beneath his bed? Perhaps they were directly by the side of Ikkesh's similarly purloined shoes. Or perhaps our Benjamin had had many other victims, murdered men (and perhaps women) of whom I had never heard and possibly never would hear. Could he have a whole collection of his victims' shoes? Could he possibly have had the idea of arranging for his assassins—supposing he had more than Dan Iddo in his employ—to bring the shoes of his victims to him as a way of securing the second half of their promised payments precisely so he could keep them as souvenirs afterwards? Or was it perhaps something that simply developed after the fact once the shoes of Benjamin Ginnethon's victims began to pile up in his storeroom? Did he simply realize at one point that he was in possession of the shoes of all his victims, one pair each, and that he could enjoy the details of their demises over and over by sleeping just a few inches above the full collection? I took my thoughts no further. I might have. I even could have. But I didn't.

As I walked through the snow, I tried to conjure up a mental image of Buki's sandals. He had been a huge man and he had had concomitantly huge feet, gigantic ones almost as wide as they were long. Everybody talked about them, but he was good-natured about the ribbing and he never appeared to take it personally. He was, as I've said many times, a good-natured fellow in general. And the fact that his girth practically invited comments, some of them far sharper than necessary, did not seem to faze him at all. Just to the contrary, actually—if anything, Buki seemed to enjoy being the center of attention and didn't seem to care at all that it was his huge belly or his gigantic feet that garnered him the attention he clearly craved. His sandals were easy to pick out, too—they were invariably the largest ones in the apodyterium, and by far. But they were easy to spot also because they were too unusually sized simply to be purchased at a cobbler's table in the shuk and had to be made especially for him. Buki, as noted, knew how to spend money. And the sandals he had made for himself were beautifully fashioned of the softest leather set out with brass or copper studs polished to a gleam and provided with sturdy soles fashioned of antelope leather treated with some sort of cobbler's paste that made them both watertight and impervious to casual damage. These were not the kind of sandals anyone would forget. But where were they now?

I told Joseph what I wanted to do. He thought it was uncertain to yield results, but when I challenged him to come up with an alternate plan, he had nothing to offer. And the plan I had hatched also had a great advantage to match the detriment just mentioned: if it did fail, it was entirely possible that Benjamin Ginnethon would not even realize that he had been targeted at all. Or at least not by us!

So part of my plan had to do with Buki's shoes. And the other had to do with a drummer Joseph and I both knew, a woman who had come to the capital several years after I had come, but who was considerably younger than I was. I had been hospitable and kind to her when she arrived. Would she agree now to help me in my hour of need? That remained to be seen, obviously. All I could do was ask!

FORTY-EIGHT

HER NAME WAS ZEBUDA bat Shimi and she was as lovely as her name. And she was talented too, not just pretty—in her day, Zebuda was one of the best drummers in the corps and by far. The Women's Drum Corps seems to have been forgotten these days by just about everybody. Mind you, it hasn't existed for quite some time, so there aren't that many of us left who remember hearing them play. (It was disbanded when the hellenizers seized the Temple and with good reason: the very last thing those self-important phonies could ever have tolerated would have been an army of dark-eyed, olive-skinned maidens banging on doumbeks and tambours, thus almost begging the assembled crowds in the Temple forecourts to feel as little Greek as possible. But when the Maccabees reseized the place and attempted to reset things to where they had been, they somehow omitted to restore the Drum Corps.) But for those of us who can remember things from that long ago, the memories are very pleasant indeed. For one thing, the *tofefot* were, to a woman, incredibly talented musicians. The rhythms they mastered weren't only multi-layered, they were *incredibly* complex and rich. And when the sound they produced combined with the style and the glamor these women were able to project almost naturally, the overall effect was truly hypnotizing.

I had no idea where to find her, but Joseph did. No one could actually make a living serving in the Corps. There was a modest salary connected with the work, but there wasn't enough of it—enough work or enough salary—to allow membership in the Corps to substitute for a real job for anyone who actually needed to earn a living. Since this was how things were for more or less every *tofefet* except for maybe the smallest handful who came from wealthy families or who had married rich husbands, it was no surprise that Zebuda had another job. And Joseph, bless him, knew what it was.

As soon as he told me, I knew that we were on the right track. I had thought to enlist her to contact Benjamin Ginnethon in the Temple where she would have found it simple to approach him with a message from someone she would say had given his name as Dan Iddo from the town of Shephem. But now a new possibility opened up, something unexpected but even better than the original plan. All that remained was for us to bring Zebuda herself on board. The rest, I thought hopefully, would just fall into place once we had her involved and willing to help.

We were washed, dressed, and back out on the street almost instantly. Evening had fallen while we were inside and the streets of Jerusalem were, if anything, even more deserted than they had been all day. The snow was still falling. Most thoroughfares were blocked either by the snow itself or by the wagons and carts people had abandoned wherever they had been when the storm had made further progress impossible. Here and there, I could see the odd shop that had somehow remained open (probably because the owners had come to work in the morning and now had no way to get home), but most businesses were shuttered and dark. Joseph hurried me along. He wasn't sure if Zebuda would be at work on an evening like this, but he thought she might be. I hoped he was right. The plan was that we had no other plan so this one had to work.

I hadn't ever been to the Blue Cormorant before. When I was married to Deborah, it had been far beyond our budget. But later on, when I could possibly have afforded to dine in one of the few local hostels that served meals to people who were not lodging there, Avital hadn't ever expressed any interest in going there and I hadn't rushed to talk her into feeling otherwise. Would it be open for business on a snowy evening? I had no idea, but it was certainly worth the effort of finding out. For one thing, it was where they all ate whenever they could afford it. Benjamin Ginnethon was widely known to appear there so often that he practically had his own table, at which was generally also seated either Naphtali ben Ahio or Zebulon ben Shashak, his two *katikolin*, or of both of them. Really, it was an inspired choice. Hadn't Ketziya more or less commanded me to confront Benjamin Ginnethon in their company? And this was precisely where they all hung out. And, if he wasn't present, we could simply revert to our first plan.

In retrospect, it's surprising that I hadn't known that Zebuda bat Shimi worked at the Blue Cormorant. She and I were acquaintances, after all, and had met on numerous occasions when the Women's Drum Corps and our brethren had co-sponsored evenings of musical entertainment. Plus, of course, our paths crossed in the Temple from time to time. But I don't believe she and I had ever discussed the question of outside employment.

The Blue Cormorant was on King Saul Road in the northernmost corner of the city near the corner of the Akra Fortress closest to the Fish Gate. It was a handsome inn, one of those ancient structures that had been rebuilt and renovated so many times that it was unclear if any part of the original edifice still existed. It was a large, airy building decorated with fine wall hangings, and its food was widely thought to be the finest in the entire country. Like I said, I hadn't ever been inside. But Joseph had. He had been his father-in-law's guest there many times, and he had gone there just with Yemima as well once or twice when he had been feeling especially flush. So it was good to have him along.

Our plan was simple. First, we'd see if the place was open. Then, assuming it was, we'd go in and order something simple that wasn't going to involve too much preparation. (That way, we wouldn't have to commit to staying until ascertaining that Zebuda was present.) Then, if BG was *also* there and it proved at all possible, we'd get her ear and ask her if she would deliver a message to Benjamin Ginnethon and lie about its provenance. That, of course, was the crucial detail. Absent the need for that specific piece of subterfuge, any waitress could surely be importuned upon— for the right sum of money—to deliver a message to a patron whose meal she was serving. Fortunately, Zebuda was the daughter of a Levite named Shimi ben Elnatan, an elderly man who no longer even came to the Temple, let alone worked there regularly, but whose name was still spoken with respect.

And so, for once, things actually worked out. The place was open. And, contrary to my other worry, it was packed. (I suppose that shouldn't have surprised me—the Blue Cormorant was a pricey inn, but most of the city had closed down hours earlier, leaving Jerusalem packed with officials and workers and all sorts of people who had no way to get home until the end of the storm.) Our luck was incredible: not only was the place open and hopping, but there was a table available in a distant corner where we would be almost invisible to almost all. We took it, ordered a jug of date beer, tried to look like weary travelers pleased to have found a place to rest. The bartender brought plates of almonds and salted fish, then our beer. For once, all felt right.

After about twenty minutes, Joseph announced he needed to step into the back alley. I relaxed when he returned, then felt my stomach tighten when he revealed to me what he had learnt on his journey to the alley and back. Zebuda was present, he said. And so was the unholy triumvirate of Benjamin Ginnethon, Naphtali ben Ahio, and Zebulon ben Shashak. The place was filled with our people, he added, so there was no reason at all for anyone to think it odd that we too were present. Where else would anyone want to be on a night like this other than in a dry, warm place where excellent food was available?

From there, things unfolded just like in a dream. When it was my turn to head for the alley, I managed to cross paths with Zebuda. She knew Joseph too, of course, but it was she and I who had at least something of a relationship, casual though it surely was, and so it made sense that it be me who approached her with the big ask. I followed her just a little bit until she stepped behind the partition that hid the doorway that led out to the servers' work area from the diners, then I followed her. She was surprised to see me, but she must have somehow read the urgency in my eyes. She said nothing, just looked at me, then turned. Clearly, I thought, I was meant to follow. So I did . . . and that is how Zebuda and I found ourselves in a chilly back room of the Blue Cormorant surrounded by about a thousand jugs of unmixed wine.

"I need a favor," I began, trying to sound like this was a normal kindness I was about to request.

She said nothing, but her eyes were trained directly on mine.

"It's . . . it's . . . it's about something that you're better off not knowing what it's about."

She stared intently at me. But she said nothing.

"I need you to . . . I want you to . . . Zebuda, I have a simple favor but it's important. I need you to deliver a message to Benjamin Ginnethon ben Baruch Hakohen. You know him, right?"

Her eyes widened slightly as she nodded. "The Ood," she mouthed silently.

"Yes," I said. "Exactly. He's here tonight."

Zebuda nodded in agreement.

"I need you to deliver a message and lie about who gave it to you."

"I'm an honest woman," she said quietly.

I knew I only had a few minutes to wrap this up. "It has to do with Buki's death," I said quietly, knowing that the opportunity to bring the murderer of a Levite would go a long way to making her eager, or at least willing, to help.

Zebuda stared into my eyes and nodded slightly. "Speak," she said.

I knew it was now or never. "Wait until he's almost done eating. Then tell him that a man named Dan Iddo came to the rear door of the restaurant and asked you to tell him that there are going to be visitors later tonight, that he needs to tidy up, that the weather is definitely *not* going to be a factor."

"That's it?"

"That's it."

"Done," she said, turning on her heel and disappearing down the corridor.

When I came back to our table, the maître d' was just announcing the day's special dishes. I can't even remember what we ordered, so totally was I focused on the scene about to unfold before me. We were seated at the other end of the dining room from the one in which Benjamin Ginnethon was holding court. But we could see him clearly, or at least I could. And so I was watching about ninety minutes later when Zebuda approached the Ood's *lectus* and delivered the message. He appeared to listen carefully, then to thank her for her trouble. He even went so far as to produce a coin or two as a tip. I saw her accept, then disappear. Benjamin Ginnethon waited a few minutes, then said something to his *katikolin* and hurriedly decamped. We had already finished our meal and paid our bill, so there was nothing at all holding us back from leaving at will. Nor did anything delay our departure. By the time the Ood was out in the street, we were right behind him.

Did he see us following him? I doubt it. The wind was howling. The snow was still falling. Because the wind was blowing towards the west while his home was several streets to the east in the direction of the Temple, he was walking directly into the wind. He was all alone, even though a man of his rank would normally travel with a bodyguard. Maybe he had sent his guard home earlier. Maybe the guard himself had never showed up for work in the storm. Maybe the Ood simply didn't like having anyone with him as he conducted his nighttime business, least of all one of us. But whatever the reason, the man was all alone. And I knew where he was going. Or I hoped I did.

The line from Amos about selling the poor for a pair of shoes flitted in and out of my mind as we walked, keeping our distance and hugging the walls of the buildings that flanked King Saul Road as we made our way eastward towards Benjamin Ginnethon's house. Of course, I had no way to know what was going to happen when we got there. Possibly, nothing at all was going to happen: he would arrive, let himself inside, and go to bed. Possibly, the house was already clean of any evidence that could link him to either murder. Possibly, he knew perfectly well where Dan Iddo was that evening . . . and understood that he was being set up, that a trap was being laid, and that whoever was laying the trap wanted him to do precisely what we actually did want him to do.

Or perhaps things would work out perfectly.

FORTY-NINE

ONE OF THE BETTER songs we used to sing on the semi-circular steps leading up to the Israelites' Courtyard starts off with the observation that Jerusalem is a town surrounded by mountains and that detail worked to our advantage that snowy night. If I had a dead man's shoes under my bed and this had all been playing itself out, say, in Jaffa, I personally would have flung the shoes into the sea and been done with it. Had this been happening in Kefar Nahum, I would have flung the shoes into the lake. But we have no harbors or immense lakes in Jerusalem, so neither option was going to present itself to the Ood as he puzzled out what to do with Buki's shoes.

I knew what I thought I myself would do. And I was betting that I was right. The good news was that, if I was wrong, I'd be no worse off. Benjamin Ginnethon would obviously hunt Zebuda down and try to wring some information out of her, but she didn't know Dan Iddo personally and all she was going to have to say was that a man who said his name was Dan Iddo had stopped her at the Cormorant's rear door and asked her to deliver the message. Who it really was, she'd say she had no idea. Nor, of course, would there have been any reason for her not to have taken the man at his word. So she wouldn't, I thought, come to any harm. And there was, I also thought, no way for him to identify me as having anything to do with anything at all. True, he could possibly have noticed Joseph and me sitting at our table. I didn't think he had. But even if he *had* noticed us, so what? There must have been eighty or ninety people dining at the same time in the same place . . . and Joseph, at least, had dined there many times previously. As far as anyone watching would have surmised, we were just two guys taking our meal on a cold night in one of the few inns still open to paying non-guests in the middle of a snowstorm . . . and nothing more than that.

Benjamin Ginnethon's home was on a narrow alleyway just west of the Temple Mount called Athalia's Lane. It was a tiny bit of a street with only a handful of houses lining its narrow length, but Benjamin Ginnethon's home would have been impressive even on a major boulevard. Fashioned of yellow honeystone and white marble, it rose three stories off the ground and was set back just far enough for there to be a rose garden in front. Ivy grew along trellises constructed by the front door, thereby giving a kind of rustic feel to the place that contrasted nicely with the exceptional luxuriousness of the house's other features. I had obviously never been inside, but I was supposing that the master bedroom would be on the second or even the third floor. Was Meirav Serach home that evening? Was little Tola? Where else would they be? It wasn't *that* late, so they could all certainly still have been awake. But the house was quiet and still as we approached it. No one greeted him at the door. Nor did he tarry on his stoop. Instead, he opened the door with some sort of key that I could not see, stepped inside, and closed the door behind him.

Two minutes later, he was back out in the street. I couldn't believe our good fortune. Joseph looked over at me, then quickly put his finger to his lips. I got the message. Sounds travel in cold air especially clearly. I said nothing.

We hung back for a moment, then set out in pursuit. The snow was falling less heavily now, but it was still coming down. The wind too had died down, so tailing the Ood was a touch riskier than it had been just half an hour earlier. Still, he seemed totally preoccupied with whatever it was he was up to. He walked slightly hunched forward, as one normally would while walking into the wind. He was clearly carrying something, something small enough for him to clutch to his chest. But I could not see what exactly it was. I knew what I thought. I knew what I hoped. But, of course, what I thought and what I hoped put together added up to . . . to nothing at all. Or at least nothing you could deposit in the Temple treasury. Still, the evening had gone so well that I could hardly believe it. Of course, our luck could obviously have turned at any moment. I resolved to be as cautious as possible, and especially now that Joseph was involved.

Benjamin Ginnethon turned south when he got to the outermost wall of the Temple Mount, then slipped inside the northernmost of the two gates named for the prophetess Hulda. We were right behind him. He was hurrying across the dark expanse as we entered the gate, then slipped through the Water Gate into the Priests' Courtyard. I could see our guy on guard in the gateway, but knew better than to ask to be admitted. And I certainly didn't want to involve anyone else in what was either going to end this whole investigation successfully or end up getting me and my brother in a huge amount of trouble.

Instead, we circled around the outer wall of the Temple itself and climbed the steps that led to the entrance to the Women's Courtyard. We passed through the gate leading inside, nodding to the Levites on guard as though we had business inside that was of no concern to them. Which, of course, was precisely correct.

The Women's Courtyard was a large square each side of which was a hundred and thirty-five cubits along. But visitors could only stand in most of the courtyard, because the corners of the courtyard were occupied by four unroofed rooms that served various functions. I've mentioned these rooms before, I think, but the one of importance for my story now is the one on the southwestern wall just to the left of the circular steps leading up to the Nikanor Gate, a kind of storage area in which huge earthen jugs of wine and oil were kept cool and ready for use. And it was also the Temple lost-and-found office, and what was mostly lost (and rarely found) were sandals, shoes, and boots. It was actually a mystery—or at least to me it was—how people could lose their shoes. It was not permitted to enter the Temple wearing regular shoes, but most people traded their sandals for felt-soled slippers at several checkpoints set up at the outer perimeter of the Temple Mount. Of course, there was no requirement to wear the slippers. Some people actually went barefoot, but this category was generally limited to the extremely pious kind of pilgrim who was hoping there might be some redemptive potential in having sore, cold feet. And some people actually showed up in slippers that they had borrowed from their hostels or lodging houses. But the bottom line was that no one who showed up at the Temple wearing shoes was admitted and the only reasonable thing to do with the shoes you were wearing was to check them and either take or not take a pair of slippers. Most people, of course, stopped back at the checkpoint on the way to return the slippers and retrieve their shoes. But there were regularly those who somehow didn't bother and it was part of our job at the end of each day to gather up the shoes left behind at the various checkpoints and bring them to the lost-and-found office on the off chance someone was going to show up to retrieve them later on.

If I personally wanted to lose a pair of shoes in a way that could more or less guarantee that they would never be found again, I'd pitch them in that southwestern storage room and forget about ever seeing them again. You have to understand, there were stored in there *hundreds* of pairs of sandals and sturdier shoes that pilgrims and others had somehow managed to leave behind when they exited the Temple complex. Occasionally, people came back to sift through the mountains of sandals and shoes to find their own.

Sometimes, they actually managed to find their own shoes too, but most of the time I think people just took a pair that fit, figured their own were in there somewhere, and called it square. But even if someone *did* locate the specific shoes I was now certain Benjamin Ginnethon had with him, there would be no way for anyone even to guess how they had gotten there.

By the time we got into the Women's Courtyard, the Ood was coming from the other direction through the little doors cut into the great Gate of Nikanor. He was still carrying his package. If he noticed Joseph and me, he would not have found it at all unusual that we were present in the Women's Courtyard. And even if he somehow knew that neither of us was scheduled for work that evening, we could surely have been present anyway to help out a colleague who wasn't feeling well or simply to help clear away the snow that was accumulating in all three Temple courtyards.

As we approached from the east, Benjamin Ginnethon headed towards the storage room from the north. It was now or never. I felt a shiver of excitement, then a surge of electricity flooding my consciousness. I broke into a run. Joseph was just behind me. He was running too.

The snow was everywhere. I was slipping as I ran. I realized that the brethren on duty were watching, but must surely have been uncertain how to respond or even whether they *should* respond. I was a well-known Levite, after all, as was Joseph. But still . . . to appear out of nowhere in the middle of a storm, to enter the Temple on a night neither of us was on duty (and so could have been spending our evenings at home around a glowing hearth with our families by our sides), and to run through the courtyard as though we were being chased by invisible demons—this must all have been well beyond anyone's ability to comprehend. And this was all happening very quickly too: the run through the courtyard could really not have taken more than four or five seconds. Benjamin Ginnethon looked up. As I leapt into the air, I could see that he recognized me. And that he knew all too well why I was flying through the air right at him.

I knocked him to the ground. Joseph slid through the snow and crashed into us both. The priest on guard in the Beth Avtinas chamber that was over the top arch of the Water Gate was there almost immediately and pulled me off Benjamin Ginnethon. In the meantime, our people were pouring into the courtyard. And so were some of the younger priests who had just been getting ready to bed down for the night in the Hearth House on the northern wall of the Priests' Courtyard but who were still dressed and awake. Finally, Joseph got to his feet and quieted everybody down. I too stood up. Surveying the crowd that had almost instantly assembled, I knew that the moment had come.

I turned sharply to the left and caught a glimpse of Ketziya in the main gateway to the Women's Courtyard, the one facing out towards the Shushan Gate through which Joseph and I had entered. In a trice, she was gone. I was on my own. All eyes were on me. And I knew exactly what I had to do.

FIFTY

AFTER I WAS PULLED off Benjamin Ginnethon, he was left lying on the ground for a moment and then helped to his feet. For a long moment, we stood there staring at each other. Uncharacteristically, he said nothing. I too was silent, but (I now realize) for an entirely different reason: he was feverishly figuring out how to escape and I was simply too stunned by my own brazenness to say a word. All around us were a motley crew of night-duty Levites, drowsy *kohanim*, and pilgrims (and not too many of them) convinced that on spending a snowy night in the Women's Courtyard could somehow help them expiate their sins. The snow was still falling, but only lightly now. The nighttime air was frigid. The stars were twinkling above in a way that felt . . . well, it sounds peculiar to say this now, but it felt like a truly cosmic moment was upon us, was upon me. I felt empowered. I felt justified. I actually felt quite good. I knew that the course of the rest of my life was about to be dictated by the events that would unfold in the next few minutes. I was totally there, totally present, totally focused. What Benjamin Ginnethon was thinking, I have no idea. He said nothing. In retrospect, I suppose he was being clever. After all, he had no real reason to think that I had connected him even *in*conclusively to Buki's murder, let alone to Ikkesh ben Tovim's. So he certainly wasn't going to be the first to speak. For all he knew, I was simply another crazy Levite too high on *ganjha* to consider the likely consequences of his actions. Did he recognize me? I thought he did. Could have possibly have been thinking that this was some sort of crazy revenge for having been abducted and held for a few days? At least for a long moment, I'm quite sure that that's exactly what he thought!

On some level, I suppose, he was glad that the jig was up, that he could begin the long process of atoning for his sins. Later on, when David ben

Levi wrote the famous lines you've surely heard, "I saw a powerful scoundrel leaving himself totally exposed like a citizen with nothing to fear, but he vanished and was no longer / I sought him, but he was nowhere to be found," he was, of course, writing about Benjamin Ginnethon. But what's missing from that great poem is the vacant, almost canine look I saw in the Ood's eyes as I stood across from him in the snow and prepared to indict him of murder. If we had been totally naked, we could not have been more exposed to each other.

For a very long moment, we just stood there. I was aware that I was out of breath and I suppose the others must have heard the rasp of my belabored breathing. For his part, Benjamin Ginnethon was also panting. But there was also fear in the air, a rancid odor I knew all too well. I realized that the next move was mine to make.

I took a step forward, half expecting the Ood to step backwards as though we were executing some sort of dance step. But he didn't step backwards. In fact, he didn't move at all. He just stood there, waiting, watching, perhaps worrying. But still he said nothing at all.

I took another step forward. A cold blast of air funneled through the courtyard bringing in its wake a flurry of snow far thicker than anything that had fallen in the previous few minutes. The assembled quickly brushed the new snow from their heads and shoulders. I willed myself to do nothing. The Ood also did nothing, preferring coolly to stare into my eyes as I came closer.

I was standing directly in front of the man whom I believed responsible for Buki's death. In a court of law, the custom is to read the charges against the defendant aloud before the trial begins. But this was not a courtroom and Benjamin Ginnethon was not on trial and so I simply reached out and took the package from Benjamin Ginnethon's hands. I could feel from the weight of the package that I had guessed right. Or at least I thought I had.

I stepped back. The courtyard was now entirely still. The wind stopped blowing. No one spoke as I unwrapped the package to reveal its contents to be a pair of giant sandals. I turned them over. On the leather soles were three Hebrew letters: two letters *beit* and a *yod*. The monogram was familiar to all of us. *Beit-beit-yod*. Bukiyahu ben Yerimoth. I was holding Buki's sandals. And of that there was no doubt whatsoever.

The rest happened quickly after that. At my signal, the Ood was seized by our people and brought to the incarceration chamber maintained jointly by the levitical security force and the municipal police force at the southwestern corner of the Temple mount. I led a small squad of officers—our men and theirs—to the Ood's house. Fortune continued to smile upon me: Tola was asleep and so I did not need to involve him in the scene that ensued, but his mother was awake. We asked for the master bedroom and she docilely led the way. And then we entered his bedroom and found beneath his bed eight different pairs of sandals of different sizes and styles, none of which could possibly have fit the same set of feet and none of which, I felt certain, belonged to the man in whose bed chamber we were standing.

I had no way to know which were Ikkesh's sandals, but that too turned out to be no problem: I simply asked Meirav Serach which were her husband's and she pointed at them without comment. Apparently, Benjamin Ginnethon had had no idea that I knew anything of his involvement in Ikkesh's death and had not scrupled to take any but Buki's shoes with him when he left the house for the Temple Mount to ditch the only physical evidence linking him to Buki's death.

In the end, he went docilely to his fate. Why exactly that was, I have never really known. He certainly didn't have to. He was a powerful man in those days. He commanded a huge security detail staffed solely by his own people. And he was intimately involved with the municipal police and served personally as the liaison between the Temple's security people and the city's. If he had wanted to, he could have started a war. But the fight was clearly out of him. Perhaps he was just weary. Or perhaps he just realized that he could still possibly be remembered for good in this world—at least by some—if he avoided a long, drawn-out trial in the course of which he would have been forced to name the many others who must have been involved in his crimes.

FIFTY-ONE

THE REST OF THE story, you probably know.

Benjamin Ginnethon confessed not only to having arranged his brother-in-law's murder *and* the assassination of Bukiyahu ben Yerimoth when the latter learned too much about his involvement in that despicable crime, but also to involvement in the murders of seven other people, four Levites who had been missing for years and three others who had vanished more recently after running afoul of the Ood. The court accepted his confession, listened patiently while the *saneigor* pled for his life, then sentenced him to death anyway.

I remember the day of his execution clearly. He looked wretched that day, actually: haggard and scared and nothing at all like the mighty Ood who took such pleasure in terrorizing our people. He was living through the last moments of his life and he was clearly afraid. I had gone in the first place because I felt I owed it to Buki to be there, but then, almost at the last minute, I changed my mind and went home instead. I'm mostly glad I did. I've occasionally thought of visiting his grave, which isn't at all far from here, but I've never actually gone.

It turned out I was right about what had happened to the scroll containing Kadmiel ben Henadad's *History of the Levites*. I'm sure Dan Iddo really did go directly to Buki's home to search for it after taking his life, but Buki had only had it in his possession briefly, having handed it over to the Great One almost immediately upon receiving it from Dan Iddo's hand and with him it had remained. Whom it legally belonged to, I'm not sure—probably some combination of Tola ben Ikkesh and Asa Gad, but the scroll itself remained in the Great One's hands for as long as he lived. I was eventually permitted to read it—the Great One said, entirely correctly, that I had earned the privilege—but I brought it back to the Great One when I was done. Whether Pachat-Moab, the Great One's son who succeeded him, has it in his possession, I have no idea. If it is in levitical hands, I can't imagine why it would not be well known by now. Maybe it was stolen. Or somehow destroyed. Or maybe Pachat-Moab is simply waiting for the right moment to spring it on the world. I don't know where you live, dear reader. But wherever you are, I can assure you that you'll hear all about it if Kadmiel's book is ever published. As long as the Temple still stands, of course, and there are people in the world other than historians who care about its politics and inner workings.

Meirav Serach was widely supposed to have been complicit in her husband's death, but no proof was ever forthcoming and she was never indicted, let alone convicted, of any crime at all. Tola inherited his uncle's mansion and Meirav Serach lived there for the rest of her life almost as a recluse. She had some sort of disease, it was widely thought, that hampered her ability to digest food. As a result, she became skinnier and skinnier, looking towards the end of her life far more like an emaciated waif you'd expect to see begging in the city gates than like the wealthy woman she truly was.

Tola also inherited his father's commercial acumen and, once he was finished with his formal education, re-opened his father's import business. He made many trips to the east and eventually became the first citizen of Judah to master Sanskrit, which accomplishment he celebrated by personally translating Panini's famous grammar into Hebrew and publishing it at his own expense as a gift to the scholars of our land. He is a man in his mid-sixties now, broad, handsome and learned, married for many years to a very engaging woman named Sigalit, and the father of three sons named Ikkesh, Tovim, and Asa Gad.

I never saw Asa Gad after he vanished about seventeen years ago. We were still in touch, still friends. And then he was suddenly gone. I tried for a year to locate him, but it all came to naught. To this day I don't really know what happened to him. Traders who spend time in the east regularly come home with reports about a tall gaunt man of Judah who lives in the land of Hind, but I have never met a single soul who had himself actually encountered the much-spoken-of individual in question. So maybe he's still alive. But it's far more likely that he's gone from the world and I've long since made my peace with not knowing.

Avital died twenty years ago in her seventy-seventh year. She became more and more beautiful as she aged, growing ever more graceful and handsome with each passing season. As do most of us, she lost some of her height as she grew older, but her skin was supple and wrinkle-free almost to the end and her hair, which she wore in a braid wrapped around her head in her older years, never lost its luminous luster. More to the point, she retained her interest in the physical side of marriage until the very end, often beckoning me to her side without saying a word, her meaning entirely clear just from the slightly heightened color in her cheeks. She was in good health until just a few weeks before she died in my arms as I cradled her and sang a lullaby she taught me in the early years of our marriage, one that she said her own mother used to sing to her as a child. I miss her to this day. Whatever I possess I would give up without a moment's hesitation to sleep another few minutes by her side. If there is a life beyond this one and she awaits me on the other side of the abyss that separates this world from the next, then this interminable wait will have been well worth the trouble.

Joseph died three years ago, but Yemima is alive still and in her eighty-eighth year. She appears healthy, but her mind is totally absent and she has no idea who I am when I come to visit. For a long while, I had continually to remind her that Joseph was dead. But now she seems to recall no longer that she ever was married and the last time she asked for him was more than a year ago. It's been more than three months, in fact, since she's spoken at all. She's alive, but not in any way that any normal person would wish to survive. She doesn't seem unhappy, though, so there's some blessing in that. I'll continue to visit. Really, it's the least I can do.

My own sons are all fine. It's hard for me to believe that Zakur is almost seventy years old, but it's true. He's a father and a grandfather, but also a widower. He visits often, finding some solace, I suppose, in the fact that he's still not the oldest living member of the family. That day will come soon enough, of course.

Yehoram never married. He is well into his sixty-eighth year, and as hale and hearty as ever. Years ago, he and his friend Aaron Itai, another confirmed bachelor, bought a home together on the coast not far from Jaffa and they seem quite content to live out their lives solely in each other's company. They seem to be enjoying their lives, so I see no reason to wish some other life for either of them than the one they have apparently manufactured for themselves.

The twins, Nathaniel and Asarela, are sixty-six years old. (In some ways, their age is even less believable to me than their brothers'.) They both married, then both divorced, then both remarried . . . and the second time seemed to bring good fortune to both of them. I like their wives, adore their many children (Nathaniel has six sons and a daughter and Asarela has three sons and two daughters), and feel wholly and fully welcome in their homes whenever I visit. They're still each other's best friend, still able to communicate a little in their secret childhood language. They still even look alike, although nowhere near to the extent that they did as young children.

What happened to their mother, incidentally, I have no idea. She stayed in Jerusalem for about six years, living briefly with a man she claimed to have met only days before our divorce came through and then alone once he (I can't help supposing) had finally had enough. When the twins were sixteen, she moved to Jaffa. She had some success there as a local artist and, for a while, she wrote to the boys almost regularly. But those letters tapered off and eventually they stopped coming entirely. Probably, she too is gone from the world. I don't miss her. I never missed her. If she's alive, I hope she regrets losing touch with our sons. If she's dead, I wish her peace.

Almost everybody else in this long story is gone. Even Zebuda herself is no more—she was the victim of a terrible fire in one of the big hostels on the coast more than thirty years ago.

And that brings me to my own story. I'm an old man now. Buki's murder was fifty-six years ago. If he were still among the living, he'd be over ninety now. Now *that* is hard to believe . . . but only because people get stuck at whatever age they are when they die, especially prematurely. So for me, he'll always be thirty-five, always hugely fat, always the same cheerful, slightly disheveled fellow he was for the years we were part of each other's lives. I didn't really know him all that well, but the fact that the investigation into his murder turned out to be the gateway I stepped through into my own life makes it feel slightly less important that we weren't *such* intimate friends in life. I've occasionally visited his grave. And him too I wish peace.

Our people, as usual, are in crisis—Prince Simon got the Romans to recognize the Maccabees as the lawful rulers of Judah, then was rewarded for his efforts by being murdered (and by his son-in-law, no less) together with his two oldest sons. The remaining son, John Hyrcanus, came to power just last year, though, and appears to be sitting reasonably tall in the saddle. We can only hope for the best. And the struggle between the priests and our holy, downtrodden, luckless people has calmed down. People are rarely ambushed, almost never beaten. A kind of symbiosis has established itself: we pay lip service to their *torah* and they pay lip service to ours, but neither side reads the other's book or grants it much credence. For better or for worse, we've settled into two solitudes, two discrete universes of spiritual discourse that can co-exist successfully only because the proponents of the one ignore the existence of the other.

How long can I have left? I feel well most of the time, but less so when the temperature drops too precipitously or when the air is too damp for too long. Otherwise, I keep to myself, look after my own affairs, boil my own porridge, wash my own tunic, see those few of my friends who are still alive. How could I have lived so long? The events out there in the world—the slave revolts in Pergamum and Syracuse of earlier this year, for example, which once would have been the most fascinating of stories for me to follow—no longer interest me at all. Nothing interests me, really. Nothing but myself, I mean . . . and my memories.

My career as a sleuth, if that's the right word, wasn't over when Buki's murder was solved. In fact, it was just beginning—the Great One asked me on so many different occasions in the years following Benjamin Ginnethon's execution to look into one matter or another that I was eventually relieved of my regular duties and allowed to devote all my time to that kind of work. As jobs went, it was a great one. I ended up travelling all over the world, seeing sights I would otherwise never have visited, meeting all sorts of people into contact with whom I never could or would have come. Some of them were even pleased to meet me, although they surely all weren't. That, however, is part of how the game is played: when you seek to solve crimes, you often meet up with criminals who are generally unhappy to be met up with. But what could I do about that? It was a living! And it was a good one too.

After Avital died, though, I retired permanently. I was in my seventy-fifth year at that point, more than ready to stop working. I had a library full of works I wished to read, and without having Avital to tell about my adventures, there hardly seemed any reason to continue having them. Maybe I was a bit hasty. Maybe not. What difference does it make now? If I thought I could solve another crime, especially one I really cared about solving, I might agree to try. But I've played the recluse since Joseph's death and I don't see myself returning to work any time soon.

The bath on the Street of the Lambs closed almost thirty years ago. It was a very comfortable place for me, but it was becoming more and more decrepit with each passing season and its owners finally decided that there was simply no point to pouring even more money into the place. Fortunately, a new place opened up a few blocks south just where Upper King Hezekiah Road ends at the top of the Rose Market. It is really very nice there, but it attracts a less homogenous crowd and it's the rare evening when our people are the only ones in attendance. Regardless, I go more or less every day to bathe, to chat, to have a cold beer in a friendly place where everybody still knows my name. Why not? An old man, even as unsociable a one as myself, still needs a place to go!

www.ingramcontent.com/pod-product-compliance
Lightning Source LLC
Chambersburg PA
CBHW072352030726
47505CB00014B/1803